THE CRIME CLUB

Mystery & Mayhem

THE CRIME CLUB

Mystery & Mayhem

Twelve
Deliciously
Intriguing Mysteries

WITHDRAWN

EGMONT

# EGMONT

*We bring stories to life*

First published in Great Britain 2016
by Egmont UK Limited
The Yellow Building, 1 Nicholas Road, London W11 4AN

ISBN 978 1 4052 8264 2

63361/5

A CIP catalogue record for this title is available
from the British Library

Typeset by Avon DataSet Ltd, Bidford on Avon, Warwickshire
Printed and bound in Great Britain by the CPI Group

MIX
Paper
FSC   FSC® C018306

# CONTENTS

# INTRODUCTION

The very word 'mystery' is exciting. It instantly conjures up visions of ruined castles, secret passageways, lost treasures, brave detectives and dastardly villains. Most of all though, it suggests an enigma – a puzzle to solve, a question that characters as well as readers are trying to answer.

From Hercule Poirot to the Hardy Boys, the Secret Seven to Sherlock Holmes, mystery stories have long been favourites on our bookshelves. Whether it's the Famous Five or Nancy Drew, it's hard to resist the fun of an old-fashioned mystery tale. But over the last few years we've seen an explosion of brand new mysteries appearing in our bookshops and libraries. With page-turning plots, puzzling clues to follow and plenty of heart-pounding action and adventure, these books nod to the much-loved mysteries of the past, but also bring detective fiction bang up to date.

If you want to get a taste of this new generation of crime

fiction, the twelve original stories in this collection are the perfect place to start. Showing just how varied and diverse today's mysteries can be, this anthology takes us from an elegant Georgian country house in Helen Moss's *The Mystery of the Pineapple Plot* to the buzzy streets of present-day Marsh Road in Elen Caldecott's *Rain on My Parade*. We visit the Great Exhibition of 1851 in Frances Hardinge's intriguing *God's Eye* and explore the streets of 1780s Soho in Harriet Whitehorn's *The Murder of Monsieur Pierre*.

These are stories that have plenty of fun with the traditions of crime fiction. Robin Stevens and Clementine Beauvais offer us brain-boggling, Agatha-Christie-style puzzles that even Miss Marple might struggle to solve; while Sally Nicholls' *Safe-Keeping* is a tribute to 'Boy's Own' style adventures. Caroline Lawrence's modern-day mystery has a hint of the American Wild West and Julia Golding's *Mel Foster and the Hound of the Baskervilles* even features an appearance from the great detective Sherlock Holmes himself.

The young sleuths in these stories can be anyone, from Kate Pankhurst's quick-thinking dog-walker Sid to my own Edwardian chorus-girl-turned-detective Lil. But what unites them all is that they are the ones smart enough to unravel the mystery, rather than the adults around them. Sharp-eyed and even sharper-witted, these young heroes are courageous, cool-headed and clever, able to follow the clues and come up with the solution even when no one else can. Susie Day's *Emily and the Detectives* illustrates this perfectly: the world believes that clueless Lord Copperbole and scientist Mr Black are brilliant detectives, but in fact it's Mr Black's daughter, the capable Emily, who's really responsible for discovering whodunnit every time.

Perhaps one of the reasons that mystery stories like these are so enjoyable is that they allow us to share the challenge of solving the puzzle. We too can experience the satisfaction of pitting our wits against the mystery, piecing together the clues and unravelling the evidence to work out what happened and why. The stories in this collection offer exactly this challenge: can you solve the crimes alongside the daring young detectives? But whether or not you manage to crack the cases, there's a huge amount of fun to be had along the way.

Happy sleuthing!

# Katherine Woodfine

# IMPOSSIBLE MYSTERIES

Sometimes crimes seem simply impossible. But intrepid detectives know that this is never really true. As Sherlock Holmes said, 'Once you eliminate the impossible, whatever remains, no matter how improbable, must be the truth.'

These three locked-room mysteries seem unbelievable, but each case can be cracked – and as soon as they are, each of them make perfect sense.

# EMILY AND THE DETECTIVES
## By Susie Day

'No, but . . .' said Emily.

'Hush, dearest,' said Mr Black – or Father, as she more usually called him. 'We are on the brink! Of a discovery! We are mere instants from revealing all – are we not, Lord Copperbole?'

Lord Copperbole – or Irritating Moustachioed Weasel, as she more usually called him – leapt back from the laboratory bench, as it erupted in blue flames.

'The clue!' moaned Mr Black.

'The clue!' howled Lord Copperbole, nursing a burnt thumb.

'The bucket?' suggested Emily, tugging a pail full of sand from beneath the bench, and dumping it unceremoniously on to the fire.

A shame. The blue flame indicated atacamite, as she had

expected from the sugary crystals gathered in the corner of the clue: an envelope addressed to Lady Tanqueray, greasy from travel, and impressed with the shape of a scarab beetle. It could not have been more obvious.

It was lucky, really, that Mary the housemaid neglected to refill the bucket with sand.

The Chinese puzzlebox Lord Copperbole brought to the house was a rare and beautiful thing: jet black, inlaid with a complex pattern of abalone shell.

'My dear friend Lady Tanqueray has again entrusted me with unlocking a mystery,' he explained, purring as he stroked his new-grown goatee. 'A gift to her eldest daughter, from an admirer. We must be discreet, Charles.'

'Of course, my dear fellow,' said Mr Black, turning it this way and that. 'But if your intellect cannot unlock it, I scarce presume to hope I might.'

This was silly, Emily thought, since her father was a very clever – if amateur – scientist, and Lord Copperbole was just a person who happened to live in a large house full of expensive things. But Mr Black was indeed outfoxed – until Emily slid the abalone-shell catch up, left, down, left and up, mirroring the castellation pattern on the lid until it clicked.

She smiled as the box sprang open.

The secret within was a large furred spider (poisonous,

clearly: anyone could identify those red markings), which scuttled out of its prison and on to the floor.

'Oh!' said her father.

'Help!' yelped Lord Copperbole.

Emily reached under the table, placed the empty bucket over the spider, and stood on top in her black buttoned boots until an eminent zoologist could be located.

The eminent zoologist revisited Mr Black's house in Richmond three weeks later, accompanied by his weeping wife.

He recounted the tragic tale of his wife's mother – an elderly seamstress, formerly of the royal household – and her purloined silver spoons. All but one had been mysteriously stolen from her private collection.

'The police are baffled, sir!' declared the eminent zoologist. 'Her eyesight failed many years ago; she only discovered the theft when she came, alas, to sell them. And she is quite distraught, the poor lady, for they were gifts given to her by her daughter, my dear Agatha: one for each Christmas since our marriage. And now there is but one left.'

His weeping wife dabbed at her eyes.

'I enjoy a mystery, sir,' said Mr Black with a frown, 'but I don't know that we are quite the right people to –'

'Nonsense!' declared Lord Copperbole, snatching up a paisley velvet scarf and knotting it with a confident flounce. 'I half see the solution already! What puzzles me is why the thief would take every other spoon, and leave only one.'

'Or,' said Emily, looking up from her book, 'perhaps there only ever was one spoon, and the daughter gave her the same one every year?'

The weeping wife stopped weeping, and attempted to leap through the window.

Mr Black gripped her by the ankle, hauled her back inside, and Emily sat on her legs until the constable arrived.

The police were not pleased to have been bested.

The newspapers, however, became terribly keen on the exploits of Copperbole & Black.

The Mystery of the Eminent Zoologist's Wife's Mother's Spoons was reported in the *Daily Telegraph*.

The Case of One-Legged Jack (who was, Emily discovered, actually Two-Legged Jill) was featured on the front page of the *Illustrated London News*.

After the Adventure of the Magician's Hatbox, their appeal extended into the society pages.

*Lord Copperbole is quite the fashionable gentleman, lately seen sporting a spotted cravat tied in a manner some have dubbed 'The Detective's Twist'. Meanwhile, in spite of his unfortunate dusky appearance, Mr Black cuts a more traditional figure, yet his habit of tucking a crocus into his lapel is also gaining regard.*

There was no mention of young Miss Emily Black's contribution.

'Or the way she wears her stockings all wrinkly about the ankle and her hair in knots,' Mary the housemaid said, finding Emily gloomily scouring the back pages. 'Fame's not all it's cracked up to be, miss. Fame brings trouble. You're better off out of it.'

Emily supposed so. Though it seemed to bring a lot of other things too.

Lady Tanqueray's favourite Parisian tailor made Lord Copperbole a new green brocade coat – 'At no charge!' said her father. 'Can you imagine? And you know Basil; he is fond of a tailor.'

Mr Black found himself invited to the Royal Society – not to join, of course, but to dine, once.

But after the Case of the Lost Prince (who happily really was lost, not dead, and thanks to Emily soon found again, in a coal cellar) mere fame changed into true regard.

Lord Copperbole and Mr Black were summoned to the palace, and each anointed with a new title: DBE, Detective of the British Empire.

*There is no crime they cannot solve*, the papers declared. *LONDON IS SAFE.*

Emily felt torn in two. One portion of her blazed with envy. Her second self glowed with secret pride.

Until one day, everything changed.

'Dearest Emily,' said her father, 'we are quite preoccupied, Lord Basil and I, with our work for Her Majesty. I know you have always enjoyed playing our little chaperone, and since your poor mother – rest her soul – was lost to us, I have adored having you by my side. But the scene of the crime is no place for a child.'

'And the daughter of the Queen's Detective should be an accomplished young lady,' added Lord Copperbole, lingering at the looking glass to tweak the pointy collar of his new green coat. 'A young lady's most *becoming* delicate qualities are not to be acquired in a laboratory, my dear.'

'But, Father,' protested Emily, 'we have work to do! Mysteries to solve! Legs to sit on, puzzle boxes to unpuzzle . . .'

*You need me*, she meant.

And – she had plenty of qualities already. She had learnt to read at four and a half from Darwin's *Origin of Species* (she liked the part about tortoises) and ever since had consumed a new book daily, sitting on the kitchen stove to ensure a warm bottom and a ready supply of toast. She knew an Erlenmeyer flask from a retort. She was a bit good at solving crimes, even if no one else noticed.

Mr Black took her hands in his. 'The former Lord Copperbole – Basil's father – was good enough to provide me my education. Now my dear friend has offered to provide for you. You are to go to Lord Basil's house in the country. He has appointed a governess for you. You'll hardly have time to miss me, I promise!'

Lord Copperbole's house was in Sussex, surrounded by rolling green hills and a lingering unmentionable smell relating to cows. It was very grand and only slightly damp. Emily had her own room and schoolroom, the run of the library (which was happily stuffed with every modern work relating to science and its principles, and a less interesting selection of magazines about hair), a stable of horses should she wish to ride, a cook to prepare all her meals, and a dog, who she called Wilfrid, because Pashmina was a silly name for a spaniel. None of which helped her heart from squeezing tight in her chest at the thought of her father, hurrying after Lord Weasel, or alone in his laboratory. Mary was bound to have forgotten to fill up the fire bucket again.

Emily resolved to make the best of it.

'I'm so pleased you're here,' she said to the governess, with her very warmest smile. 'I love learning. Especially chemistry, and botany, and mathematics.'

'We will study the pianoforte, conversational French and watercolour painting,' said Miss Hethersmith, who wore a bun, and spectacles, and a mouse-like expression.

'Of course we will,' said Emily brightly.

And she proceeded to spend her time at the piano, or the easel, or with her French text on her knee.

'Oh yes, sir, she has been a most attentive student,' Miss Hethersmith assured Mr Black, when he and Lord Copperbole visited on Friday evening.

It was not a lie. She had indeed been attentive: to the pamphlet on poisons tucked into her French vocabulary; to the careful detail in her watercolour portrait of the human anatomy and its vulnerabilities to violent attack; to the composition of a baroque piano solo, using a substitution code to spell out *I AM BORED AND WOULD LIKE TO DO SOME DETECTING*. And, of course, to the newspapers, which had begun to report what they were calling the Case of The Deadly Bedchamber, a mystery so bewildering that there was no question who must be called upon; a case so baffling that the police were 'probably, like, not even going to bother', according to a source. Copperbole & Black had been summoned at once, and were now investigating the most mysterious murder of Viscountess Lucetta von Fromentin.

The facts of the case were plain.

The Queen received Viscountess Fromentin, a widow from Austria, for tea on September 12th. The Viscountess had taken a liking to London on a previous visit, and that day had moved into a small but well-appointed house in Marylebone, which had been decorated to her very exacting instructions: carpeting from Constantinople; blown-glass vases from Venice; an extensive range of Austrian cheeses in the larder.

She was noted by her lady's maid, Bertha, to seem especially pleased by the appearance of her bedroom: a comfortable reading chair, an antique grandfather clock, and all decorated in wallpapers, curtains and bedlinens from Paris, in the latest fashionable green.

('I am always rather ahead of the tide,' said Lord Copperbole, swishing his striped green coat-tails in case they were not noticeable enough.)

After leaving the palace, the Viscountess dined in a hotel in Kensington on soup and stewed guinea fowl, and consumed a single glass of Medoc which she insisted came from a bottle which no one else would drink; the sommelier recalled pouring it away (with a tragic sigh; it was a very good year) in front of her, to be certain.

('Most curious,' noted Mr Black. 'Though the contents are lost I should very much like the bottle, for testing.')

Bertha took her a small bottle of soda water as was her habit shortly before ten that night, and noticed the Viscountess looked pale and dishevelled. She later recalled hearing a terrible noise in the night, like the thumping footfalls of some monster. The lady's maid also swore she had heard the bedroom's grandfather clock strike thirteen. And then she had gone back to bed, because that was scary.

The following morning, Bertha found herself unable to enter her mistress's room: the Viscountess had locked the door from inside, and the golden key was still wedged into the keyhole. Her knock received no answer. The windows, their green Parisian curtains still drawn, were bolted shut on the inside.

Fearing her mistress had been taken ill – or worse – the lady's maid roused the cook, who roused the underbutler, and they hurled themselves at the locked door until it gave way.

What they saw then was quite impossible.

On the bare floorboards beneath the grandfather clock was written, in ominous blood-red letters, the word 'hare'.

The green linens of the bed had been rent and torn, as if by claws.

The soda bottle was smashed.

And on the bed lay the still, white body of the Viscountess in her Parisian nightgown, quite dead.

('A tragedy,' pronounced Lord Copperbole, wiping his brow with exaggerated sorrow. 'Such exquisite taste in decor, and she had barely one night in which to appreciate it.')

All this was recounted to Emily over *limande sole au beurre* (buttered lemon sole; Emily was learning all her *poissons* alongside her poisons) at Lord Copperbole's dining table on Friday.

'I feel we have barely scratched the surface of this most enticing case, dearest Emily!' said her father, eagerly squeezing a lemon over his fish. 'One week into our investigations and so many clues still to unravel! So many theories present themselves . . .'

'I maintain the Lady's maid is prime suspect,' sniffed Lord Copperbole. 'Sole witness. First to find the body. One should never be too trusting of a servant, Miss Emily,' he added meaningfully, as a footman held out a platter of potatoes. Somehow the footman did not tip them all upon his head.

'Ah, now, I have my eye on the sommelier still, sir!' said Mr Black. 'The wine was surely poisoned. Although how he would have profited from the murder, I have yet to draw together. And that does not explain the significance of the *hare*.'

'Then there is the matter of the torn bedlinen . . .'

'And the clock which struck thirteen . . .'

Mr Black drank deeply, and smacked his lips. 'Indeed! It is a remarkable case. One for the history books, if we can but solve it! Tell me, dearest Emily, what do you make of it?'

Emily dropped her fish knife (into all her other knives – there were at least six) in surprise. He was smiling benevolently at her, sincerely curious as to her mind. She felt suddenly aglow. Perhaps, at last, he saw her.

She stole a glance at Lord Copperbole, waiting for his lip to curl ready with dismissal – but he was staring listlessly at his plate, pushing his *limande sole* about. He had not touched either of the soups, nor the kickshaws of pickled herring (*hareng mariné*, she remembered) and horrid oysters (*les huîtres horrible*) he typically pounced upon.

She recognised the expression; her father often sank into similar despondency mid-case. Unless Lord Copperbole was realising he was shortly to be replaced at her father's side . . . by herself?

'Well,' she said eagerly, pushing her plate away. 'I think – that is to say, what I make of it is –'

Her voice faded to a croak.

Emily, for the first time in her life, had no idea how the crime had been committed.

Usually she was able to see each clue, each suspect, each moment of importance in her mind as if they were chessmen on a board – and played a swift and confident game until the only piece remaining was the solution. For the first time, for every pawn she took, there was another jostling for attention. For the first time, it seemed the murderer had left *too many* clues to his identity, not too few. And all while seemingly committing the crime from inside a locked room – and vanishing.

Her shoulders drooped. Perhaps she was not worthy of royal patronage after all.

'Oh dearest, in my excitement I've overtired you with this unpleasantness,' said her father. 'We shall not speak of it again.'

Emily opened her mouth to protest, but it stretched itself into an unbidden yawn. She was sent up to bed at once, and the next morning her father and Lord Copperbole returned to London to pursue the case.

'Today, we shall paint this vase of lovely flowers,' said Miss Hethersmith.

Emily was so dejected, she obeyed without argument.

The rest of the week was spent pressing flowers, reciting poetry, and improving her deportment.

On Friday evening, the Queen's Detectives returned to Sussex, aflow with new theories.

At least, her father was.

'The Viscountess's Venetian glass was purchased from an antiquities dealer in Amsterdam,' he explained in an excitable gabble. 'However! It is a fake. I surmise that the Viscountess had discovered the lie, revealed it in conversation with Her Majesty, and in doing so inadvertently revealed that the royal house too had fallen prey to such fakery. She was murdered to prevent a scandal!'

'It is a bit *more* of a scandal now, though, isn't it?' said Emily, thinking of the stack of newspaper cuttings in the library, and shifting one chessman across the board.

Mr Black tapped his chin. 'True. Perhaps instead it was the antiquities dealer himself, fearing exposure, who killed her!'

'He'd need to enter the room, though,' said Emily, 'and come out again, and to come all the way from Amsterdam to do it with no one noticing, and to kill her with a weapon no one has yet found.'

Another pawn was discarded.

Mr Black nodded thoughtfully. 'Very well. I propose the key clue is the word "hare" and that it is a bookmaker that we must pursue! Perhaps the Viscountess was prone to gambling on hare-coursing, and the murderer wished to . . . er . . . send a clear message to all other hare-gambling enthusiasts who had not paid their debts, by writing the word in blood!'

'Do you really think so?' said Emily.

Mr Black sighed. 'No. The Viscountess had no unpaid debts. And the bookmaker too would need to enter the room and get out again: the police are adamant the bolts inside the windows were quite secure, and the door locked.

Then there is the clock striking thirteen. Unless . . . was there a bee, perhaps? A killer bee, which stung the poor woman? Or, or – Basil?'

Emily had almost forgotten Lord Copperbole was present.

He was still moustachioed, and as weaselly as ever – but there was no flounce or flourish to the wilting knot of his cravat. Even his famous coat hung loose from his narrowed shoulders. And the food that whirled around the table – *truite aux amandes* (trout with almonds) and cucumber salad – seemed to interest him not at all.

'Lord Copperbole is taking the challenge of this case to heart,' confided Mr Black to Emily, in a kind low voice. 'We are working so terribly hard, you see.'

Emily did see.

Unfortunately, the newspapers saw too.

*QUEEN'S DETECTIVES OUTFOXED?*

*NOT SO CLEVER NOW, SIR! COPPERBOLE AND FRIEND REMAIN PERPLEXED*

*MURDERER ROAMS STREETS AS QUEEN'S TOP 'TEC TURNS PEAKY*

Emily redoubled her efforts.

While Miss Hethersmith urged her to paint a bunch of violets, she traced the letters of 'hare' in her paintbox in Cadmium Red, over and over.

She spent hours in the library, poring over Lord

Copperbole's books.

She stared out at the green cow-smelling downs, as a spider crawled across the windowpane and began to spin its web.

At that, the final chessman shifted into place.

Now the queen was in play, and the game was on.

'I shall need to send a telegram to London,' she announced, in the large empty hall, as Wilfrid skittered across its tiles leaving small muddy prints. 'Hello?'

But no footman or housemaid appeared.

She hurried to the schoolroom, but Miss Hethersmith was not there. All she found was a copy of the *London Times*.

### COPPERBOLE & BLACK TO FACE THE DEADLY BEDCHAMBER!

*These pages have remained firm in the conviction that the Queen's own Detectives are to be offered every courtesy and respect while they unravel this notorious mystery – now entering its fourth week. It is with much hope that we report that Lord Copperbole – despite his recent ill health – and his dusky companion intend to stay one entire night in the Deadly Bedchamber itself, to expose its secret at last.*

Emily's heart pounded.

It was yesterday's edition.

The time was now past three. Her father and his colleague were to lock themselves into the Deadly Bedchamber at nine that very evening – and she knew, now, with terrible certainty that if they did, she would never see either one alive again.

Lord Copperbole might be a weasel and a peacock with a curly lip, but she did not wish him dead.

And her father . . .

Her dear papa . . .

There was no time to waste.

Emily dashed to the library to collect one slim volume. Then she made for the stables, rode headlong for Brighton, and boarded a steam train.

She was alone, and rather muddy, and, as the darting eyes and whispers were quick to note, also unfortunately dusky. But she kept her head high and her chin firm, and made sure to find a compartment filled with people reading newspapers, so they would not stare.

After an agonisingly slow journey, the train pulled in at London Victoria.

For a moment she quailed: would a carriage driver take a small muddy brown girl, all alone? But all it took was a confident jingle of her purse, and the driver cracked his whip for Marylebone.

It was not hard to find the correct house. A crowd had gathered, all eager to see the famous detectives. A ring of bobbies was attempting to hold them clear of the front steps, and Emily found herself crushed against warm smelly bodies and hairy coats as she tried to press through the throng.

'Stand back, ladies and gents, no pushin'!' bellowed a policeman.

'How are we to know they'll stay all night long, eh?' yelled one voice.

'And who's going to solve it if they both pop off?' called another, to a ripple of laughter.

'I will!' shouted Emily, finding herself pressed against a red pillar box at the edge of the pavement, and scaling it at once. 'I have solved the mystery of the Deadly Bedchamber!'

She stood awkwardly on the domed top of the pillar box, slipping in her muddy boots, and waved the pamphlet from Lord Copperbole's library excitedly above her head – but the crowd jeered and booed.

Emily looked imploringly at the line of policemen, but they only had eyes for the crowd.

She tried calling out: 'Father! Papa, I am here, come out at once!' but her voice could not carry.

She could not draw him out alone. But she was not alone.

Thinking fast, Emily crouched down on her pillar box perch.

'I don't think they're even in there,' she said, to no one in particular.

'Darlin', I saw them go in myself,' said a woman hotly.

'They could've slipped out of a back entrance,' said Emily casually.

''Ere, that's a point.'

'How do we know they're still in there?'

'Oi! Show yourselves, Lord La-di-dah and Wotsisface!'

The crowd took up the cry. 'Show yourselves! Show yourselves!'

To Emily's joy, a pair of curtains on the first floor were thrown back, and a sash window lifted.

Mr Black leant out, looking rather irritable. 'Sirs, ladies, it is rather a challenge to solve a locked-room mystery; more so if you will not allow us to keep it locked.'

'Papa! Father, over here! It's Emily, I'm here!'

This time Emily's voice was heard. Mr Black almost fell out of the window in surprise at finding his daughter, in London, alone, standing on a postbox, but she shook off all his demands for an explanation.

'No time, Papa! You must get out of there at once, both of you! The room is deadly!'

'We know that, dearest,' said her father, gently.

'No – *the room itself* is deadly.' She took a deep breath, trying to calm herself. 'Father – Lord Copperbole has been unwell. Has he taken a turn for the worse since entering the room?'

Mr Black looked furtive, as a gaspy choking sound issued from behind him. 'Er. Possibly?'

'I know why. And it is what killed the Viscountess Fromentin!'

The crowd, which had fallen silent, began to mutter.

Emily brandished the pamphlet triumphantly above her head, almost slipping from her perch.

'Why are you waving a fashion catalogue from Paris about, dearest?'

'Paris Green!' she called back. 'The Viscountess was not murdered by a vanishing monster, or an invisible bee. She was poisoned.'

'By the wine, I knew it!' yelled someone.

'Nah, son, it was that guinea fowl.'

Emily shook her head. 'No! What poisoned her was the wallpaper, the curtains, her bedlinens – all handmade in Paris, to the popular shade, exactly like Lord Copperbole's *coat*. Paris Green. Also known as *copper acetoarsenite*.'

'Eh?' said the crowd.

'But . . . that's toxic . . .' said her father, his face falling as he glanced at the curtain by his side.

'Oooh,' said the crowd.

'Ordinary exposure will result in a slower reaction,' Emily continued. 'That's why Lord Copperbole has been unwell! His coat has been very slowly poisoning him. But

– the room, the furnishings: I think they must have been *super-impregnated* with the compound. Sleeping in that room, in a bed, coated in the same poison – that takes only one night to kill.'

There was stillness for a moment.

'Wait. What about the torn bedlinen?'

'It was a new bed, new linens. I believe the sheets were torn before she slept, to give the impression of an assailant in the room. The maid either did not notice when she made up the bed, or feared blame if it were mentioned.'

The crowd grumbled.

'Why did the clock strike thirteen?'

'I believe the mechanism was tampered with, to add confusion.'

'What about the wine that got poured away?'

'Oh! That was just wine. And a viscountess being mean.'

'All right, all right, I buy it all so far,' yelled one of the policemen. 'But who or what is that *hare* all about?'

Emily's throat was beginning to hurt from shouting, and her boots really were slippery, but to be called upon by an officer of the law urged her on to reveal her proudest deduction.

'That,' she said loudly, 'holds the vital clue to *why* this crime occurred in this way. After all, if you want to kill a viscountess, there are quicker ways than selling her curtains super-impregnated with poison. The word "hare" does not mean *hare* as in furry rabbity creature, but the beginning of another word. *Hareng*. It is the French word for "herring", written in blood. A *red herring*. I think it was written on the floorboards before the Viscountess moved into the room, and covered up with a rug. The missing letters were wiped away by footfalls - or perhaps missed out all along, to prolong the mystery. For this is why the Viscountess died: to preoccupy the Queen's Detectives with an impossible case. To give them too many clues to solve. To humiliate them with failure - and to draw them into the same trap. The Deadly Room - which is killing them both while I'm talking! Father? Papa? Please, *please* come down?'

The crowd's faces turned up to the window, to the forgotten Mr Black above.

Emily met his bright eyes, and saw her father's chest swell with pride at last.

'Oh! Yes, at once,' he said, coming back to himself. 'I mean to say - oh - Lord Copperbole will need a doctor! And no one is to come into this room!'

Lord Basil Copperbole made a full recovery, and acquired a new coat (demure grey, though the lining was pink and yellow stripes) in time to accompany Miss Emily Black and her father to the palace, where she received a gallantry award for services in the prevention of crime.

'Perhaps some time back in the country, until all this fuss has died down, hmm?' said Mr Black, peering anxiously from their carriage as they drew up to the old Richmond house and laboratory, to find the usual crowd gathered to catch a glimpse of the Queen's Detectives and their young protégée.

'A little Sussex air . . . some shopping, of course,' said Lord Copperbole, clapping his hands.

'Indeed, sir, indeed!' said Mr Black.

'Aren't we going to finish the case first?' asked Emily.

'But you solved it, dearest Emily!' said her father, squeezing her hands. 'All those clues . . . solved the lot. Even the ones that weren't really clues.'

'Yes. Very clever,' said Lord Copperbole, his cheek twitching with the effort.

'Um. Well, we know *how* the Viscountess died, Papa. But we haven't caught who arranged for her to furnish her home with super-impregnated poisonous bedlinen then laid a false trail of clues, all in order to entrap the two of you in the same room and kill you,' said Emily, quite slowly, to be sure it went in.

'Oh. Oh dear,' said her father.

'Good heavens,' said Lord Copperbole. 'And now we have no clues to go on at all!'

'Apart from the tailor you visited in Paris who made you your coat,' said Emily. 'And whoever recommended him.'

She looked Lord Copperbole in the eye.

Lord Copperbole clutched his lace handkerchief to his lips. 'But – you can't be suggesting . . .'

'She did give you a puzzlebox containing a poisonous tarantula. And I think a cursed scarab beetle before that. I don't think she intended for it all to help you become a famous detective. Is it possible she doesn't like you very much?'

Lord Copperbole's moustache wilted.

'Don't worry,' said Emily. 'Mary knows Lady Tanqueray's second footman. If she's fled the country, he'll know where her cases have been sent. Shall we go?'

Her father smiled at her with great warmth.

'My dearest Emily,' he said. 'You are becoming quite the detective!'

# RAIN ON MY PARADE
## By Elen Caldecott

It felt just like mini sparklers were fizzing in Minnie Adesina's arms and legs and elbows and knees. She couldn't stay in her flat above Mum's salon on Marsh Road, not with fireworks exploding from her fingers to her feet! Today was Carnival! Car-ni-val. She drawled the word slowly, the way Bernice, one of Mum's assistants, did in her Kingston accent. Those three syllables turned the road upside-down and left-side-right every year. The regular market was swept away by a swell of sound and colour. She rushed downstairs, ready to see it all.

It was still early, the summer sun hardly heating the ground, but already the street was full. People in high-vis jackets swung barriers like giant paddles; food vans' fried onions and spices made her mouth water. At the end of the road, a camera crew and technicians swarmed a temporary stage, tweaking the spotlights on the lighting rig, adjusting the legs of tripods and moving monitors. That would be where the bands played into the evening. But already there was music. From speaker stacks the size of cars, from tiny portable radios, from everywhere, rhythms that made her shoulders leap and roll throbbed and thrummed. Marsh Road was alive with it all.

'Minnie!'

Flora, one of Minnie's very best friends, hurtled down the street towards her and grabbed her elbows. Minnie and Flora were part of an investigating team who'd solved more than one mystery on Marsh Road, and seeing her always meant fun and excitement. Then Minnie noticed Flora's twin, Sylvie, strolling behind. Minnie sighed. Sunny days came with shadows. She smiled at one half of the twins.

'Isn't this exciting?' Flora asked, her red hair bouncing as she leapt up and down. 'I can't believe Bernice wants us to help her get ready! We're going to be right at the heart of Carnival this year, with one of its very best costume makers.'

Minnie glanced at Sylvie. She hadn't been part of the plan.

Flora noticed the look, but Sylvie was too busy smiling at the camera crew.

'Is it all right if Sylvie comes too?' Flora ground the tip of her trainer into the pavement. 'She didn't want to be left out.'

Sylvie never wanted to be left out. And she was often loud and pushy enough that it was impossible to ignore her. Sylvie even helped with the Marsh Road Investigators' cases, when it suited her.

But today was too nice a day to make trouble. Minnie sighed. 'You can both come. More hands make light work, Mum always says.'

'Girls!' The word was yelled so loud that it made a man carrying a barrier drop it on his foot and swear. 'Girls!' Bernice waved with both hands. She looked amazing – she must have been up before the sun to do her hair; it was teased into a huge pile on her head, streaked red, yellow and green with extensions. Her gold nails sparkled as she waved. She pulled Minnie into a tight hug. 'I've got an extra helper, have I? Good. My costume is the best yet, like a parrot fought a glitter factory and won. Today you three are my right-hand girls. Come on, the dress is waiting at the lock-up.'

The lock-ups were down a narrow footpath behind Marsh Road, under the railway tracks. A span of arches had doors set into them, creating workshops and storage spaces, vaults of red brick. As they walked, Bernice kept up an excited commentary. 'Mind your step, this part is a bit overgrown. Careful of the nettles. I've been working on this costume for a month now, every spare minute I get. It's going to knock the shoes and socks off everyone! Ooh, wasp. I don't like this path, but the lock-up is so cheap, and it's dark and cool, perfect for storing costumes. No one can even peek inside. Watch out, this bit's muddy.'

Finally they were in front of Bernice's lock-up. The smartly painted blue door, with a polished letter box, was padlocked shut.

Bernice took out a key.

She turned it in the lock.

The door swung inward. Minnie caught a scent like charring before Bernice flicked on the light.

'No!' she cried. 'Oh no!'

Minnie ducked through the small doorway, the twins clambering after her. 'Bernice? What is it?'

With one look it was obvious what was wrong.

Standing on a dressmaker's dummy in the middle of the space was the ruin of Bernice's costume. The base layer of Lycra was in place, but the tatter of feathers surrounding it was hideous. The spines were bald without their fluff, the broken quills ugly as road kill. Whatever had happened to the costume had taken all its grace and beauty and left behind a horror.

'My costume,' Bernice whispered. She stepped forward robotically. As she reached to touch the few remaining feathers, they crumbled to dust under the pads of her fingers.

Brittle pieces flaked to the ground.

Minnie stepped further into the room, with the twins close behind her. They moved slowly, the way hospital visitors might walk into an intensive care ward.

But it was too late for the costume. It was already dead.

'What happened to it?' Sylvie asked. 'It's awful.'

'I . . . I . . . don't . . .'

Minnie glared at Sylvie. 'Bernice, I think you need to sit down. Here.' Minnie grabbed a wheeled chair from beside the desk and pushed it towards Bernice.

'Wait!' Flora said suddenly. 'We shouldn't move anything.'

Minnie froze. Her hands tightened on the back of the chair. Was Flora suggesting what she thought she was suggesting? 'You think this is a crime scene?' Minnie whispered. Could this be a case for the Marsh Road Investigators?

Flora gave a firm nod. 'Bernice, the costume didn't look this way when you last saw it?'

Bernice shook her head, whipping her extensions back and forth. 'No – no way. It was fine last night.'

'And could this have happened by accident?'

Again, Bernice shook her head. 'No, child. The temperature is just right. The place is kept dark. There are no insects, or mice, no chemicals or anything that could do this damage. This is no accident.' Her eyes widened as she realised what she was saying. 'Someone did this on purpose! Someone doesn't want me to walk in Carnival!'

'Who?' said Sylvie.

'*How?*' said Flora.

Minnie saw exactly what Flora meant. There were no windows in the lock-up at all. The door was the only way in, and it had definitely been locked.

'Bernice, who else has a key to the padlock?' Flora asked.

'No one. There's only one key and I've had it safe in my purse all night.'

Minnie watched as Flora did what she always thought was one of the most exciting things in the world. She opened her ever-present backpack and took out a pen and a notebook. It was the signal that they were about to begin a new case. They had investigated several crimes before now, and each time the details went into Flora's notebook – every clue, every witness statement, everything – until there was enough information to help them catch the culprit. They had to do the same for Bernice. No one was going to hurt their friend and get away with it.

'Bernice,' Flora asked, 'does anything look unusual? I mean, apart from the costume?'

Bernice glanced around, taking in the dummy, the clean workbench, the perfectly arranged shelves of bright material. 'No,' she said finally, 'nothing.' Her voice shook as she spoke.

Minnie was horrified to see tears glistening in her eyes.

Bernice turned away and faced the wall. 'I'm just . . . going to call . . . I have to let people know . . . officials, maybe . . .'

Minnie felt a hand on her arm. It was Flora. 'She needs a minute,' Flora said. 'She's probably in shock. Let's help the best way we can, by finding out what happened.'

Minnie knew Flora was right.

Minnie left Bernice to make her calls. She had to concentrate on the clues. Clues could be anything: anything that disrupted the pattern, anything that looked out of place.

Who or what could have ruined a costume inside a vault-like room?

Minnie examined the walls, while Flora looked at the costume on the dummy. Sylvie wandered outside. Had she lost interest already? Typical.

Right. Ignore Sylvie too. Clues.

The walls of the lock-up were filled to the rafters with carefully arranged colour and texture: silks and sequins, taffeta and tulle, in reds and greens and blues and purples. There were ribbons, glitter, tissue paper, craft paper, crepe paper and tracing paper – if it was paper, then Bernice had some, as well as jars of feathers and lace and fringe, arranged according to the colours of the rainbow. Minnie let her eyes wander over it all. Was any of this technicolor craft equipment a clue? It all looked like it belonged.

Flora had moved away from the dummy to look for entrances and exits. She scanned the ceiling, looking for vents, she clattered the letter box to see if she could fit more than her hand through (she couldn't) and she searched the floor for a trapdoor. 'The door is definitely the only way in,' she said finally.

'What about the costume? Any clues there?' Minnie asked.

'I'm not sure. Only the feathers have been affected. But then, the costume is ninety per cent feathers. Bernice has already given us a good idea of the things that damage feathers – insects, mice, chemicals, heat and light.' She scribbled something in her notebook. 'Let's see what Sylvie's got.'

Sylvie was outside, crouched with her back against the lock-up doors, staring at the ground.

She glanced their way as they climbed out of the doorway. 'There you are. Have either of you found a clue?'

Flora shook her head.

'Well, it's a good job I came along today then. Look at this.' Sylvie spread her arms to point at the ground at her feet. 'Careful – don't stand on them.'

All Minnie could see was dirt. She bent lower.

'There!'

Minnie could see them now. Tiny square-ish dimples in the dirt. Heel prints? She counted six of them, in a pattern, as though someone in high-heeled shoes had stood still, but changed position a few times.

Rats.

Sylvie had found the first clue.

And her smug smile was infuriating.

Sylvie pulled out her phone and snapped photos.

Just then a huge man with arms and legs like logs lumbered past. He paused, noticing Sylvie taking snapshots of mud. He stopped. Minnie knew him – it was Big Phil. He had a lock-up a few doors down. She managed a smile, but she felt a bit embarrassed. She still remembered the time they'd had him down as a suspect in one of their cases. It had been understandable – after all, he sold fake designer perfumes that smelt of hamster wee, and diet pills that did absolutely nothing, and he wore a leather jacket and an air of menace. But they'd found out that underneath his macho exterior, Big Phil was a teddy bear.

'Morning,' he said in a deep voice. 'Bernice all ready for Carnival, is she?'

'Not really,' Sylvie said. 'Her costume looks like a toddler made it in the middle of a tantrum.'

'But her costumes are always great,' Big Phil said, confused. 'Best in the whole parade. She's the best designer in town.'

'Not this time. Something happened to her costume and now it's ruined. I don't suppose you know anything about it? Were you here last night?' Sylvie asked.

Big Phil raised one end of his monobrow. 'Ruined? Oh, poor Bernice. Is she all right? Is there anything I can do to help?'

'Yes,' Sylvie snapped. 'You can answer the question. Were you here last night? Did you see anything suspicious?'

Big Phil's face reddened. 'I *was* here, as it happens. In my lock-up. I can be there any time I like – there's no law against it.'

'Did you see anything? Or hear anything strange?' Flora asked.

'Nothing suspicious. But there was something a bit strange. I was bothered by three of the biggest moths you've ever seen. No idea how they got in.' He gave an involuntary shiver. 'Horrible things. You know they get stuck in your hair?'

Big Phil was entirely bald.

Sylvie rolled her eyes. 'Moths? Is that it? You didn't hear any strange sounds? Or notice any unusual visitors?'

Big Phil shrugged. 'No. Sorry. I had the radio on – I

couldn't hear anything over Soft Rock Classics. Love that show, I do.' His eyes went a little misty. Then he seemed to remember himself. He squared his shoulders. 'Well. I can't stand here talking about sparkly frocks. Tell Bernice I say hello.' He wandered off in the general direction of his lock-up.

Sylvie put her phone away. 'Might he be involved? He had the opportunity – he was here last night.'

Flora shrugged. 'What's his motive, though? Why would he want to hurt Bernice or her costume? I don't think he can be a suspect really.'

'And there are these marks,' Minnie added. 'It was probably a woman, don't you think? Was she standing here in high heels trying to pick the padlock?'

'Maybe,' Flora said. 'But she didn't succeed.' Flora tilted the padlock that hung clipped to the door frame and examined it. 'You can't pick a lock without scratching the metal, and this lock is clean.'

They went back inside and shut the door behind them. Bernice was off the phone and had made herself a mug of tea. They watched as she spooned in three sugars.

'It's not for the shock,' Minnie whispered. 'She just likes three sugars.' Then, a little louder, 'Do you want me to call my mum, Bernice? She might know what to do about your costume.'

'There's nothing that can be done. Someone has ruined it. I won't walk in the parade. The saboteur has got what they wanted.' Bernice had stopped looking upset and was looking angry instead.

'We found some footprints outside,' Flora said.

'*I* found some footprints,' Sylvie corrected.

'Yes, Sylvie found them,' Flora continued. 'They look like someone in high heels stood outside the door. Do you wear high heels? Or have you had a visitor who does?'

Bernice shook her head. 'I come here to build. Sensible shoes only until parade day. And no one has visited either – I wouldn't want to spoil the surprise for the people watching the parade.'

Minnie caught Flora's eye. Who was it who'd been standing outside in heels, if it wasn't Bernice?

'Do you have any enemies, Bernice?' Sylvie asked abruptly.

Bernice stirred her tea, clinking the teaspoon hard against the sides of the china. 'Enemies? Why would I have enemies? I'm not James Bond, I'm a hairdresser and costume maker! I'd been hoping this would be the year I could finally go full-time as a designer. But I guess that won't happen now.'

Just then, there was a knock on the door. It opened without waiting for a reply. 'Bernice! Bernice, sweetie, is it true? Carol heard from Ash, who heard from Billie. Your costume? Gone?' A tall woman with straight-as-a-die black hair and soft brown skin skipped inside. Her hands gestured wildly as she spoke.

Bernice sighed. 'Yes, Jasleen, it's true.'

Jasleen gasped. Then she saw the costume and gasped again. 'It's hideous!' she said.

Jasleen sounded like she was the same sort of friend as Sylvie.

'Thanks, Jasleen,' Bernice said softly.

'You can't walk the parade in that!'

'I know.'

Jasleen circled towards the dummy, her lip curled softly. 'Carol wondered what you're going to do. She said I should take your place at the front of the line, but I couldn't do it without seeing you first.' Jasleen looked down and took a few paces, as though she was thinking carefully about what to say next. She gave an exasperated sigh. 'Listen, I still have the costume I made for myself last year, if you'd like to wear it? I know I'm not such a well-known costume maker as you, but lots of people admired it.'

'Your costume? I can't wear someone else's work, you know that. A designer who's wearing someone else's design? No one would ever employ me again. I would ruin my career. I'd rather not walk than wear a costume I didn't make.'

Jasleen prickled. 'Suit yourself. I was only trying to help.' She dusted some imaginary flecks off her blouse. 'Right, I can't stay. My boyfriend is filming the parade for television and if I'm going to be at the front, I want to look my best. Oh, sorry. That was very insensitive. Give me a call if you change your mind about the spare costume.'

Before she walked out of the door, Flora held out her hand to stop her. 'Jasleen, do you ever wear high heels?'

Jasleen gave a little laugh. 'Honey pie, I'm six foot two. Of course I never wear high heels.' Then she was gone.

Flora laid her notebook on the workbench. The details of the crime were written down: Bernice left the lock-up securely padlocked last night. Sometime between then and eight o'clock this morning, someone had broken in, somehow, and ruined the costume. Someone in high heels.

'What about the moths?' Minnie asked. 'The moths that frightened Big Phil.'

'What about them?'

'Bernice, didn't you say that insects damage costumes?' Minnie asked.

Bernice nodded vigorously. 'Oh, yes, moths can do terrible damage to clothes. Especially silk and wool and feathers. They eat them!'

'But,' Sylvie said, 'someone would have to get a whole load of moths in here, and then get them back out again without leaving a trace. Bernice, I don't suppose you were sent a mysterious package yesterday that you left in here unopened, did you?'

'No,' Bernice said. 'There was nothing out of the ordinary.'

Flora wrote: 'MOTHS??' in big letters. Then, in smaller letters, 'Trained moths?' Then, in even smaller letters, 'Trained clothes moths???' Then, with a sigh, she scribbled it all out. 'Clothes moths are tiny, not like the ones Phil saw. You definitely couldn't train them. And my pen's running out,' she said in a very despondent voice.

Sylvie bent down and handed Flora a stray stick of charcoal. 'Here.'

Three sharp raps came from the doorway. All four heads inside the lock-up turned to look. An anxious-looking white woman poked her head inside.

'Amber?' Bernice said. 'What are you doing here? Come in. Girls, Amber works for the council. She's their Community Liaison Officer. Amber, these girls were supposed to be my wardrobe assistants – Minnie, Flora and Sylvie.'

Amber squeaked a hello. 'I had to come as soon as I heard,' she said in a voice that was hardly more than a whisper.

'That's kind of you.'

'It's no problem. Are you all right?'

Bernice gave a tight shrug and gestured towards the

ruined costume.

'I see,' Amber said, suddenly sounding brighter. 'I wondered whether you wanted to lodge an official complaint?'

'Against who?'

Amber opened her briefcase and pulled out a blue sheet of paper. 'Against the Carnival. Any disturbances associated with the Carnival have to be recorded. They are used to determine whether it should be allowed to continue.'

'Well, of course it should be allowed to continue!' Bernice said indignantly.

'Of course!' Minnie agreed. She was getting a bad feeling about Amber.

Amber slid the blue form along the workbench. 'I agree, if the Carnival runs smoothly. But if there are unpleasantnesses, like the terrible vandalism that happened during last year's parade, then it should be reduced in scale, or stopped altogether.'

'That wasn't vandalism! Those trees were yarn bombed with knitted bunting!'

'Fabric dyes can be very toxic to plants,' Amber said. 'It's getting more and more difficult to control that sort of thing. If there were enough complaints, then the council would have to take my concerns seriously.'

Minnie glanced down at Amber's feet. She was wearing sensible black shoes, with the laces tied in a double-knot.

'Do you ever wear high heels?' Minnie asked.

Amber frowned. 'No. I don't know how anyone can walk in them. I wear these, or my vegan boots. Why?'

'No reason,' Minnie replied.

Amber tapped the blue form that lay on the workbench. 'Can I count on your support?'

Bernice didn't pick it up.

'I'll be reporting this incident anyway,' Amber said. 'Even without your testimony the council will have to realise that the Carnival brings out the worst in people.'

Bernice glared at Amber. 'I think you'd better go, don't you?'

Amber shrugged and tucked the form back in her briefcase. 'You know where I am if you change your mind.'

They watched her leave in silence.

Well, all except Sylvie. 'That woman is a witch!' she said loudly. 'She turns up here looking all sweet and shy but really she wants to stop Carnival just because she thinks people are having too much fun! Oh! You don't think she would have ruined your costume, do you? To give Carnival a bad reputation?'

They all looked at the dummy.

'She *is* vegan,' Minnie said. 'Maybe she hates feathers. When they're not on birds, I mean.'

'And she's always going on about the litter and the noise

pollution,' Bernice said softly.

Flora wrote Amber's name in her notebook. As she pressed, the charcoal stick snapped in two. A dark line scored its way across the page. 'Rats!'

Then Flora tilted her head. 'That's weird,' she said. 'Look at this.' She held one half of the charcoal and tilted it so that the others could see. The very centre of the charcoal stick was pale wood. It wasn't singed all the way through, the way that charcoal was supposed to be.

'It isn't real charcoal!' Minnie said. 'Otherwise it would be burnt all the way through.'

Flora tapped her notebook a few times and watched the dark flakes fall. Then she grinned.

'I think I know how the costume was ruined,' she said.

'How?' Bernice asked.

'Sylvie, where did you find this charcoal?'

Sylvie waved vaguely towards the ground. 'Just there.'

'Under the letter box?'

'I guess so, yes.'

'Is it yours?' Flora asked Bernice.

Bernice shook her head.

Of course! Minnie saw at once what Flora was getting at. Everything in Bernice's workshop was neatly ordered! Each object had its place. Even though it was a riot of colour, the riot was organised. It was the same at the salon. Bernice was always tidying, sweeping up locks of hair. There was no way she would leave charcoal lying around. Especially not fake charcoal. The charcoal was the thing that didn't belong! Which meant it had to be a clue.

Flora moved over to the letter box and pulled up the flap. 'Imagine you wanted to make the letter box stay open. You might use a stick wedged up like a clothes prop. And, if that stick spent a long time, hours, being heated, then it might get scorched and start to look like charcoal.'

Minnie stepped closer to the letter box too and peered through the rectangle of light. She could see the dirt road and the footpath outside the lock-ups.

'But what would make a stick that hot?' Sylvie asked.

'Burning!' Minnie said suddenly. 'That's what I smelt when you first opened the door. It was burnt feathers! They smell as bad as burnt hair. Bernice, if someone directed a heater into the space, and left it on all night long, what would happen to your outfit?'

Bernice turned to look at the manky creation on the dummy. 'Well,' she said, '*that* would happen.'

'So,' Sylvie said, 'someone in high heels stood outside the letter box with a heater?'

Flora shook her head. 'Not exactly. A really powerful lamp would generate lots of heat, and if you positioned it properly you could focus an intense, boiling-hot spotlight on one place.'

'And,' Minnie said with a grin, 'a really powerful lamp left on overnight would attract some really big moths too! *That's* why there were moths in Big Phil's lock-up!'

'But who?' Sylvie said. 'Who was the lamp-holder in heels? Do you know?'

'Yes! Because the marks on the ground weren't high heels at all,' Flora said. She marched back to the table. Minnie joined her. With half of the fake-charcoal Flora drew six dots on her pad, just like the marks they'd seen outside. She joined three of the dots to form a triangle, then joined the remaining three to form a second triangle.

'A tripod!' Minnie said. 'Like the ones we saw by the stage on Marsh Road! Someone with a strong light on a tripod did this! Someone set it up, but wasn't happy, so they moved it to get just the right angle. They could have left it there for hours without having to do anything else.'

'It was Jasleen,' Flora said. 'Her and her boyfriend. He works with the filming crew. They use spotlights all the time.' Flora rolled the charcoal piece along the workbench. 'This must have dropped inside the letter box, instead of outside, when the crime was done. Jasleen hoped we wouldn't notice. I think she came back here to try to get it. Remember her looking at the ground? She was hunting for this!'

'But why did she do it?' Sylvie asked.

'She's a costume maker too,' Bernice said. 'She isn't as good as me, but she's not bad. If *she* walks at the front of the parade and *I'm* nowhere to be seen, then everyone will order their costumes from her next year.' Bernice caught sight of her own sad, sorry costume and gulped back a sob. 'My reputation will be as ruined as these feathers.'

'But how can we prove it?' Minnie asked. 'There won't be any prints on the charcoal now we've touched it. And finding any witnesses will be difficult, if not impossible. Big Phil was worse than useless.'

'Hey!' a bass voice said. 'I heard that.' Big Phil stepped into the room, carrying a huge suitcase.

'Sorry,' Minnie said, feeling her cheeks redden.

'I heard everything. And I don't think you need to prove she did it,' Big Phil said, 'you just need to prove that it *doesn't matter* that she did it. You need to show her that you won't let anything stop you.'

'But I can't take part in the parade dressed in that!' Bernice said, pointing to the wreck on its stand.

Big Phil smiled shyly. 'I bought this a little while ago.' He gestured with the suitcase. 'I was going to say it belonged to Marilyn Monroe and sell it on at a profit, but I thought it might fit you.' He opened the case and pulled out a red sequined dress, with a huge spray of ostrich feathers at the shoulder. 'You can alter it, if you want. I don't mind.' Big

Phil hugged the dress in his huge hands. 'You can have it. I think you'll look beautiful in it.'

Bernice took a deep breath. 'You're right,' she said. 'No one's going to rain on my parade. I'll show Jasleen that she can't stop me, whatever she does. Pass me the frock. Minnie, fetch my scissors. Twins, we'll need all the lace you can find. I've got three hours to make a showstopper. Thank you, Philip!'

As she took the dress from his hands, she dropped a quick kiss on his cheek. Big Phil blushed redder than the fake Marilyn gown.

At noon precisely, the steel drums launched into their first tune: crackling bass notes first, then trilling top notes and a surging rhythm that made everyone who could hear it start to bob. Minnie grabbed Flora's hand and lifted it up and down in time to the beat. 'It's starting!'

Then the parade swung into view. Dancers led the way, stepping forward and to the side, forward and back, repeating the pattern in time to the music. Like butterflies, like flowers, like birds of paradise, the colour and sound moved closer.

There was Bernice! Looking wonderful in red ostrich feathers reaching to the sky, gold paint on her neck and arms, and a smile spread like warm butter from ear to ear.

And keeping pace with her in the crowd was Big Phil,

looking pleased as punch.

But where was Jasleen?

Minnie raised herself on tiptoe.

There!

Right at the back of the line. With no one looking at her, or smiling, or dancing at her side.

'I guess everyone has heard what she did,' Flora said. 'I don't suppose anyone will be ordering their costume from Jasleen again.'

'And moany Amber has nothing she can complain about,' Sylvie said.

Minnie forced the shadow that Jasleen had tried to create from her mind. 'Doesn't Bernice look wonderful?' she asked.

'Big Phil certainly thinks so,' Sylvie replied.

As the drums gave way to a brass ensemble, the pace of the bobbing grew more insistent. Minnie found her feet moving whether she wanted them to or not, her hands clapping. She was dancing in the street, like a proper performer! Other hands joined in. Flora, Sylvie, the people beyond them, all dancing in time.

And it seemed to Minnie that in that moment everyone in the parade, in the audience, everyone in the whole world maybe, was full of fireworks.

*

*Read more about Minnie, Flora and Sylvie in the* Marsh Road Mysteries *series! Available from Bloomsbury now.*

# THE MYSTERY OF THE GREEN ROOM
## By Clementine Beauvais

'I know I *said* Mrs Feather looked like she wanted to kill Mrs Whistlewell, but I didn't mean it *literally*,' whispered Amy. 'I just thought she was throwing her weird glances, like *this*.'

Amy threw Joseph a weird glance like *this*, and it was frankly terrifying. 'Well, you were right,' I said. 'Mrs Whistlewell is undeniably dead. She's been slaughtered. By Mrs *Feather*.'

I picked up poor Mrs Whistlewell from the floor of the cage. She was already cold. Mrs Feather chirruped approvingly to see her victim taken away; she was clearly very proud of herself. We buried the murdered canary in the garden, behind the well. Digging a hole was tricky, because the earth was stone-hard, blades of grass locked together by frost.

51

Little Jazz was devastated. 'Do you think she'll go to Heaven?' she sniffled.

'No,' I replied. 'There's no Heaven. When you die, you just become molecules of nothing.'

This made Jazz cry. 'Does that mean Uncle Lucian is just mollicles of nothing now?'

'Absolutely.'

(Jazz cried even more.)

Our great-uncle Lucian Leroux had died three days previously, triggering this impromptu family reunion on his island off the coast of Brittany, in France. There weren't many houses on the island, and *la maison de M. Leroux* – Mr Leroux's house – was the biggest, spread over parrot-green lawns and hidden by high hedges and trees. The rooms of the mansion – the ones, at least, that hadn't been entirely eaten up by black rot and mushrooms – were now occupied for the weekend by the four adults and four children of the family.

None of us were very sad; we hadn't seen Uncle Lucian in ages, and by all accounts he hadn't been a very nice person. I barely remembered him. When I thought of him, I simply saw a boring old person's face. But I also remembered light and darkness; the last time I'd seen him, when I was a young child, he'd set up a magic lantern for me, which threw moving, shuddering shadows on the walls. That was a good memory – my only good memory associated with Uncle Lucian. He'd made that magic lantern himself: he was an inventor, although, as far as we knew, he'd never invented anything important.

'Mum's calling us,' Amy shouted, waving at her mother – my aunt Pris – who was standing at the door of the house.

Night was falling already, darkening cherry-red the pinkish bricks of the mansion. I wished it were summer – February is a rubbish time to be reunited with your cousins in a place like this. I'd have liked to stay up all night in the garden. And catch up with Joseph. He was so tall now, so big – I didn't feel as close to him as I had when we'd been kids. Three years hadn't been such a difference when I'd been seven and he'd been ten, but now I was eleven and he was fourteen . . .

'You know,' I told him as we walked to the house, 'since you started high school, we've drifted apart.' I liked how adult an expression this sounded. 'We've drifted apart,' I repeated. '*We have drifted apart*, Joe.'

Joseph wasn't listening. 'Who's that in the car?' he asked.

*That in the car* – a big brown sedan that was pulling up to the mansion, farting loudly – was an old man I was not sure I knew. Aunt Pris, however, clearly recognised him. And it didn't look like she was expecting him.

'Uncle Bill!' she stuttered as the old man got out. 'We

didn't know you'd be joining us, we . . .'

'I've had a phone call from Lucian's lawyer,' said the man. 'Apparently there's something for me from my *dear* brother in the will.'

The way he said 'dear' suggested that Bill thought there was nothing *dear* about Lucian. Aunt Pris looked astonished. 'Something for *you*? But . . .'

'Surprising, I know,' said Bill. 'I suppose sibling resentment weakens as death approaches . . .'

And he pushed past Aunt Pris to get into the house.

'Erm . . . all right,' she whispered, stunned. 'Well, I suppose . . . Joseph, would you mind preparing the green bedroom on the first floor for Uncle Bill? Just make the bed and turn on the heating.'

I was a bit upset she hadn't asked me. Clearly Joseph seemed more responsible. But I was even more upset that *he* didn't suggest I helped him. *We've drifted apart*, I thought again, watching him walk up the big staircase.

The reading of the will happened that evening. Everyone was invited, even Jazz and Amy. They were pretty polite, I thought. Jazz was picking her nose very discreetly.

'Wake me up if it turns out I'm inheriting the mansion,' I told Joseph.

No luck, unfortunately. But I did wake up when the lawyer

announced, 'Finally, my client bequeaths to each person in this room one object that he made himself. The objects are in labelled boxes, in my car. It is my client's request that the boxes be opened by each family member on their own, as they contain personal notes.'

The parents mumbled, amused. 'This is the kind of thing old Lucian would do,' my dad smiled. 'He wasn't the most likeable person, but he always enjoyed surprises.'

We went down to the lawyer's car, which was packed with square metal boxes, roughly big enough to fit a football. My box was bright yellow, and said 'Marcel' in lovely cursive.

'Danielle Darzac,' said the lawyer. Uncle Lucian's carer, a middle-aged lady who'd been crying for three days, picked up her box and ran off.

'Bill,' said the lawyer next, and Uncle Bill came to collect his box.

'I can't believe *Bill*'s getting a box,' my aunt Myriam whispered to my mum. 'Lucian *hated* him!'

After dinner, we were allowed to go up to our bedrooms to open our boxes.

On the wallpaper in my bedroom, the little dark-blue shepherdesses on swings seemed to jitter as I flicked open the golden lock which kept the box closed. A little metal roll popped out of the lid, aligning six wheels of scrambled letters, and a small engraved message above them: 'Who are you?'

I smiled. Clearly, grumpy old Uncle Lucian had had a dramatic, secretive streak to his personality . . . I carefully twisted the little wheels to spell out my name: M-A-R-C-E-L.

*Click!* The box opened, and a note swirled down to the floor.

'*I know you liked this as a child, Marcel. Maybe you'll still like it now. I wouldn't want anyone else to have it. Uncle Lucian.*'

In the box was the old magic lantern. It had a rash of rust and the paper was yellowed, but my skin tingled behind my ears; for the first time – ever – I missed Uncle Lucian.

Suddenly the door creaked open . . .

'What did *you* get, Marcel?'

Little Jazz, and Joseph, and Amy, in their pyjamas, cradling their boxes.

'I got a toy car,' Amy marvelled.

'A pocket watch.' Joseph said this as if it wasn't a big deal, but you could tell he was proud. He kept putting it into his pocket and drawing it out to read the time.

'A teddy bear,' Jazz whispered. 'With *lice!*' she added, picking a moth out of its dusty fur. (Clearly the lice were the best part of the heirloom.)

'He wasn't such a boring old person in the end,' I said. 'No one who takes the time to pack all those things for his

great-nieces and great-nephews is an *entirely* bad person.'
And I wished he could see us now, piled up on my bed,
handling the objects he'd made and handed down to us.
I almost felt like, in a way, he *was* there; or at least, that
he'd *imagined* how it would go. That he'd *pictured* his family
opening the boxes, and . . .

*BANG! BANG! BANG!*

Dry, hard thuds resonated down the corridor.

Joseph and I exchanged a glance, and popped our heads
out of my bedroom door. At the end of the hallway, Danielle
the carer was knocking heavily on the door of the green room.

'Mr Leroux?' she asked. Then, louder: 'Mr Leroux!'

We walked down to her. 'What's going on, Danielle?'

'Mr Bill,' she said. 'He's not answering his door. He
asked me to bring him his tea, but it looks like he's locked
himself in.'

'Maybe he's asleep,' I said.

'He'd have to be pretty comatose not to have heard those
knocks and calls,' Joseph scoffed, rolling his eyes at me.

Joseph's dad, alerted by the noise, had joined us at the
door. He knocked as loudly as he could. 'Uncle Bill? Uncle
Bill!'

No answer came. He looked through the keyhole. 'Looks
like the key's in there. You don't have another key, Danielle?'
She shook her head.

'Then we need to break down the door,' Joseph concluded. I beamed at him: it was the most exciting thing I'd ever heard.

His dad just replied, 'Indeed.'

The three of us began to give the door sharp, hard blows with our shoulders, like in the movies – once, twice, three times – until . . . *BROOF!* It blew open, sending bits of wood and metal everywhere.

We peered inside. And for a moment there was silence.

Until Danielle's piercing shriek.

'*He's dead!*'


Uncle Bill wasn't just dead – he'd been *killed*. *Horrifically.*

He was sitting up in his chair at his desk, a metal arrow in the middle of his chest.

'This is disgusting,' Joseph said with discernible delight.

'Oh my goodness,' his dad gasped. 'Kids – get out of here!'

But he was too busy shouting the names of all the adults in the house to make us leave. On the floor next to Uncle Bill's body was an empty box.

'Joseph, look – whatever was in his heirloom box isn't there any more. It must have been stolen by the killer!'

'Are you sure?' He dived to the floor, looking under the bed and under the desk, brushing aside staples, pens and a rubber that must have fallen off the desk, and lots of little bits of metal that must have come from the broken lock. 'Yeah, you're right. Nothing I can see . . .'

'What the . . . Joseph! Marcel! You should *not* be here!' Mum gasped behind us. 'Out! Out of this room!'

'Oh, Mum!' I implored. 'There might be clues!'

'*Get out of here!*' she screamed.

'Wait, Mum, listen! Uncle Bill's been killed because the killer wanted whatever was in his box!'

'*Get out!* Someone call the police!'

We tumbled down the marble staircase. 'Wow,' Joseph sighed. 'That was the most horribly amazing thing I've ever seen.'

The staircase resonated with hiccoughs and sobs: Danielle was sitting on the bottom step, blowing her nose on a sheet of kitchen roll.

We sat down on either side of her. 'Danielle,' I whispered, 'who else had the key to the green room?'

She stared at us as if she didn't understand. Then she said, 'No one. There's no other key.'

'Well, *someone* must have a key. The killer must have run away and locked it behind him.'

She shook her head, and blew her nose hard. 'The key was in the lock, inside.'

Joseph and I exchanged puzzled glances. 'Then maybe

the killer went through the window,' I suggested.

'It was closed,' Joseph remembered.

*Rrrring!*

The doorbell made Danielle leap up like a cat that's heard the hoover being taken out of the cupboard. Behind us, the parents came running down the stairs. They opened the door, and the only local policeman walked in.

'Brigadier Gaston Mabille,' said the policeman. He looked tired, and clearly in complete disbelief that a serious crime could have happened on the island. 'I doubt it's a murder,' he said as he walked down the corridor to the green room. 'I'm very sorry for your loss and all, but we often jump to conclusions when, in fact, there's generally a very simple explana-'

Silence as he pushed the door open, and then: 'OK, we've got a murder case.'

'We've got more than a murder case: we've got a *locked-room* murder case,' I added.

'Marcel, for Heaven's sake! You're still here?' Dad exploded. 'A *locked room* is where you and Joseph are going to end up right now. With a murderer on the loose . . .'

All the other adults shuddered – they hadn't thought about that. A few minutes later, Joseph and I had been locked by Dad into my yellow bedroom. Infuriating, but we knew we could easily exit through the window.

And we immediately did.

'The first thing to do is to figure out how the killer got in,' said Joseph as we landed in the freezing, coal-black garden. 'We need to check if the ivy outside Uncle Bill's window looks like it's been climbed on.'

We ran down to the path below the green bedroom window. There was no ivy at all on that external wall: just hard, sleek brick. And because the garden was sloped, first floor windows were much higher up on this side of the house than the other. It would be difficult, if not impossible, to climb . . .

'Is it possible,' I suggested, 'that Uncle Bill opened the window to get some fresh air, got shot in the chest by an arrow, and then closed the window again and sat down at his desk?'

'Sure,' sniggered Joseph. 'And then he clipped his nails, phoned his best friend, played the guitar and finally decided it was time to die . . .'

'All right, it was just a hypothesis,' I grumbled. 'So the killer was definitely *inside* the room – perhaps standing opposite Bill with a bow and arrow. *That's* really weird. Who would use a bow and arrow to kill someone?'

Joseph twitched. 'Actually,' he muttered, 'that rings a bell . . . Come on!'

He grabbed my arm and we ran deeper into the garden, towards the old wooden cabin at the bottom of it.

'Do you know this place?' he asked.

'Uncle Lucian's laboratory! Dad's told me about it.'

'That's right. I was wandering around the garden yesterday and had a look.'

He pushed open the door, and switched on the light.

The place was a wacky scientist's dream: chock-full of random objects, bits of metal, wood shavings, electronic paraphernalia, piles of stained paper, plans of rockets, cars, catapults, mini-carousels, levers, washing machines. More metal boxes. And a pristine coffee machine, near a tower of dirty cups.

After taking in the mess, I spotted an archery target on the opposite wall. And the arrows stuck in it.

'The *same* arrows,' I whispered.

'Yeah.' Joseph nodded. He wrenched one from the cork target. Like the one that we had seen in Lucian's chest, they were slim, stainless-steel, short arrows.

'What are they doing here?'

'I guess Lucian must have been an amateur archer. The murderer didn't need to look too far for a weapon . . . Hey, look at that!'

In a box on the table lay three arrows, snugly hugged by tight-fitting foam, with another seven empty slits next to them.

'And only six arrows in the target,' I said. 'So one arrow is missing.'

'I think we know where that one is,' Joseph murmured. 'Hmm . . . anything else that strikes you?'

It was a bit like doing a spot the difference, but one orchestrated by a murderer.

'Yeah,' I said, scanning the small, messy room. 'There's no bow, is there?'

'Not that I can see,' Joseph agreed.

'Blimey. Where is it?' I shuddered. 'With the murderer, you think?'

'Yeah. Probably.'

'Should we tell Brigadier Mabille about this?'

'I guess,' said Joseph reluctantly. 'He'll send us straight to bed . . . but it would be helpful to the investigation. Let's get back and see what he's up to.'

I picked up an old-fashioned electric torch from one of the work benches and switched it on as we stepped outside. It threw a weak, vomit-yellow beam on to the grass. Three diamond-bright pairs of eyes stared at us for a second, and then the rabbits ran off.

'Hey, Joe,' I said, 'remember that big hide-and-seek game we played in the woods a few summers ago at Granny's? There were rabbits everywhere!'

'Were there really?'

I cursed myself. Of course he didn't remember. It was such a childish thing to say.

We walked into the house. The dining-room door was ajar. Inside, Mum, Dad, Aunt Pris and Joseph's dad, Uncle Quentin, were sitting at the long table, across from Brigadier Mabille. We crept up to the doorway.

'Thank you for answering my questions on this distressing night,' said Mabille. 'I hope you understand that, however abhorrent this may sound, you are all, tonight, suspects in the murder of Mr William Leroux.'

Joseph and I listened in. My mum was the first to speak. 'That's absurd. None of us knew that Uncle Bill was even coming tonight. We hadn't seen him in years.'

'Why not?' asked Mabille, busily taking notes.

'He'd had a row with his brother, Lucian,' explained Aunt Pris. 'Ten years or so ago. Lucian was always closer to his sister, our mother, Pauline, so we stayed in contact with him, not Bill.'

'Do you know what the row was about?' Mabille interrupted.

The adults frowned. Joseph's dad, Uncle Quentin, said, 'I think it was mostly sibling jealousy. Lucian was a failed inventor living off his inheritance, Bill a successful businessman making his own money. Lucian didn't like that.'

Mabille nodded. 'What about Danielle Darzac, Lucian's carer? Do you know anything about her? Her past? Previous employers?'

'My goodness!' my dad cried. 'You're not suspecting that nice lady, are you? She's been looking after Lucian for years! Why on earth would she kill his brother?'

'I'm *very much* suspecting that nice lady,' Mabille said. 'Being close to Mr Leroux, she could very well have resented Bill as well. She would also have known what was in that box. If it was precious, she might have coveted it.'

The adults shuffled uncomfortably. 'I don't know anything about Danielle's past,' said Aunt Pris, 'but this hypothesis is ridiculous. Danielle, shooting Bill with a bow and arrow? Absurd!' The other adults nodded vigorously.

'Not ridiculous,' said Brigadier Mabille. 'I have interrogated Danielle. She says William Leroux went to his room at eight in the evening. She did household tasks until nine, and then brought him tea. That leaves a window of an hour for the crime to have been committed. The police team coming from the mainland tomorrow will give a more precise estimate of the time of death, but I have to ask you: where were you all, between eight and nine?'

Uncle Quentin immediately replied, 'We were still having dinner between eight and eight thirty. All of us, adults and children. We were all in this room.'

'And then?' asked Brigadier Mabille.

'Then, at eight thirty, Pris suggested we opened our heirloom boxes. Lucian had specified we needed to do this separately, so everyone went to different rooms. As far as I'm concerned, at nine I was in the kitchen, playing with the little radio Lucian had left me.'

'Right,' Brigadier Mabille said. 'So there's a half-hour window when anyone could *say* they were in a room opening their box, but could in fact have been in Bill's room. Now, don't get angry,' he added quickly. 'I'm just stating *facts*. Does anyone remember seeing Danielle at any time between eight thirty and nine?'

Silence. Then, 'No,' 'No,' 'I don't think so,' went the adults around the table, slightly awkwardly.

'Interesting,' Brigadier Mabille said. 'Very interesting.'

'Wait a minute,' said Uncle Quentin, suddenly standing up. 'If Danielle *could* be the murderer, why on earth have we left her in charge of Jazz and Amy?'

Joseph and I barely had time to step away from the door and hide behind the staircase – the door swung open, and the adults rushed up the stairs. Two seconds later, we heard a scream:

'The children are fine!'

And then another:

'But Danielle isn't here any more!'

Brigadier Mabille, who'd only just left the dining-room, crossed his arms and took his phone out. 'Looks like someone's got a guilty conscience. Listen, I don't think she'll strike again – clearly she wanted what Bill had, and left with it. She'll probably try to take a boat to the mainland. I'll call the harbour.'

'What do *we* do?' Aunt Pris asked.

'Nothing. You all stay here. The team from the mainland will be here at ten in the morning. We'll keep you updated if we find Ms Darzac.'

And he was off.

'Well,' I whispered, 'that was a bit of a slapdash deduction, wasn't it?'

Joseph scoffed. 'Oh, was it, Sherlock? Come on. Running away is a sign of a guilty conscience.'

'Really? She left the mansion. Big deal.'

'Yes, big deal! Why would you do that if you weren't guilty?'

'Why would you do that if you *were* guilty? If she had any sense, she'd stay and avoid looking suspicious.'

'Oh, Marcel,' sighed Joseph, rolling his eyes. 'Stop talking nonsense. Listen – we need to find Brigadier Mabille and tell him about the arrows. He needs to know she's probably armed.'

'She's only got a bow, not even an ar–'

'Hurry *up*!'

But Brigadier Mabille's car was already pulling out of the driveway.

And to the left of the mansion, at the bottom of the garden . . . was a *fire*.

'*Fire*!'

We sprinted down the long lawn towards the bright yellow light. It was a small, controlled fire, in a pit in the ground. Clearly visible against the flames, like a . . . yes, like a magic lantern character, was a black silhouette – Danielle, doubtlessly.

She threw something into the fire, and slipped off into the woods.

'Quick, let's get that before it burns!'

We ran to the pit. Joseph rolled up his shirt and coat sleeves – I gaped at his much-bigger-forearms-than-mine – and picked up a branch from the ground. Swiftly, he pulled the burning object out of the fire.

It was a notebook, blackened and crumbling.

'We can't open it here,' I said. 'It'll fall to pieces. And we won't be able to read a line in this darkness. Let's go back to the house.'

Joseph wrapped the notebook in his scarf. But before we could get to our room, we saw my mum and Uncle Quentin heading our way.

'Shall we give them the notebook?' I asked.

'No way. We'd be told off,' Joseph replied. He meant he wanted to see what was in it first – which made me guiltily happy.

But there was nowhere else to go in that corridor, to escape the parents, other than *right into the green room*.

So we opened the door, and slipped under the red string which had been half-heartedly hung as a poor excuse for a DO NOT CROSS cordon.

U ncle Bill's dead body wasn't a pretty sight.

'Don't touch anything,' said Joseph.

I rolled my eyes. 'I know, Joe, I'm not an idiot.'

I sat down on a chair, and scanned the floor of the room. 'I think Bill's gift was something mechanical.'

'Oh yeah?' muttered Joseph. 'How d'you know that, then?'

'There are bits and bobs left on the floor from where the box fell, look. A coil there, near the window, and a little metal bar nearer the desk. And . . .'

'It's bits of *lock*, Marcel. Remember we broke the door? Hey, look at *that*.'

Joseph was standing in front of a big, old portrait on the wall, right by the desk where Bill was sitting. A portrait of an old-fashioned lady with a dog.

'What about it?'

'There's a hole in it.'

There was indeed: right in the face of the poor oil-painted lady. I'd mistaken it for a mole.

'It wasn't there earlier,' Joseph said.

'Earlier when?'

'When I helped Uncle Bill move in. I know, because he said it was their grandmother's portrait. So I looked at it, and it definitely didn't have a hole in it.'

Forgetting his own injunction not to touch anything, Joseph picked up from the desk a slim letter opener and inserted it in the gash.

There was a *tzing!* and he pulled out . . .

'A spring.'

A slim, steely spring, roughly the size of my middle finger.

'What's it doing here?'

'Oh, blimey . . .' whispered Joseph. 'I *think* I know.'

He walked to the broken door opposite the desk, which still had its lock half hanging off its screws and the key inside the keyhole.

'I've seen this in a film. Look, if you coil the end of the spring around –' he showed me – 'the handle of the key . . . and then you stretch the spring down to the bottom of the door . . .' (It didn't quite reach.) 'OK, then you tie something like an elastic band to make it longer –' he picked up a rubber band from the desk organiser and did it – 'and you pass it under the door. Then as you leave the room, you pull the band hard until the spring makes the key twist in the lock on the other side. And voila! The door would lock itself. It would look like it's been *locked from the inside*.'

He tried it on the open door. It sort of worked, but took a long time and a lot of tugging. Ultimately, the key turned, and the spring . . . sprang out, limply.

'This is how the murderer made it look like the door had been locked by Uncle Bill himself.'

'The spring doesn't jump all the way to the portrait, though,' I murmured.

'Yes, Marcel, *thank you* for your extraordinary insight. Have you noticed the lock's *broken*?' Joseph said. 'And that I've tried it with the door not in the same place? Course it would jump further. And no one would notice a little spring just lying on the floor. 'Specially as it'd mingle with bits of the door we broke.'

'OK. Seems like a lot of trouble for a murderer, though. I mean, personally, I'd just murder and then run away. Why make it look like the room was locked anyway? Anyone can tell Uncle Bill didn't kill himself . . .'

'Marcel! *Hello*! This is a *murderer*. They don't reason like us.'

'But –'

'Come on, let's find the adults and call Mabille to tell him . . .'

'Wait, didn't you want to look at that notebook?'

'Oh, I'd forgotten. Yeah, I guess.'

He sat down, and perfunctorily opened the blackened notebook. It was a kind of diary, with blueprints, drawings and notes, by Uncle Lucian. Joseph flicked through them.

'Hey, slow down, we need to read it properly . . .'

'Let's just cut to the chase,' he grumbled, flicking through dozens of pages with diagrams and maps. 'Ah-ha! Here we are: an entry about Uncle Bill! This is dated . . . two weeks ago! Yep, damning evidence.'

Among a page of notes rambling about – as far as I could tell – death, illness and old age, there were a few sentences: '*And Bill – that rat – that's another one I won't miss in whatever wretched place I end up in beyond this life. But at least he won't survive me long anyway, if my faithful servant executes my orders as planned. Let's just hope we're not sent to the same corner of hell.*'

'Oh my *goodness*,' I whispered. 'Uncle Lucian wanted to kill Uncle Bill!'

Joseph tried to laugh, but it sounded more like a cackle. 'Yes, Uncle Lucian planned Bill's murder before he died! *Uncle Lucian asked Danielle to kill Uncle Bill!*'

He stared at me. 'High five! We've got our killer and our motive. Now let's go tell the parents.'

At five o'clock that morning, Danielle Darzac was arrested off the coast of the island, trying to escape in a small dinghy. No bow was found on her, or anything that could have been in Uncle Bill's box, and at first she denied everything.

But then she admitted a few things: *yes*, she'd tried to burn the notebook; Uncle Lucian had asked her to burn it before he'd died but she'd forgotten all about it until last night, and then . . . she'd read it and realised what it contained.

But she claimed her innocence again and again. She had no idea how Bill had been killed, or by whom. Lucian must have asked someone else to do it – another 'servant'. It wasn't her, it wasn't her, she swore.

This is what murderers do, sometimes, Brigadier Mabille told us. They lie.

But I *didn't* find that explanation satisfactory.

As everyone was packing the next day, I stayed in my bedroom and watched the magic lantern turn.

I couldn't get my head around that case.

We knew that Uncle Lucian had organised Uncle Bill's murder.

We knew that Uncle Bill had been killed by one of Uncle Lucian's arrows.

We knew that Danielle had run away, and had known

about the contents of the notebook.

But . . .

But it didn't quite *fit*. Not for me.

'Joseph,' I said as my cousin walked into my bedroom, carrying his bag. 'I don't get it. I don't understand why Danielle would make it look like the room had been locked from the inside, when it was so obvious that Bill hadn't killed himself. I mean, if she'd wanted to, she could have set it up as a suicide scene. And I don't understand why she'd use such a weird weapon. I don't understand where the stolen object is. Where's the bow? *Where is the bow?*'

'She probably got scared and chucked it into the sea, or something,' said Joseph. 'You're such a kid sometimes! Getting all "Why? And how? And when?" We've *got* an explanation.'

My face was hot and my eyes annoyingly prickly as I gathered my stuff. I walked out, and down the corridor, and was about to take the staircase when I heard a pitiful squeak from the library.

I opened the door. Mrs Feather the canary was lying on the floor of her cage, dead, although her wing was still fluttering.

'Oh, blimey – who did that to you?' I opened the cage and picked up the warm bird.

She looked just like Mrs Whistlewell had the day before. What could have gone through the bars of the cage? I tried to dislodge the water dispenser near the feeder to clean the bird's wounds and see them more clearly.

'Ouch! What the hell is *that*?'

*That* was a long and sharp metal pin, supposed to hold the water dispenser in place. It had come loose – and injured my finger. I realised that it sprang out if weight was applied on a specific spot of the little perch.

'*That's* what it was! Poor birds. They were just trying to drink, and got speared by that thing. Sorry we thought you were a murderer, Mrs Feather. It did *look* like she'd been mur– *Wait a minute!*'

A minute later I was running towards Uncle Lucian's cabin.

And two minutes later, I had proof.


'I have proof that Danielle Darzac did not kill Uncle Bill.'

The whole family, across the table, stared wide-eyed at me. 'Marcel,' Mum said, 'don't be silly.'

'Uncle Bill wasn't killed for what was in his heirloom box,' I said.

'Do you *know* what was in his box?' Uncle Quentin whispered.

'Yes. I'll get to that soon. First, the murderer. Uncle Bill was killed by Uncle Lucian. By Uncle Lucian *alone*, with no help from anyone.'

'Oh, really? He's still alive, then?' Joseph sniggered.

'No. He didn't need to be. His faithful servant did it for him after his death, as he'd said.'

'His faithful servant isn't Danielle?'

I picked up the metal box I'd brought from Uncle Lucian's cabin. 'No. It's this.'

Mum sighed. 'What do you *mean*, Marcel?'

'Want to open it, Joseph?'

Joseph raised an eyebrow. He got up, walked around the table, and opened the box.

*SHPLINK!* A cotton bud flew straight in his face. 'Hey! What's *that?*'

'A kind of catapult box. Uncle Lucian wasn't practising *archery* in his laboratory. He was designing a box that could fire an arrow when opened. No bow was found anywhere because there was never any bow.'

I showed them the inside of the box. 'I found this one in the shed. Looks like a prototype. Look, it's got all sorts of springs and bits of metal. You insert the projectile right here, and close the box, which tenses the springs. They're still in place now, because I've only put in a light cotton bud instead. My guess is that they're much more tensed when they're holding a heavy metal arrow. So when the box is opened and the arrow fired, the whole thing would probably just . . . disintegrate. Throwing coils and springs around.'

'You mean that the spring we found in the portrait . . .' Joseph whispered.

'. . . was just a loose one from the box, yes. Like the ones that were lying around and that we thought were bits of the door. The room *had* been locked from the inside – by Uncle Bill himself. No one else was ever in it. Uncle Bill simply opened his heirloom box. It fired an arrow at him. He died. The box fell on the floor. It looked empty – and it was – but it wasn't empty because its contents had been stolen. Its contents were all over the room, including right in the middle of Uncle Bill's chest.'

Uncle Quentin dropped his head in his hands. 'So you mean that what Uncle Lucian bequeathed his brother was . . .'

'Death. Pretty much.'

Little Jazz gasped. 'Mollicles of nothing,' she murmured.

As our parents called the police *again*, Joseph came up to me, frowning.

'This is crazy. Who would wish their brother *dead*, even after their own death? What could Bill possibly have done to Lucian to make him resent him so much?'

'We can only guess. It was probably Bill's fault too. Bill was probably mean to Lucian. He must have underestimated him and dismissed him and didn't listen to him. He must have thought himself better than him. Those things can hurt.'

77

Joseph looked at me, and nodded.

'Yeah,' he said. 'I'm sure they can.'

And he tapped my shoulder with his fist. 'You did well, mate. You did really well. I'm sorry we've drifted apart. I'm sure that can be fixed, no?'

I smiled, and tried to look cool.

'Yeah, I guess.'

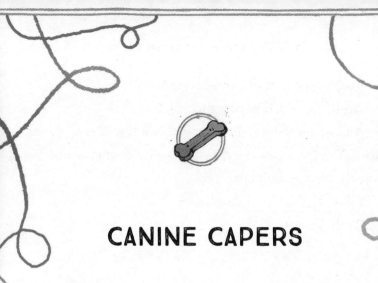

# CANINE CAPERS

**D**ogs can be a detective's best friend – they're loyal, they're brave and they're excellent at sniffing out clues. So when a canine goes missing, it's catastrophic.

These three doggy puzzles have three very different endings – can you solve a monstrous mystery on the moors, a dogwalking disaster and a Wild West crime?

# THE MYSTERY OF DIABLO CANYON CIRCLE
## By Caroline Lawrence

In England, summer holidays last six weeks, but in America they last for three whole months. My older brother Cliff said summer vacation was the best thing about our move from London to California last year, but I was dreading it. Those ninety days stretched away to the horizon like an empty road going through a desert full of bleached cow skulls.

Cliff and I are opposites: I like school and he hates it.

I like movies set in the Wild West; he prefers *Dr Who* and *Sherlock*.

I like American food such as burritos and hot dogs, but he misses bangers 'n' mash and Marmite on toast.

The one thing we both agreed about was that we wanted to spend part of the summer holiday at Lake Arrowhead

Camp. I wanted to go because there were Western activities like horse riding, canoeing, archery and sitting around a campfire at night. Cliff wanted to go because lots of his friends would be there. And also there would be girls.

But Dad said we couldn't afford it this year, so we would just have to make our own fun like pioneer kids did in the olden days. (Dad likes Western movies too; he was the one who got me started.)

On the first day of the summer holiday, my mother was trying to get Cliff out of bed.

'Come on, Cliff,' she said. 'Rise and shine. Look.' She pointed at me. 'Darcy is already up.'

'Mum! It's Saturday. And it's the holidays!' Cliff grumbled. 'I want to sleep some more. It's not like we have anything to do.'

'I'll drive you to the park later,' she said in her firm voice. 'I want you and Darcy to play outdoors before it gets too hot. I want to get in an hour of writing while Rochester is having his nap. He's been up since the crack of dawn.'

'Come on, Cliff!' I urged. I was already dressed in shorts, my *True Grit* T-shirt and flip-flops.

'No!' Cliff put his pillow over his head.

'If you come now,' said Mum, 'I'll make buttermilk pancakes with maple syrup and nice crispy bacon.'

Half a minute later, my brother was up. Half an hour

later we were tossing a Frisbee back and forth.

When my mum says she wants us to play outdoors, she means in our back yard. Now that we live in America, she will not allow us to go out front and ride our bikes or scooters on the street.

It's not even like we live in one of those dangerous towns you see on the news. We live in a quiet neighbourhood of a pretty town called Santa Clarita in sunny southern California. Some people call this area 'Hollywood's Back Yard' because this is where they used to film all those old Western movies. These days they mostly make crime dramas here, but there is still a film ranch that looks like a Wild West town.

In London we used to walk all the time, but nobody walks here. They drive everywhere. My dad says it's a car culture. If you walk on some of the streets, the police will stop and ask if you are all right.

So we were out in our back yard, which has an awning over a concrete patio and a patch of grass with a half-inflated paddling pool in it. For the first five minutes Cliff and I enjoyed throwing my Frisbee back and forth. Then he got grumpy.

He threw the Frisbee carelessly and it hit me in my chest.

'Ow! That hurt, Heathcliff!'

Cliff's name really is Heathcliff, but I only call him that

when I'm mad at him. He hates it and usually rewards me with a punch.

So when he charged me, I threw the Frisbee back hard. It hit him in the stomach.

'Darcy, you idiot!' he yelled.

He picked up the Frisbee and spun it as hard as he could out over the fence and the roofs of the houses beyond.

'Cliff!' I yelled. 'That was my limited edition *Rango* Frisbee. Go get it!'

'You go get it,' he snarled, and he stomped inside, slamming the back door behind him.

I heard Rochester crying and then Mum yelling at Cliff.

I ran to the fence and pulled myself up high enough to look over. No sign of my Frisbee.

Then I went to the garden gate and opened the latch. The door swung open and I hesitated.

Mum had told us never to go out without asking permission, but I could hear her yelling at Cliff and I knew if I asked permission to go look for my Frisbee she would say no.

So I quietly stepped through the garden door and closed it behind me with a gentle push.

It was a beautiful morning, with a high blue sky. Later it would be blisteringly hot but at that moment it was still fresh. I could hear the chunter of sprinklers and the buzz of someone's lawn mower. I caught a whiff of newly cut grass.

I crept down the driveway hugging the half wall where it met our neighbour's fence, then slipped around the corner. The street sign said Diablo Canyon Circle. I had lived in Santa Clarita for nine months but I had never been here before.

I could see six houses in a kind of semicircle. A narrow path between the middle two houses led to a hill, the crest of which we could see from our house. I once asked my dad about that hill and he said it was a natural refuge for native grasses, weeds, oak trees, coyotes and rattlesnakes. My mum said it was more likely a tick refuge and told us that California grasses harbour a tick that can give you Lyme disease. I'm guessing it does more than make you turn lime green.

Anyway, I scanned the six houses of Diablo Canyon Circle and spotted my Frisbee right away. It was lying on the lawn of one of the houses on my right. The sprinklers were going, and the sun made rainbows in the mist. I picked my way among them; the fine spray of cool water felt good on my bare legs. As I bent to pick up my Frisbee, a woman's voice said, 'Get off my lawn, kid!'

It was an old lady in a pink tracksuit, standing in her doorway. Mum has told me never to use the F-word here in America, so I will just say she was heavy.

I held up the Frisbee. 'Sorry!' I called. 'Just getting my Frisbee.'

As I started back home, a picture of a dog on a lamp post caught my eye.

I went to have a closer look. The dog had a squashed nose and silky cream and tan fur that only partly hid his big button black eyes and nose. He was so cute he would have made a tough movie cowboy like John Wayne say, 'Awwww!' There was writing on the sign. It said:

LOST DOG! REWARD!
HAVE YOU SEEN SHANE?
SMALL MALE SHIH-TZU, WHITE AND TAN
$2500 REWARD OFFERED FOR HIS RETURN
OR INFORMATION LEADING TO THE
RECOVERY OF THIS BELOVED PET
ABSOLUTELY NO QUESTIONS ASKED!

There was also the phone number and the date he went missing, which was Wednesday night three days earlier.

'Goldarn dog!' The voice made me start. I turned to see the big lady in pink who had yelled at me to get off her lawn. She had crept up behind me as quiet as an Apache scout.

'Used to poop on my lawn every goldarn day.' The lady was scowling at the sign. 'I hope he's dead.'

I said, 'You want that cute little dog to be dead just because he pooped on your lawn?'

The woman shrugged. 'Maybe not dead. Maybe just gone on vacation. A long vacation. Who are you, anyway?'

'My name is Darcy Day,' I said, holding out my hand as I had been taught. 'I live around the corner. My brother threw the Frisbee over on to your lawn, not me.' 'I'm Polly.' She gave my hand a firm shake. I guessed she was about my grandmother's age.

'Pleased to meet you,' I said.

She cocked her head. 'You got a funny accent. You from England?'

I nodded. 'London. My mum is American and my dad is English. He's a film editor,' I added.

'Santa Clarita Studios?' she said.

'In his dreams,' I replied. 'He's freelance at the moment, working on a job in Burbank.' I pointed at the poster of the cute dog. 'Is that the dog we can hear barking at night? My dad calls them yapper dogs.'

'That's the culprit,' she said. 'The only time he's not barking is when Madz lets him out so he can poop on my lawn and annoy the other neighbours.'

'We can hear him when the air-conditioning is off,' I said.

She said, 'I don't mind the barking so much; I can take out my hearing aid. But I do mind the mess.'

'So he lives in one of these houses?'

Polly nodded. 'Yup.'

'Which one?'

She cocked her head. 'You thinking of looking for him? You want the reward?'

I nodded vigorously.

She looked at my *True Grit* T-shirt. Then she looked at the limited edition *Rango* Frisbee in my hand. 'You like Western movies?'

I nodded.

'Then you tell me where he lived.' She gestured at the other five houses. 'Be a detective. Look for clues.'

I turned and looked at the other five houses. They were all one-storey houses just like ours: three bedrooms, two bathrooms, one garage. They were either beige or cream with dark red or brown slate roofs. But although the houses were similar, their front yards were distinctive.

House One across the street had some clumps of pampas grass, some eucalyptus trees and some rose bushes near the front door. Its grass was pretty dry. There was a pickup truck in the drive.

House Two had a trimmed hedge around a well-kept lawn. I could see five pink balloons on the door and a pink scooter lying on the driveway near a Mercedes and a white Ford.

House Three had two motorcycles in the driveway. Also, the garage door was open and I could see another motorcycle in there, partly in bits.

House Four had no cars in the driveway, a covered-up barbecue on the porch and a few small rose bushes around medium-green grass. There was a basketball hoop over the garage but it was rusty. Six newspapers lay on the lawn near the front door, still in their plastic wrappers. It looked like whoever lived there had been away for nearly a week.

Then I looked at House Five, the one next to Polly's, and my jaw dropped.

The whole front yard looked like something out of a Western movie.

Instead of grass it had yellow and tan pebbles with little round cactus plants poking up and also some of those spiky shaggy-trunked yucca trees like in the movie *Rango*.

There was a pink jeep and a vintage red convertible Mustang in the driveway. Instead of having a number on the mailbox, it had the name *Rancho Vaquero* burnt into a piece of wood above it. I knew 'vaquero' was Spanish for 'cowboy'. I guessed the people who lived there must like cowboys a whole lot.

Then I remembered something. Shane is the name of the main character in a classic Western movie called *Shane*.

I pointed to the house with the desert garden. 'Shane's

owners live there,' I said. 'Right?'

'Correct,' she said, making it sound like two words. 'An actress named Madz Caramel lives there. She is crazy about Westerns. And cowboys,' she added under her breath.

I went to have a closer look, leaving wet flip-flop prints on the smooth white sidewalk. Then I saw something that made my blood run cold.

I pointed at a small white animal skull lying by a round cactus. 'I think I have found Shane,' I said. 'Or all that is left of him.'

Polly came hurrying up but when I pointed out the grisly remains, she laughed.

'How could that skull belong to the missing dog?' she said. 'Shane has a little squished face like he was chasing a car and it stopped all of a sudden. That skull has a narrow, pointed muzzle. If you want to be a detective, you've got to use your eyes and your brain,' she said. 'Observe and think.'

I looked at the skull and nodded. 'You're right,' I admitted. 'That was sloppy detective work.'

We both bent over to examine it more closely.

'I wonder what animal it belongs to?' I said.

'That there,' said a gravelly voice, 'is a coyote skull.'

We both looked up to see a tall and skinny old man in a cowboy hat shuffling across the street towards us. He was coming from House One. He had his newspaper under his arm, still in a plastic wrapper to keep it dry from sprinklers.

'A coyote?' I said. Western movies have taught me that a coyote is a kind of wild dog they have here in America, sort of like a fox in Britain. The local paper recently had an article about how urban coyotes were getting to be a nuisance – stealing pets and raiding garbage.

'What is a coyote skull doing here?' I asked. 'Where is the rest of it?'

The old man snorted. 'I reckon they consider it landscaping.' He pointed a trembly finger at the sign on the mailbox. '*Rancho Vaquero!*' He snorted again and shook his head. 'They should call it *Rancho Gringo.*'

I knew from watching Westerns that a *gringo* is what people in Mexico call a foolish white person who does not know the ways of the west.

I looked at the old man. He wore a battered white cowboy hat, a brick-red shirt and dark-blue jeans. He had thick glasses and one of those bolo neckties which looks like a shoestring with silver tips and a clasp that goes up and down to make it tight or loose. His skin was as tan as leather.

'Hello, Mr Colachi,' said Pink Polly. 'How are you today?'

'Better than I have been in a long time,' he said. 'And so is my Rose. Thanks to a few good nights' sleep without that yapping dog.'

'What's going on here?' said a third voice. It was a man

in running shoes, shorts and glasses. He had jogged over from House Two, with the hedge and the balloons on the door. 'That dog still missing?' he said, pulling his earbuds out. 'Good riddance. He chased my Chelsea last week and made her fall and scrape her knee.'

'Is Chelsea your five-year-old daughter?' I asked.

'Why yes! How did you know?'

'Five pink balloons on your door,' I imitated a Western drawl so that he wouldn't get distracted by my English accent. 'I'm guessing her birthday party is this afternoon?'

The man nodded and Polly gently elbowed me in the ribs. 'Good detective work,' she said under her breath. Her encouragement made me bold.

'What do y'all think happened to the dog?' I asked them. I kept my American accent because it made me feel more like a detective.

'I think it was petnappers,' said Chelsea's dad. 'It's a growing industry here in the valley. 'Look how much they are offering for that mutt, no questions asked. It's an invitation to the criminal class.'

His T-shirt said 'CRIME DOESN'T PAY' in big letters.

Underneath, in small print it said 'UNLESS YOU'RE A LAWYER'.

I guessed he was a lawyer.

'But there hasn't been a ransom demand,' said Pink

Polly. 'I know because Madz told me so this morning when she was picking up her paper.'

'They don't have to ask for ransom,' said a big man in black leather. He had a beard and a ponytail and was coming from House Three, the one with the motorcycles. 'I saw a documentary about it. Those dognappers just turn up with the dog and say they found it wandering in the hills or by the side of the road. They get the reward with no questions asked. But they usually show up within forty-eight hours,' he added, 'so I think it is good news for us.'

'You didn't like Shane either?' I said.

He shook his shaggy head. 'Hell no!' he said. 'That mutt was always chasing our motorcycles, and once he nearly made my old lady crash.'

I spotted the coyote skull and that gave me an idea.

'Maybe a coyote got him,' I said. 'You can hear them sometimes at night.' I pointed towards the little golden hill peeking up from behind the roofs. 'I think one lives up there on the hill behind your house,' I added.

'Yup,' said Motorcycle Man. 'I see her sometimes just after dark. She is pretty mangy.'

Old Mr Colachi said, 'Yes, coyotes check their territory at dawn and dusk. But it is unlikely that a coyote took a family pet. They prefer to rummage in the garbage for old burritos and half-eaten hamburgers.'

I almost reminded him that the newspaper had just been urging residents to keep their pets inside because of the threat of coyote attacks. But maybe an old cowboy like him knew better.

Then I noticed something by a cactus. 'Could that be coyote poop?'

Old Mr Colachi rested his bony hands on his knees and bent forward. 'My eyesight is not so good these days,' he said. 'Is it furry?'

'Furry?' I said.

'Yup,' he said bluntly. 'Coyote poop looks just like dog poop, only furry, on account of any critters it might have eaten like mice, rats or voles.'

'That is most definitely Shane poop,' said Pink Polly. 'I have cleaned it up enough to recognise it. He usually waits till Madz isn't looking to do it on my nice soft grass.'

'Does he ever come out without Madz?' I asked.

'Nope.'

'Is there any way Shane could have got out on his own?'

'I reckon not,' said Motorcycle Man. 'They have a big door like the rest of us.'

We all looked at the door to the back yard. It was made of solid wood and painted white with a hint of pink like the rest of the house. Suddenly it opened, almost as if our stares had power.

'Oh my gosh!' gasped Pink Polly. 'It's him!'

A man was coming towards us. He was barefoot and wearing jeans, a faded grey sweatshirt and a white cowboy hat. He was broad in the shoulders and slim in the hips. He had dark hair and dark eyes and was probably the best-looking man I had ever seen in my life.

Chelsea's dad nodded. 'It's that sheriff from *High Noon in Hollywood*. He's been dating Madz.'

Hogg grinned. 'He was here last weekend too. I know because he drives the same sixty-five convertible Mustang he does in the TV series.'

I looked closer and saw that red convertible. Sure enough, it was the very car from the TV show about the Arizona sheriff who is reassigned to Hollywood. Even Cliff likes that show. My family watches it every Saturday once Rochester is in bed.

'Be still my beating heart,' said Polly.

I did not think I would be star-struck, but my heart was thumping too.

'Please tell me you got some good news of that dog,' drawled the star of *High Noon in Hollywood*. 'My girlfriend is beside herself with worry.' Then he smiled, showing the whitest teeth I have ever seen. 'I'm Jake Wyoming,' he added.

'We know,' breathed Polly, her cheeks as pink as the rest of her.

'Pleased to meet you, sir,' stammered Motorcycle Man. 'I love your TV series. Never miss an episode. I'm Hogg,' he added. 'With two Gs.'

'Aaron Nebbish,' said Chelsea's dad. 'Big fan,' he added. I noticed that the tops of his ears were red.

'Luis Colachi,' said the old man, holding out his hand. 'Don't have a TV and never heard of you, but it's a pleasure anyways.'

Jake Wyoming shook the old man's hand. 'They told me a real cowboy lived around here,' he said. 'That you?'

'Yup,' said Mr Colachi. 'I am one of the last of the vaqueros.'

Jake Wyoming touched his hat. 'I might come to you for advice, if you don't mind.'

'It would be my pleasure,' said old Mr Colachi. I noticed his leathery skin had taken on a ruddy flush too.

The famous TV star turned to me and raised his eyebrow. 'And you are?'

My hand was trembling but I stuck it out. 'My name is Darcy Day,' I said. 'And I am going to find your dog.'

He shook it firmly. 'Well, Darcy,' he said, 'if you can find poor Shane, dead or alive, I promise the reward is yours.'

'Dead or alive?' I echoed.

He gave a solemn nod. 'I'm afraid Madz will not move on until she has proof he is alive or dead. She needs closure. We were not there that night – we were at a movie premiere, and Madz blames herself.'

I said. 'Do you mind my asking if your house is secure?'

'It's not a fortress,' he said. 'But it's as secure as the others around here.' He gestured at it. 'Six-foot-high wooden fence all around.'

I nodded. 'And was there any way that Shane could have got out on his own?'

'Nope,' said Jake Wyoming. 'Come see.'

We all followed him up his driveway and he showed us a garden gate like ours which you could only open from the outside if you reached over to undo the latch.

'Madz never lets him out at night,' he said, 'on account of the coyotes.'

'Jake?' said a woman as he opened the gate. 'Have they found Shane?'

My jaw dropped again. A woman stood there. She wore a checked cowboy shirt of pink and baby blue tied above her tan belly button, and faded denim shorts and little pink cowboy boots. Her yellow hair was scraped back into a ponytail. She had been crying but even with no make-up and swollen eyes she was beautiful.

'Have they found my Shane?' she asked.

'Afraid not, sweetheart,' said Jake Wyoming. He put his arm around her and gave her a squeeze. With his free hand he gestured at me. 'But young Darcy here is going to do a little detecting.'

'Please find him!' She gripped my hands in hers. She had long fingernails with pearly pink nail polish on them.

I swallowed hard. 'I will do my best,' I told her. 'May I have a quick look around your back yard? To see if there are any places that Shane could have got out?'

'Sure.' She nodded. 'But you won't find any.'

She had a really nice back yard with a swimming pool and everything, but she was right: there was no way for a dog to get out or a coyote to get in.

I hurried back home and quietly let myself in. Thankfully Mum didn't even realise I had been gone. She was dressing Rochester for an afternoon in the park. Cliff was slouched on the sofa, playing a game.

'May I use the computer?' I asked her. 'It's homework. Mrs Wilmer asked us to do a big project about Santa Clarita history.'

'If you're sure you want to work today,' she said. 'We'll be back around four. Make yourself a peanut butter sandwich for lunch. You've got your phone. Text me if you need anything. You know the drill.'

'Yes, I do,' I said, and waved vaguely in their direction. 'Have a good time.'

I finished doing my research about noon.

I had a theory but I would have to go outside to test it out.

Even though it was now about a hundred degrees out there I put on double socks and long jeans and my Wellington boots from England. I changed my *True Grit* T-shirt for a long sleeved shirt. Finally, I took my dad's old beekeeping hat and Mum's cream leather gloves that she had worn on her wedding day.

'Just let a Lyme tick try to bite me,' I said to myself as I went out the back door of the house.

It was hot enough to fry an egg on the sunny part of our patio, but my research had told me that coyotes like to sleep during the day, so I thought it would be best to go up to Coyote Hill now.

I stretched to unlatch the garden gate and was careful to close it behind me. Somehow, leaving the house by the garden gate didn't seem as bad as leaving by the front door.

I went around the corner into Diablo Canyon Circle. It was deserted with no sprinklers or sign of life, just the hot sun beating down. As I went up the path between Hogg's house and House Four, I saw those newspapers on the lawn again. I realised the people who lived there could not have been involved – they had already been away for three days on the night Shane went missing.

There was a dirt path leading up to a hill of golden dried grasses. It was just like being in a Western movie. I could smell the spicy, dusty smell through the net of my beekeeper's hat. I could hear crickets throbbing. I found a hollow in the ground by an oak tree where someone had made a fire. I saw some empty beer cans and an empty packet of Doritos.

It didn't take me long to find the coyote hole. It was right there in the hillside, a little dark circle in the brown dirt half hidden by golden weeds.

Then I saw something else. Right beside the trail was some coyote poop; I know because it was furry.

The fur was Shane coloured.

Outside the coyote hole was something that made my blood run cold. Some little half-chewed bones. They might have belonged to a rabbit or a bobcat. Or Shane. I needed one more piece of proof.

Then I found it.

It was a little dog tag shaped like a blue bone with a spot of rusty blood on it. It said 'SHANE' on one side and had a phone number on the back.

I had brought a couple of clear plastic sandwich bags in case I found clues. I put the evidence in them, sealed them and put them in my backpack. I was glad I was wearing my mum's gloves so I did not have to touch those things. While

I had my backpack open, I lifted the veil of my beekeeper's hat and took a long swig from my water bottle.

I felt sad and also happy. Sad that I had discovered poor Shane's fate, but happy that Madz Caramel could have closure. As I came back into Diablo Canyon Circle, I stopped right in the road and looked at the houses, and I knew that I had only solved part of the mystery.

The coyote had killed poor little Shane. But she must have had a human accomplice. Someone must have opened the latch of Madz Caramel's back gate and let Shane out around the time the coyote did her rounds.

Four of Shane's neighbours had the motive and means to open that gate.

Pink Polly hated the way the dog pooped on her lawn.

Old Mr Colachi hated the way Shane's barking kept his sick wife awake at night.

Aaron Nebbish hated the way the dog chased his little girl.

And Hogg hated that Shane almost caused his wife to crash her motorcycle.

Jake Wyoming might have secretly wanted the dog dead, too, but I had eliminated him as a suspect because I had found pictures on the internet of him and Madz at the movie premiere on the evening Shane had disappeared.

Then a voice said, 'Sweet Jesus, what are you got up as?'

It was Old Mr Colachi across the street. He was checking his mailbox.

I pulled off my beekeeper's hat and stuffed it in my backpack along with my mum's gloves. 'I'm armed against ticks and rattlesnakes,' I said. 'I was exploring that little hill up there. I found a coyote hole and nearby some furry poop and chewed dog bones and Shane's bloody dog tag. I guess now we know what happened to him.'

Mr Colachi crossed himself like they do in the movies and shook his head sadly. 'Poor little critter,' he said. 'He has gone to a Better Place.' Then he looked at me. 'I don't suppose you would you like to come inside for a glass of soda pop?'

I hesitated. Mum would have a fit if she knew I was outside. She would have a triple fit if she knew I was going into a stranger's house. She would have a mega-meltdown if she knew I was going into the house of a suspect in a crime case.

Then I had an idea. 'Sure,' I said. 'Just let me text my mum.'

'Quite right,' he said.

I took out my phone and typed:

*Mr Colachi from 22342 Diablo Canyon Circle around the corner invited me for a soda. May I go?*

A moment later I got a text back: *You are OUTSIDE?*

*Yes*, I texted. *He is an old cowboy and is helping me with my project.* I did not tell her that the project was the case of the missing shih-tzu.

There was about a minute's pause. Then I got this reply: *All right, but first send me a picture of him.*

'She wants me to send her your picture first,' I said.

'Wise woman,' he said and tipped his hat back on his head so I could see his face. 'Snap away.'

I took a photo of him with his house in the background and sent it to my mum.

My mind was calm but my body was a little scared and my heart was pounding. But I felt better once I was inside his house. It was dim and cool. There was a propeller fan on the ceiling. Mr Colachi gave me a glass of root beer with ice.

'Come meet my wife, Rose,' he said. 'She should be awake by now. She would like to see a young person.'

I followed him into a room. An old lady was lying in a bed propped up on pillows. She was reading a book.

'Who's this?' she said, looking over her glasses and smiling.

'This here is Darcy,' said Mr Colachi. 'Darcy, this is my wife, Rose.'

'How do you do?' said Rose Colachi. She lifted her hand a little so I politely stepped forward and gently gave it a shake. Her fingers were cool and soft. She smelt like baby powder.

'Sit down,' she said, gesturing to an armchair.

I sat in the room with her. Mr Colachi went out and then brought in a tray with some persimmon cookies he had baked himself. I had never had persimmon cookies before. They were delicious.

Mr Colachi sat in a chair on the other side of the bed and they told me stories of Santa Clarita when it was still canyons and dry creeks and golden hills and the railroad. They told me about a famous bandit who lived near here called Vasquez. They finished each other's sentences and smiled at each other a lot.

Later, when Mr Colachi walked me to the front door he said, 'The doctors say Rose will probably not last the summer. It has been a long time since I saw her so happy.' He shook my hand. Behind his thick glasses his eyes were full of tears.

I waited until I was outside on his porch with Pink Polly watching from her doorway and Hogg cleaning his bike in the shade of his garage and Chelsea waving goodbye to some of her party guests with Mr Nebbish beside her. Then I turned back to him.

'The coyote killed Shane,' I said, loud enough that everyone could hear. 'But somebody opened the gate and let him out just before she did her rounds. I am going to tell Madz and Jake about Shane and the coyote after dinner. But

I am not going to tell them who opened the gate.'

Mr Luis Colachi blinked at me. Then he hung his head and nodded. 'Understood,' he said. He looked up at me and gave a wobbly smile. 'Maybe you could visit us again tomorrow?'

When Dad got home that evening I told my family all about my day.

'You know that dog that barks all night?'

'The yapper dog?' said my dad.

Mum said, 'I haven't heard it recently.'

'It belonged to an actress who is dating Jake Wyoming. She lives just behind us in Diablo Canyon Circle. The dog was called Shane and he went missing Wednesday evening,' I said. 'Today I figured out what happened to him and I am going around after dinner to collect the reward.'

'A reward?' said Cliff, his face lighting up. 'Tell us!'

I told them about the suspects and showed them the grisly clues.

'You went up into the tick refuge?' my mum cried.

'Yes, but I was well protected,' I said. 'The coyote killed Shane, but she had a human accomplice.'

'What's accomplish?' asked Rochester, who is not quite four.

'It means a helper,' I said.

'Who was it?' cried Cliff and my parents.

'All four had motives,' I said. 'But three of them are innocent. The culprit is the person with the strongest motive.'

'Oh, I know!' said Cliff. He whispered in my ear.

'Yup,' I said.

'Give me one more clue,' said Dad.

'It is the person who told me a coyote would probably not take a household pet, even though reports of that have been in his newspaper, and then admitted that coyotes have furry poop because they eat small critters.'

'Old Mr Colachi?' cried Mum, covering her mouth in horror.

'Yup,' I said. 'Polly may not have liked Shane, but she was helpful to me – the culprit would never have done that. And Shane did not actually hurt Mr Nebbish's daughter, or Mr Hogg's wife. The only person he really upset was Rose, Mr Colachi's wife. I reckon that's why Mr Colachi decided to get rid of him.'

'You spent the afternoon with a man who would do such a thing?' she gasped.

'His wife is dying,' I said. 'I think he would have done anything to make her last days easier.'

'Are you going to tell Shane's owner?' asked Cliff.

'I am going to tell Jake and Madz the coyote did it, but

not who let Shane out. It is up to Mr Colachi to tell them about his part in the crime, and I think he is going to do it.' I looked at my dad. 'If you come with me after dinner you can meet Jake Wyoming and maybe mention that you are a film editor.'

'Oh, Rupert!' cried my mum. 'Imagine working on *High Noon in Hollywood*!'

'Also,' I said, 'that reward money means Cliff and I can afford to go to summer camp up at Lake Arrowhead.'

'How much is the reward?' Dad asked.

When I told them they all stared at me.

Then Cliff said, 'You'd share your reward money with me? Even after I threw your Frisbee away?'

'Of course,' I said. 'If you hadn't thrown my Frisbee over the fence I'd never have met our neighbours or got the reward for solving the mystery of the missing lapdog.'

My brother grinned.

'Darcy,' he said, 'you are a darn good detective. And also the best sister ever.'

# MEL FOSTER AND THE HOUND OF THE BASKERVILLES
## By Julia Golding

Mel Foster gazed out of the window at the sleet splattering the London pavement. Slush heaped in the gutter, piled there by the crossing sweeper. A most unpromising day, but that was something he was determined to change. Mel drum-rolled his fingers on the sill.

'Eve, I want something to happen.'

Eve Frankenstein looked up from her sewing. At over seven feet tall, she was making a dress for a ball at Buckingham Palace from a bolt of green velvet. She would look like one of the towering firs in the Queen's gardens when she put it on, but Mel was too tactful to mention that.

'What kind of thing, Mel Foster?' Eve asked.

'An adventure.'

'Is living in the headquarters of the Monster Resistance not enough adventure for you?' When Eve smiled, her oddly stitched together face lifted in one place and pulled in another, showing where her creator, Frankenstein's monster himself, had connected spare body parts. When Mel first met her during a voyage to the North Pole, he had found this alarming; now he just grinned back. Until a year ago, when Londoners found out that monsters existed side by side with common folk and the Monster Resistance had become famous for saving the Queen and the Empire from certain doom, Mel had always thought himself an ordinary boy. Then he had discovered both his monstrous talent for zapping things with electricity and his knack for solving extraordinary crimes, and his life had become one adventure after another. Now it was time for a new one.

'But everyone else is busy.' He counted his friends on his fingers. 'The Jekyll twins are investigating a rogue werewolf in Whitechapel. Viorica has gone to visit her vampire relatives on the Orient Express, and the monster fairies have gone with her to sample this year's Paris fashions. The raven is in moult. Even the mummy is busy, repairing the motorcar. That just leaves us.'

'You're supposed to be doing your schoolwork.' Eve gestured with her needle to the books on a side table.

Mel tugged at his stiff shirt collar. He still missed dressing as an urchin. 'Being with you, Eve, is an education all by itself.'

Eve laughed, and tucked a lock of her long black hair behind her ear. 'Charm won't get you top marks in your arithmetic test.'

'But it can't do any harm either, can it?'

'Tell that to Abel Jekyll when he marks your paper.'

Mel sighed. But then a noise outside made him throw aside his unopened schoolbook and race downstairs, just beating their ghost butler to the door.

'Allow me, Mr Marley.'

Mr Marley gave way with a little moan of 'Doom,' wrapped his chains and cashboxes around him, and continued dusting surfaces with his spectral breezes.

Mel opened the front door. 'Can I help you?'

A stout gentleman stood on the step, hand still reaching for the knocker, his black eyebrows raised like exclamation marks in a sensational headline. 'Have I come to the right address?' By his accent Mel could tell he was from North America, which might explain why he thought it acceptable to wear a red-tinted tweed suit in London.

'That depends. Who are you after?'

The man's gaze searched over Mel's shoulder. 'Monsters. I need some monsters.'

Mel stepped back. 'Then you've definitely come to the right place.'

'But you're not –'

111

Why did people never see the monster in him? Mel held up a finger. 'Don't say it.'

'I was only going to remark that –'

'Exactly. I'm Melchizedek Foster, member of the Monster Resistance. Who might you be? And, more importantly, how did you know where to find us?'

Eve appeared on the landing and the gentleman's face cleared. 'Ah, I *am* in the right place!'

'Is everything all right, Mel Foster?' Eve called over the banister.

'Fine. I was just going to invite our guest inside, *once* he has given me his name.'

'Forgive me. My name is Sir Henry Baskerville.' The man bowed.

Eve came down to join them in the foyer. She tapped her cheek thoughtfully. 'Did I not read about you recently? You had a little problem with a dog?'

Sir Henry winced. 'A hound, madame, and it was far from little.'

Mel now remembered the story. 'A monstrous hound was terrorising you and your household – but Sherlock Holmes solved the mystery and stopped the creature. The hound is dead.'

'So we thought.' Sir Henry ran his hand through his hair. 'I'm at my wits' end. Although that should've been the end

112

of the matter, we are now being plagued worse than ever. Boots are going missing, the villagers are being terrified – somehow the hound seems to have come back! Has it returned in ghostly form, or is it another beast entirely – and what does it want? No one dares go out at night on Dartmoor for fear for their life. I want you to find out what is going on and stop it.'

'And Mr Holmes cannot help?' asked Eve.

Sir Henry shook his head. 'No, he says this isn't a problem for him.'

'But he can solve any mystery given enough time with the facts,' said Mel, upset. Mr Holmes was one of his heroes, and Mel followed his exploits in the newspapers.

'I have to admit to being disappointed that he refused the case, but Mr Holmes told me that the world is full of obvious things which nobody ever observes. He said that this time around, a monster mystery needed to be solved by a couple of monster detectives. He recommended the Resistance for the job and told me your address.' Sir Henry examined them both. 'Well, I suppose one monster will do at a pinch. You, mademoiselle, look very capable.'

Mel bridled at the implied insult. He knew he was just as much a monster as the rest of the Resistance. But Eve came swiftly to his defence.

'We work together, monsieur. What makes someone a

monster is more than skin-deep.'

Sir Henry frowned. 'But you'll take the case?'

'A monster hound loose on Dartmoor – danger – mystery?' Mel grinned at Eve. 'We're in.'

The train pulled into the wayside station of Grimpen Village. Mel, Eve and Sir Henry were the only passengers to get out. If anyone else had been thinking of descending there, seeing Eve on the platform had changed their mind.

'It's a long walk to Baskerville Hall so I've asked my new man Crichton to bring over the carriage. Ah there he is – on time as ever.' Sir Henry led them to a wagonette driven by a handsome servant, tall where his master was short. Crichton's steady gaze did not falter once on being introduced to the giantess. *He must be made of steely stuff*, thought Mel.

'I've brought us the monster detectives as promised, Crichton. Please give them the run of the house and help them with their investigations.'

'Very good, sir.' The manservant sniffed, a hint of disapproval. Someone wasn't pleased to see detectives arrive. Did Crichton have something to hide?

'While Crichton manages the driving and whatnot, I guess I should tell you more about the hound.'

'That would be most useful,' agreed Eve, making the springs creak as she took a seat behind Crichton. The servant silently shifted to counter her weight and clicked the horse into a walk.

'It all started with a dastardly ancestor of mine, Hugo Baskerville. He was a cruel lord of the manor. The legend says that one day he went too far – gave his soul over to the Powers of Evil if they would help him chase some unfortunate girl across the moor. But both man and girl were found dead, and Hugo seemed to have got his comeuppance at the jaws of a giant hound. The uncanny events investigated by Mr Holmes proved to be a monster dog, possibly a descendant of that original hound, trained to terrorise me – but it is dead, and that should've been the end of the story.'

'But something has come back?' asked Eve.

'Exactly. I've heard howling from Grimpen Mire, the very spot where my ancestor met his end.'

Mel frowned. 'So the hound has come back as a ghost?'

'Perhaps – but more physical signs have been spotted as well. Villagers have seen a great shape on the horizon in the moonlight: a four-legged creature as big as a bear.'

'You do not have bears in England?' asked Eve.

'No, we do not, not since Norman times. And in the yew alley in my garden, I saw them.'

'Saw what?' Eve asked breathlessly.

'The footprints of a gigantic hound!'

'Oh!'

'We must see those,' muttered Mel.

'And I believe that it can assume bodily form,' continued Sir Henry, getting quite carried away by his own story. 'While I was leaning over the prints, I felt a hot breath on the nape of my neck. I froze. Something leapt on my back . . . I screamed . . . there was a shot and I turned, but too late.'

'It ran away?' That was a surprise.

'I think Crichton scared it off.'

'Mr Crichton, what did you see?'

'I did not see a hound. I heard Sir Henry's shout and rushed out of the house,' the servant replied in his stiff manner. 'I shot a rifle in the air to alert Sir Henry that I was coming, and in hopes of scaring off any ne'er-do-wells.'

Sir Henry patted Crichton on the back. 'I owe this man my life.'

'I strive to give satisfaction, sir.'

Crichton seemed rather too pleased with himself. Had he set up the incident, revived the story of the hound to make Sir Henry grateful, Mel wondered? No one had actually seen it clearly. Could there be another explanation – could someone be using the legend for their own ends again? Such things as footprints and silhouettes on the horizon were possible to fake. Crichton wouldn't be the first servant Mel had met who had taken over his employer's life by making himself indispensable.

The wagonette travelled along high-banked roads with their tangle of frosted ferns and blackened stalks of cow parsley, and emerged into a different world of bleak moorland, broken by stone outcrops and tumble-down sheep pens, patches of snow lingering in hollows. Grey clouds scouted the horizon looking for spots on which to dump the next fall of snow.

'Dartmoor!' said Sir Henry. 'I lived in Canada most of my life, so coming here felt like coming home.'

Mel had lived in some grim places – in an orphanage, on a ship, in the slums – but he thought this might be the very worst. He preferred a noisy city street any day.

'*Magnifique*,' said Eve, resting her chin on her hand, lost in fond memories. 'It reminds me of the home I shared with my father in the Arctic Wastes.'

'Then you understand – it's the desolation that gets you here.' Sir Henry thumped his chest.

Mel noticed Crichton raise his eyes heavenward. Evidently the manservant shared Mel's view of country versus the comforts of town. Perhaps he wanted to frighten his master into returning there?

The wagonette entered an oak plantation. Chimneys poked above the treeline. They passed through a gateway flanked by statues of two cats holding shields: the entrance to Baskerville Hall.

'Stop a moment!' called Mel, spotting claw marks on the gateposts. 'Eve, come with me. We have some detecting to do.'

Leaving Crichton and Sir Henry in the carriage, the two friends poked around the bottom of the plinths.

'Do you see this?' Mel asked Eve softly so as not to be overheard.

'*Oui*. Both statues have their tails broken off.' She held up the fragments. 'And they have been bitten to dust. This cannot be the work of a ghost.'

'That happened last night,' called Crichton from the wagonette. 'I'm sorry I haven't had time to have them mended again, sir.'

'Again?' asked Eve. 'How many times have they been broken?'

'Sixteen, miss. Always the tails.'

Mel brushed the dust from his fingers, keeping his back to Crichton. 'Something's not right here. The hound only attacked Sir Henry last time – so why is it wasting its time on stone statues now? Maybe Crichton is doing it himself to worry Sir Henry?'

'Then we must watch him like hawks.' Eve's eyes swivelled alarmingly, blue pointing up and brown focused on Crichton.

'Don't let him suspect anything.'

They got back into the wagonette. Rounding the last bend, they came into sight of an ivy-draped house with twin towers at either end of a steeply pitched roof. Baskerville Hall looked so old it had to be riddled with secret passages and hidden doors – the best place to play hide-and-seek, but also the perfect place to pretend there was a monster.

'You have rooms prepared, Crichton?' asked Sir Henry, leading the way into the house. The entrance showed its origin as a baronial hall: stained-glass windows with heraldic symbols and hunting trophies.

'Naturally, sir. I have put the lady in the Chinese bedroom and the young master next to her, in Sir Hugo's old room.'

That brought Sir Henry to a stop. 'But that room hasn't been used since the hound did for him. The servants say it's haunted.'

Crichton raised a brow. 'But you said that our guests were monster detectives, unafraid of anything, sir.'

'So I did. Are you happy with these rooms?'

Mel rubbed his hands. Was Crichton trying to scare them off too? If so, he had miscalculated. Mr Marley was a ghost and Mel had several more friends among the undead. 'Don't worry, sir, we'll be right at home.'

'Then I'll see you at dinner.' Sir Henry hurried off to his library and shut the door with a bang.

'Allow me to show you to your rooms,' said the manservant.

'That would be admirable. Thank you, Crichton,' said Eve, giving him one of her inimitable smiles. 'I would like, how do you say, to raise my feet?'

'I think you mean *put up* your feet, mademoiselle.' Mel detected a flicker of a smile on the manservant's face.

The room Mel had been allocated was spotless. Unless ghostly Sir Hugo did his own dusting like Mr Marley, the staff had been in here recently to polish the heavy oak furniture and air the red velvet curtains. He knocked on Eve's door.

'I think we should find out more about Crichton and explore the grounds. Are you coming?'

'Of course. I only said I would rest to put him off the scent. We do not want him following us.'

'Good thinking, Eve.'

Heading downstairs, they sneaked through a door to the domestic quarters. Halfway along the flagstone passage, Eve held up a finger – Crichton was speaking nearby.

'Jim, that's another boot gone missing: the fourth this week! And as for the mangled bit of leather you showed me, it was hard even to recognise it as Sir Henry's shoe! This is unacceptable.'

'I know, Mr Crichton. I line them up in the boot room

each night, polished for the morning, but when I goes to fetch them the next day, they're gone. Whoever stole them must be able to pass through walls because I keep the only key to the door on me.'

*Or maybe there are secret passages Jim doesn't know about,* thought Mel.

'I could understand if it were a pair – then I would say thieves were behind it – but to steal a single boot each time, it smacks of an ill-timed jest,' said Crichton.

'I'm not playing no joke, sir. It must be the hound!'

Crichton clucked his tongue. 'As I've told you before, the monster hound was killed.'

'But Sir Henry says –'

'Understandably, Sir Henry believes that it has returned in ghostly form because of the family legend; but we below stairs should not be influenced by such superstitions. Monsters and ghosts are rare; vandals and thieves are not. It is up to us to keep our heads in a crisis. I for one will keep my rifle loaded and double-check the locks each night.'

'Yes, sir.'

'Jim, lose another boot and you lose your job. Keep them with you tonight in your room. That way no one will sneak in and steal them, will they?'

'But what if the boots attract the monster to my room?'

Crichton gave an exasperated sigh. 'In that unlikely

event, then you are to defend them with your life. Am I understood?'

Peeking around the corner, Mel saw the gangly red-haired boy of his own age nod his head miserably. Crichton marched off, leaving Jim alone.

'Afternoon.' Mel stepped out so Jim could see him.

'Afternoon . . . Aargh!' Jim had spotted Eve.

Mel scowled at him to mind his manners. 'We're the monster detectives.'

'Really? I'd never've guessed.' Jim had to be recovering from his shock to manage sarcasm.

'Sir Henry has asked us to get to the bottom of the mystery about the hound,' said Eve.

'So I've been told, m . . . miss.'

'How long has the boot theft been going on?' asked Mel.

'Over the last few months. I think it's come back to haunt us as revenge for its death. You should see the state of the boots I've found half-buried in the garden – bitten to pieces! It must hate us.'

'Interesting,' said Eve. 'Could a ghost hound chew them?'

'You never know what wicked things these monsters can do, beg pardon, miss.' Jim blushed.

But ghosts had great difficulty handling physical objects; they could manage spectral breezes, but mangling things in their teeth, no. It seemed less and less likely that they were dealing with a ghost. Had Crichton been taking the shoes himself, or was this proof that there really was a new monster? Mel couldn't decide. They needed more concrete evidence. 'Give the boots to us tonight,' said Mel. 'We'll look after them.'

'That's awfully brave of you, sir,' said Jim.

'It's Mel please, Jim. Deliver the boots to my chamber later.'

'Righto.' Jim gulped. 'Tonight.' White-faced, he bolted for the kitchen.

'Curious,' said Eve. 'Mr Crichton did not talk like a man who believed in the monster. If he was making it up, surely he would pretend to believe it himself?'

'Unless it is a double bluff. He would be the last person suspected of inventing it. Let's go and look at those footprints.'

They went out into the grounds to ask a gardener for directions. They found one sweeping up leaves in the dark alley of the yew walk.

'Just here they were, sir,' said the craggy-faced gardener. He pointed to a patch of bare earth where the faint outline of a paw could be seen. Mel spread his hand; they were of a size.

'Big, but not exactly monstrous,' he told Eve.

'They are partly washed away. Let us go and ask the

villagers if there are any clearer prints,' suggested Eve. 'Which way to Grimpen?'

The gardener pointed out a shortcut across the moor, which cut out a great loop of the road. 'But you'd best keep strictly to the footpath. The moor is full of bogs. Stray on to Grimpen Mire over yonder –' he waved to a suspiciously greener patch on the moor – 'and you can disappear below the surface, no one the wiser as to what happened to you.'

This confirmed Mel in his belief that cities were safer than the countryside. London pavements might be crowded and occasionally cracked but they never swallowed anyone whole.

In the village Mel and Eve walked along the main street, admiring the whitewashed houses. Some houses had paper cut-outs of snowflakes on the glass, a reminder that it wouldn't be long till Christmas. The brightest lights shone from the village shop, already illuminated against the twilight of the short day, and the nearby pub. Mel thought it might be best to split up, to find out exactly what the villagers knew. He dug in his pocket, came up with a sixpence.

'Eve, why don't you ask locals about the footprints while I see what the shopkeeper knows?'

Mel smiled as Eve headed for a group of brawny farmers standing outside the tavern. They fled like sheep before a collie. It might take her a while to round them up.

Inside the shop, jars of sweets were ranged on the shelf behind the counter, an Aladdin's cave of treasures. A black kitten played by the owner's feet, testing its claws on a ball of wool. The grandmotherly shopkeeper put aside her knitting. 'Can I help you, young man?'

Mel's eyes jumped from sherbet lemons to aniseed twists to chocolate drops. 'Might I have a pennyworth of strawberry shoelaces and another of liquorice?' The latter were Eve's favourites.

She reached up to take down the jar of pink sugar-strands. 'Soon these shoelaces will be the only ones left in the village.'

Mel pounced like the kitten on the subject he had been hoping to raise. 'Why's that?'

The lady shook out the sweets on to her scales. 'Haven't you heard? That hellhound's back to haunt us.' She glanced up at him, her pale-blue eyes stern. 'Nothing's sacred, just as you would expect from the devil's dog. It's worse this time – even the parson's boots have gone missing. It got the right one of my Sunday pair too. I'm fair shaking in my shoes just thinking about it.' She spun the white paper bag by the corner to twist the edges closed and started on the second order.

'Have there been any other signs of the hound?'

'Stop it, you. This baby is such a menace.' The shopkeeper

toed the kitten away as it started chewing on the hem of her dress. 'Well now, Mrs Jameson's chickens have all gone, as has a duck from the village pond. And then there were the Golightly children.'

'What? It's taken children!' Mel thought this news rated rather ahead of chickens and ducks.

'Not taken, dear – it chased them! They were out on the moor, even though they knew better.'

'Where?'

'By the Druid's stepping stones – they're on the edge of the mire but you mustn't go there – terrible place. They said that the creature bounded out of the dark and headed right for them. They ran for their lives and made it back home just before the monster slammed into their door. They swore they could hear clawing at the planks and howling outside.'

'Where's their house?'

'Last one on the edge of the moor.'

Mel rejoined Eve outside, and they compared notes. The terrified farmers had all sworn on their life that the creature was real, but none of them had seen any more concrete sign of it than Sir Henry had.

'We should go and look at the claw marks on the boys' door,' Mel suggested, handing Eve the packet of liquorice.

The damage was plain for all to see: great gouges taken

out of the wood. Sucking on a strawberry shoelace, Mel pondered their options.

'So is this a new monster hound, or just someone wanting us to believe the legend has returned?'

'And if it is a monster, what does it want? It doesn't just seem interested in Sir Henry – it's attacking the village!' said Eve.

'It doesn't add up,' sighed Mel. 'But I think we have done all we can for one day. We had better head back.'

They hadn't timed their journey very well. Night was falling. Mist swirled, hiding the landmarks that had guided them on the way out. Fortunately someone had placed white stones along the edge of the path, a beacon showing the shortcut past the edge of the mire. Then the mist cleared and some way off to the right they could see some larger grey stones set close together.

'The Druid's stepping stones?' Mel wondered aloud, his voice sounding odd in the quiet of the moor. 'The beast was seen there too.'

'Let's go and look.' Eve stepped off the path and her boot immediately sank below the surface up to her ankle. Mel grabbed her arm and helped pull her free, staggering as her foot came out with a jolt.

Eve might be almost indestructible but there were still some things that could harm her, Mel realised. Drowning in a bog was one of them.

'Eve, I think you're too heavy for that path. Wait here while I look.'

Reluctantly, Eve let him go alone. Leaping from tussock to tussock, Mel made his way to the rocks, which stood like the last outpost of a forgotten empire. A wind rattled the dry grasses and an unfamiliar bird cry scratched at the air. Everything smelt rotten. He looked over his shoulder, the lights of Grimpen Village twinkling in the distance.

'No!' he gasped. There on the brow of a nearby hill was the creature – far bigger than any dog Mel had ever seen, a hulking blackness in the night. It threw back its head, howled, then, scenting Mel, bounded towards him.

'Help!' Mel raced for Eve, but he had to be careful not to step into the bog. The hound leapt, sure-footed, gaining on him. 'Eve!' As a final thought, he threw the sweets behind him. Running flat out, Mel made it back to the path and collided with Eve who was running towards him. He landed in a puddle.

'Mel Foster, what is the matter?'

'The hound of the Baskervilles is real, and it's after me!'

Eve looked over his head. 'But I see nothing.'

Mel turned. Mist had moved in again and there was no sign of the creature. 'Trust me: you don't want to. But it does exist – not a hoax, not a ghost, a real-life monster hound!'

'What do we do now?'

'We try to catch it. Jim is bringing us the boots this evening – it seems to like vandalising them so if it comes for them we'll be ready.'

Eve lifted him up and brushed him off. 'Then we'll do that.'

'It got my sweets.'

She hugged him. 'Better it has your sweets than you for its supper.'

The trap was prepared. Mel sat up in the bed, single candle lit on the nightstand as he guarded the household's boots, lined up in the middle of the room. Eve was keeping watch in the corridor outside. No one would get past her.

Around midnight, there came a scratching, but not at the door. Mel's skin stippled in goosebumps. It seemed to be coming from behind the skirting board. What if there was a passageway there too? Mel threw back the covers but then the noise stopped.

'I must be imagining it,' he murmured.

Then, to Mel's horror, a section of the wall near the fireplace nudged open. A nose appeared, accompanied by the smell of rot, then a monstrous snout, sniffing towards the boots. Two huge black eyes deep-set in wrinkled skin followed, its yellow-white fangs and red tongue visible. With a chilling growl, it took a shoe in its mouth and began to crunch, mincing it to pieces in seconds.

'Eve!' Mel's voice was a rasp, carrying no further than his feet.

But the hound heard and looked over at the bed with an unmistakably possessive gleam in its eye. It bared its teeth, bootlace trailing.

Mel scrabbled for the door, but the dog had settled on new prey. Dropping the mangled boot, it charged and knocked Mel flat. This was the end! The dog's dire breath fell on his face. Reaching for his monster gift, he zapped it with electricity. Knocked back, it yelped and then crouched for a renewed attack. 'Eve! Now would be good!'

Eve burst into the room. '*Diable!*'

Too late: the monster was already on top of him. But what was this? No teeth sinking into his neck, no pain? Maybe this murderous hound was not really so murderous after all. Mel's hand went tentatively to the creature's chin, not to zap but to scratch. Its back leg shivered with pleasure as Mel found just the right spot to rub.

'That is nothing but a puppy!' exclaimed Eve, trying to heave the dog off Mel as it smothered him with licks and wagged its tail.

Mel rolled free. 'I said you were an education for me, Eve. Of course, you're right: the smallish paw mark, the urge to play chase with everyone, the chewing of shoes and stones! I bet it's started teething, which is why it came out of hiding now. Get down, you great lump.' Mel pushed the hound away.

The dog howled.

Sir Henry and Crichton appeared in the doorway.

'Shoot it!' bellowed Sir Henry. 'Crichton, your gun!'

'Don't you dare!' shouted Mel, wrapping his arms around the dog's head. Eve hoisted Crichton off his feet so he was left running in mid-air, gun pointing at the ceiling.

'Can't you see it's just a baby?' said Mel. 'You killed a monster hound, but did none of you stop to wonder if she might have left a monster puppy behind?'

Sir Henry gaped. 'But Sherlock Holmes – '

'I think he deduced it from the clues, when you came to him a second time. That was why he sent us. Our mission wasn't to hunt it, but to rescue it.'

'It's so sweet!' sighed Eve, stroking the creature's rough snout as it slobbered on her.

Patting the dog that was now sitting obediently, Mel faced the last Baskerville. 'I suppose this is your hound, as it was found on your land. Do you want a new dog, Sir Henry?'

'Me, take on that creature?' Sir Henry went pale.

'It'll make a mess on my clean floors,' moaned Crichton.

'Thought not. So, Eve, what do you think about the Monster Resistance getting a pet?'

'You think he'll make a good p-pet?' Sir Henry spluttered with horror.

Mel shrugged. 'Monster Resistance – and a monster hound of the Baskervilles. It's a perfect fit.'

A few days later, back in London, Mel and Eve received a letter. They almost didn't get to read it – the Baskerville puppy had got to the envelope first. Rescued from Basker's jaws, Mel shook out the mangled note.

*Dear Master Foster and Mademoiselle Frankenstein,*

*May I congratulate you on your swift solution to the case? I deduced that only those who know what prejudice monsters face could save the young creature from the hunters' guns. I am delighted I was right. Greetings to the hound.*

*Yours,*

*Sherlock Holmes*

*P.S. My housekeeper, Mrs Hudson, says she will send you all of our leftover bones in hopes of saving your shoes. I fear, however, it may be too late.*

Mel looked at the hole in his boot where his toe was peeking through and grinned. 'I'd say that's elementary, my dear Eve.'

\*

*Read more about Mel and Eve in the Mel Foster series, available from Egmont now!*

# DAZZLE, DOG BISCUITS AND DISASTER
## By Kate Pankhurst

Charlotte McCarthy, the Princess of Year Eleven, thinks of herself as a delicate poodle. But as I listened to her upstairs in McCarthy Mansions it sounded like a bulldog had been let loose in a cake shop. Her footsteps thumped around above our heads, rattling the crystals of the living-room chandelier.

'DAZZLE? DAZZLE! Are you there?' Her panicked voice echoed down the stairs.

'DAAAZZLE?' Charlotte's mother, Margot McCarthy, screamed from another bedroom. But their dog, Dazzle, was nowhere to be found.

Dazzle's owners, the McCarthys, might be the most awkward customers of my mum's dog-care business, the Dog House, but Dazzle isn't like that at all. He's a bichon frise (bee-chon free-zay, as Charlotte explained to me once), but he doesn't let that get in his way. Among all of the dogs Mum walks, he's the leader of the pack.

I wish I had a bit more of his attitude sometimes. It might help me deal with stroppy show poodles like Charlotte McCarthy.

In school, when I'm with Fliss (my dog-obsessed best mate) we can laugh off the looks of disgust she flings our way. Fliss even does a spot-on-hilarious ponytail-swishing impression of Charlotte. But when I drop off Dazzle I have to face Charlotte alone, on her territory, and she gets her kicks finding new ways to make me feel as if I should apologise for darkening her doorstep. She sneers at my *so-hideously-uncool-it-pains-her-to-look-at-it* dog-walking cagoule and sniffs at my tatty old trainers and too-short jeans.

I can put up with Charlotte, though, because the rest of being a Junior Assistant Dog Exerciser is brilliant. I've spent every school holiday for two years helping Mum out, ever since we moved out of Gran's, adopted our scruffy dog Bacon and Mum set up the business. For two years life's been, well, amazing. But now we might be about to lose everything.

Charlotte had flung open at least five doors by now, and every time the sound drummed the same unspoken statement through my head: *SID TAYLOR, DAZZLE IS MISSING AND IT'S ALL YOUR FAULT.*

It wasn't. It couldn't be. I knew I hadn't left the back door open.

But with each slam my hopes that Dazzle would be found inside the house, violating all the rules by shedding dog hair on Charlotte McCarthy's bedspread, faded.

Charlotte had never shown much interest in Dazzle before – apart from to shout at him when he slept on her designer clothes or buried his dog treats under her neatly stacked pillows – but now she seemed really upset.

She had watched us search the downstairs of her house, as though she thought that the scatty dog walker from the Other Side of the Park (Mum), her helper (Jane), her Year Eight son (me) and his weirdo mate (Fliss) were about to make off with her mother's soft furnishings stuffed under our cagoules. It didn't help that my (supposedly trained) dog Bacon wasn't helping sniff out Dazzle. He was more interested in the sofa cushions.

We aren't sure what breeds of dog Bacon's ancestors were, but hopefully there's some sniffer dog in there somewhere. I've tried to teach him to be able to sniff out missing people, like police dogs do, but so far the only concealed items he's discovered are bacon-flavoured Frizzle crisps.

Fliss, who was searching under the enormous white-leather sofa assisted by Bacon, turned and shot me a worried expression. Confirmation, as if I needed it, that things were really terrible. Fliss is hardly ever serious. I knew she meant: *Sid, you're done for!*

And I knew that, if we didn't find Dazzle and prove I hadn't had anything to do with his disappearance, she'd be right.

I replayed the scene again, remembering what I'd done half an hour before, just like I was part of one of the crime reconstructions on *Crim-Catcher*, the TV programme me and Fliss watch every week. The police always urge the public to come forward with information – anything could help solve a real-life crime, even it if doesn't seem important.

So what could I remember about Dazzle's disappearance?

1. After our walk was over that afternoon, Mum stayed outside McCarthy Mansions in the Dog House van with Fliss, while I went in. McCarthy Mansions is the joke name me and Mum have given the McCarthys' over-the-top house, with its sweeping driveway and roaring stone lions on the gateposts. It's actually number ninety-two, Newton Park Avenue, on the Nice Side of the Park. (Fliss is always around because she doesn't have a dog of her own. Her mum says she's having a laugh to even think one could live in their tiny flat above her family's newsagent business, but she's just as mad about them as I am. So, during school holidays, she helps me and my mum with the Dog House.)

2. Mum couldn't drop Dazzle off herself because she was taking a call from somebody who had heard about the Dog House's high-quality dog whispering, walking and watching services: bad behaviour therapy, walks and dog sitting.

3. In the McCarthys' sleek kitchen (the same size as our entire flat) I followed Margot McCarthy's stupid Dazzle Drop-Off Routine. *No mud to be left on the kitchen floor. Fill Dazzle's water bowl with chilled mineral water. Dazzle may have three Hortnum and Hoffarty dog treats but no more.* I knew that if so much as a dog biscuit was out of place when she got back from yoga it would mean a long lecturing phone call to Mum.

4. Charlotte came into the kitchen, ignored Dazzle (as usual) and gave me a look that said: *Hurry up and leave, dog dweeb.* She threw a plate in the sink and headed back to the living room. That suited me. I shut the back door as I left – and I *know* I wiggled the door handle three times, like always, to make sure it was locked.

5. We waited in the van while Mum dropped off Barnibus the labradoodle up the road from the McCarthys'. We were about to head home when Mum's phone rang again. It was Jane. 'I was dropping Rufus off at number eighty-three and saw Margot in the street

calling Dazzle's name . . . Charlotte says Sid dropped off Dazzle but left the back door open . . . We can't find Dazzle anywhere. He's gone!'

6. We drove back to McCarthy Mansions in a rush. Fliss kept saying that I didn't have to convince her of my story, but Mum didn't say very much at all. That was probably the worst bit of the whole disaster, that it felt like Mum was thinking: *Dazzle could be squashed under a bus by now, and it's all because Sid didn't shut the door properly.*

Now, I had my suspicions about what might have happened to Dazzle. I wondered what would happen to Charlotte's regal poodle pose if I ran upstairs and told her what I thought:

'Bit weird, isn't it, that I know I dropped Dazzle off after his walk and locked the back door, and then he somehow escaped when only you were in the house? Or maybe it isn't weird. I know you don't like him. Maybe you let him escape because he chewed one pair of your designer shoes too many? Because he peed on your school bag again?'

I was desperate to discuss my theory with Fliss, but her usual approach of charging in head first and thinking about the consequences later wasn't going to work. I knew I needed solid evidence before I could say anything. One bad word from Margot McCarthy at the Newton Park Residential Committee meeting and faster than you could say, 'Custard cream?' Mum would find herself out of a job. The Dog House would be done for.

Maybe I was overestimating how cold Charlotte was. She didn't like Dazzle, but would she go so far as to deliberately release her mother's adored pet?

I thought some more, and realised that there was another possible explanation for Dazzle's disappearance. He was a pedigree with wealthy owners – and that made him the perfect target for a dog snatcher who wanted to make Margot pay a fortune to get him back. But there was just one problem with that. So far, I hadn't spotted a ransom note.

*DOOF! DOOF! DOOF!*

By the angry thud of footsteps now coming back down the stairs, I judged Margot and Charlotte had still not found Dazzle.

Bacon took refuge under the coffee table. I wished I could join him.

'Dazzle!' Mum called hopelessly, sticking her face under the chaise longue. But I knew it was pointless. Dazzle might look like a walking pompom, but there was absolutely no way that we just hadn't spotted him because we'd been mistaking him for a decorative scatter cushion.

Mum stood up, and Jane squeezed her shoulder. I guessed that panic had set in for Jane. She must have known that the Dog House could be about to go the same way as Waggy

Tails, the company she had run before she came to work for Mum. Lots of dog walkers in Newton Park struggled to keep the fussy customers from the Nice Side of the Park, and loads of companies had failed.

Then Margot McCarthy swept into the living room, and if looks could kill, the withering one she shot Mum would have caused instant death. Mum looked like she wanted to run for cover, her face as red as her dog-walking fleece.

'Dazzle can't have gone far. We'll get him back,' Jane said, stepping in as pack leader on Mum's behalf. Jane is more pug than greyhound, a walk-to-a-park-bench-and-throw-a-ball-while-eating-a-Kit-Kat dog walker rather than a-four-mile-circuit-of-the-park one, so she must have quickly deduced there was no escape.

'Too right you're going to get my dog back!' snapped Margot without taking her eyes off Mum. 'Or I'll see that everyone round here knows that you rely on children to help run your business, Lisa Taylor!'

Hold on! This wasn't Mum's fault!

I had to prove to Margot that Mum's business wasn't to blame. And Dazzle, the innocent victim, had to be found. It was time to take action.

Five minutes later, Fliss, Bacon and I were outside. Pressed against the ivy-covered back wall of McCarthy Mansions,

I signalled to Fliss for silence and hissed at Bacon not to yap at the water feature he was sniffing (a marble mermaid squirting a trickle of water out of her mouth that Dazzle liked to wee on whenever he got the chance).

I had explained my suspicions to Fliss, and she had totally believed me. She agreed that the best place to search for clues relating to our options, Dog Snatching or Deliberate Dog Release, would be around the mysterious self-opening back door.

Mum, Margot and Charlotte had gone to Newton Park, across the road from the front door of McCarthy Mansions. It was where Dazzle was bound to be, if he was still nearby. But Jane was only a few doors away. We could hear her calling Dazzle's name into a neighbour's garden.

Had she heard us? I knew that Jane, like Mum, would only say it was stupid and irresponsible to further infuriate Margot McCarthy by snooping around, even if what we were doing was trying to prove that I hadn't been so stupid and irresponsible as to leave the door open.

Seconds passed, but Jane seemed not to have noticed us. We were safe.

I waggled the door handle, like I had earlier. It was locked.

So the door couldn't be faulty! I studied the lock more closely. Surely if it had been forced, there would be some scratches. The golden handle and lock gleamed. I wondered if Margot McCarthy's cleaner buffed it? Probably.

'No signs of a break-in,' I said to Fliss. 'It's not conclusive evidence, but it fits with Charlotte opening the door herself and letting Dazzle run off.'

Before Fliss could answer there was a crunch from behind us.

My heart skipped a beat as I turned, expecting to see Margot McCarthy nipping back for a Hortnum and Hoffarty dog treat to tempt Dazzle with, but it was only Bacon. He was chewing something, and at his feet were a few broken crumbs of what looked like dog biscuit. I knew it could be important.

'Bacon! DROP!' I said.

Bacon let go of it guiltily. I frowned at him. There was clearly more training to be done. Police sniffer dogs should sit patiently next to potential evidence, not eat it.

I examined the fragments of broken orange biscuit. 'This isn't the brand Margot buys! Mum gets these from the pet shop on the high street,' I said. 'And it couldn't have fallen out of my pocket. I've been using other treats today. I suppose Mum might have, yesterday, but it's weird that Dazzle didn't sniff it out when I brought him back to the house this afternoon.'

If there is so much as half a cold chip by one of the bins in the park Dazzle is always the first dog to snaffle it.

'So, the question is, who dropped it? And Sid, are we ruling out *dog snatching* too soon?' Fliss asked.

She said 'dog snatching' in the same tone of voice she uses to read out the most sinister-sounding *Crim-Catcher* crimes from the TV guide. But I wasn't finding any of this exciting – not when I was the one branded guilty.

'That treat could have been used to lure Dazzle out of the kitchen by the dog snatcher, so he wouldn't bark and attract Charlotte's attention,' she added. 'The lock doesn't look like it's been forced – what if it wasn't? The thief could have had a key.'

I was about to say, 'Come off it.' People who live in mansions filled with expensive stuff don't leave a spare key under a plant pot. But then Fliss looked horrified, like she'd realised something majorly important.

'Sid. Maybe I'm being ridiculous, but we're supposed to consider everything, right?' She paused then continued in a rush. 'What if your mum realised she could make more money by taking Dazzle than she does running the Dog House?'

*What?* We'd just watched Mum get torn to pieces by Margot, and now Fliss wanted to waste time making stupid accusations. I felt like she wasn't taking the possible demise of the Dog House seriously.

'Can I just remind you we're meant to be saving Mum

from disaster? I can't believe you'd say something like that!' I snapped.

Fliss doesn't like being told she's wrong. So I was surprised that she didn't explode back at me, in one of the Fliss-frenzies I've seen when her brothers dare to change the channel during *Crim-Catcher*. Instead she stared at her wellies and took a deep breath before speaking calmly.

'Sid, I don't want to say this stuff. I really like your mum. I'm just pointing out the facts. You said yourself that we've just found a brand of biscuit your mum uses outside a door that she has a key to. She was gone a while dropping Barnibus off – she could have done it then and hidden Dazzle somewhere before she came back to the van. I wouldn't blame her for being driven to doing something mad. Sid, you know she needs money!'

I was really mad at Fliss for suggesting it, but I realised it wasn't a completely stupid motive. Mum tries to hide it, but I can tell she's worried about the bills that land on our doormat, the ones I've seen her shove behind the bread bin and ignore.

'Maybe so,' I said. 'But I just can't imagine Mum doing it! She wouldn't frame me, or risk the business she's built up. It's as stupid as suggesting that Jane did it, or I did. After all, I have a key too. You've only got my word that I haven't turned into a dog snatcher.'

'OK! OK! I just think it's a good idea to, you know, consider all angles,' Fliss said, apologetically holding up her hands. 'Anyway, we should definitely follow up on the Charlotte McCarthy angle. Whatever happened, she was in the house when Dazzle disappeared, and we know she is a definite Dazzle-disliker. She might slip up and say something that incriminates her. Or even if she didn't do it, she might have heard something important.'

I nodded, glad to be focused again.

'If we speak to Charlotte and record the whole conversation as evidence, Margot will have to believe it,' I said, pulling my mobile phone from my pocket.

'Secret recording and entrapment?' Fliss said. 'I like it.'

Charlotte was still in the park, not far from the house. She was calling Dazzle's name and trying her best not to get mud on wellies that looked like they'd only been used for high-class shopping trips until now. As Fliss and I approached I fumbled with my mobile, trying to hit the record button, and . . .

'CHARLOTTE! Charlotte!' a breathless Jane called out from behind us. 'I need to speak to your mother, urgently!'

She was jogging across the park and she looked frantic. My first thought was: *Jane, running?* Then my mouth went dry, as if I'd eaten a dog biscuit. Whatever news she had did not look like it was good, and I still had no evidence to prove I hadn't left that door open.

Charlotte put her hands to her face and turned pale. Why this sudden burst of concern? Was she feeling sorry for setting Dazzle free?

'I've seen Dazzle!' Jane continued. 'In the wasteland, behind the supermarket. But he was spooked and he wouldn't come to me and . . .'

She paused, and looked at me. Then she dropped the bombshell. 'He ran through the bushes on to the motorway.'

I had a slow-motion image of a terrified Dazzle cowering on the hard shoulder and then darting haphazardly across the carriageway while horns blared, cars whizzing by at seventy miles an hour.

If it was true, Dazzle was a goner. Charlotte knew that too. She didn't look like show-poodle Charlotte any more. She looked like a hurt puppy.

'Dazzy? It can't have been him – he wouldn't have gone that far. When I found the door open I knew he'd come back. He loves Mum and me, doesn't he? He's got to come back – he wouldn't leave me!' Charlotte said. Then she started to cry, the sort of sobbing where you can't breathe and your whole body shakes. She didn't even try to push Bacon away from her leg as he nuzzled sympathetically against it.

If Charlotte was acting it was Oscar-winning. But I

knew she wasn't. This grief was real. And that meant that Charlotte wasn't guilty of Deliberate Dog Release.

Fliss stared at her feet. I knew that, like me, she felt sorry for Charlotte, and devastated for Dazzle.

Jane looked like she might cry too. 'If we get the search party over there now we still might be able to save him.'

Through her tears, Charlotte pointed over towards Margot. Jane guided her away.

My head raced like a car speeding in the fast lane. Now that Dazzle had been seen running free, could he really have been snatched? It didn't make sense. And if Deliberate Dog Release *and* Dog Snatching had been ruled out . . .

Charlotte was in the clear. But I still wasn't.

I replayed the afternoon again, this time with new scenes. Scenes where I slammed the door behind me without realising it had bounced open. Scenes where I dropped a dog biscuit on the ground and didn't pick it up again.

I was glad Fliss hadn't said out loud what we both knew: that the only explanation for Dazzle escaping was that I hadn't closed the door properly.

But could this still end well for Dazzle? If the search party left now, how long would it take for them to get to the motorway? It was at least a mile and a half away. Eight minutes in the van. Fifteen at a human sprint. Maybe five if you were a greyhound.

A mile and a half there. Three miles there and back.

Wait.

I looked again at Jane, walking away with Charlotte. She seemed to have recovered quickly from what was probably the first three-mile sprint she had done in her whole life. Come to think of it, she wasn't even sweaty.

How long would three miles have taken at her pug speed?

Longer than had passed since we had heard her calling Dazzle's name outside the McCarthys' house about twenty minutes ago.

Jane would never run that far – she'd always take her van. But Jane's Dog House van, printed with photos of cheerful dogs poking their heads from windows of an enlarged Dog House logo, was parked only a few doors down from McCarthy Mansions – where it had been since she had dropped off Rufus at number eighty-three and called us to say Dazzle was missing.

My heart raced.

'Fliss. When was the last time you saw Jane break into a sprint?' I asked, not taking my eyes off Jane.

'Sprint? Jane? What?' Fliss said, looking at me like she couldn't believe I was making casual conversation at an inappropriate moment. 'Never!'

'Exactly,' I said. 'So that means Jane is lying. Or at least I think she is. She can't have got to the motorway and back on foot since we last saw her. And why lie, unless she's up to something?'

When I said it out loud I knew I wasn't going crazy. Fliss didn't think so either. I pointed at Jane's van. Fliss stared from it and back to Jane, wide-eyed.

'There's an easy way to check out her story – come on,' Fliss said, pulling my arm. We reached the van, and Fliss pressed her hand on the bonnet.

'Cold,' she said to me. 'It hasn't been moved. And you're right, Jane couldn't have got to the motorway and back on foot.'

An anguished cry came from the park. Jane had broken the news about her mysterious and, if I was right, impossible motorway sighting of Dazzle to Margot McCarthy. I could see Jane and Charlotte supporting her. Margot was half collapsed with shock. Mum was standing a few metres from them, head in her hands. I knew what she was thinking – that all of her business dreams were slipping through her fingers like crumbs of broken dog biscuit.

Watching Jane comfort Margot the same way she had earlier with Mum made me question myself. Maybe she *could* sprint three miles if a dog was in danger? Was I just desperate not to be blamed for Dazzle's demise?

And Margot might have been awful to Mum, but seeing her, seeing anyone, being told their dog might be gone forever gave me the urge to hug Bacon. Wait. Where was Bacon?

I saw with a surge of relief that he was at the back of the van, standing on his hind legs with his front paws resting on the back doors. His head tilted to one side. He let out a short sharp yap, and pawed at the door.

Had our training sessions worked after all? It was just like the signal I had been teaching him to use to tell me he had located something important.

Fliss looked at me, then at the van doors, printed with the Dog House logo. I could tell she was thinking the same thing I was.

*Could Dazzle be inside? But if so, why isn't he barking?*

I pressed my ear to the cold door. The only sound was my own blood, pulsing in my ears.

But wait – there *was* a noise, a faint whimper. Fliss heard it too and gawped at me.

Then we both jumped, as someone shouted, 'Sid! Get into your mum's van. I'll take Margot and Charlotte home.' Jane was with a distraught Margot and Charlotte, in official Rescue Coordinator mode. Mum trailed behind them like a lost stray, unsure where to go or what to do.

Fliss and I were frozen to the spot, but Bacon yapped again, his eyes fixed on the van and his ears twitching.

'SID! Come on,' Jane called, letting go of Margot and

Charlotte and taking a few steps in our direction. She clearly didn't want us anywhere near the van – and that made me suspicious all over again.

I tried the back door handle – it was locked. Fliss didn't need telling – she'd already lunged for the handle of the other door. Also locked.

'SID! Honestly, don't you care that it's your fault a dog is missing? Don't you care that –?'

*SMASH!*

Fliss had hit the driver's side window with the metal hook of Bacon's lead, shattering the glass, just like one of the quick-thinking heroic bystanders who save the day on *Crim-Catcher*. Covering her hand with her jacket sleeve, she reached inside and pressed the door release button on the dash. The locking system opened with a *pop*.

I pulled open the van doors – and I swear my heart actually stopped for a second. Jane fell silent.

Dazzle lay limply, a deflated pompom, on a blanket scattered with the same orange dog biscuits we'd found in the back garden. His tongue dangled pink against his fluffy white fur.

What had Jane done to him? And why?

Jane was running now, at full (pug) speed, falling over her own feet to get to us.

'My dog! My Dazzle! What have you done to him?!'

Margot McCarthy screeched behind her.

Fliss dragged Dazzle, paws lolling, from the van, pulling the blanket he was lying on with him. Dog biscuits, a glass medicine jar and a pile of leaflets fell out of the van behind him.

Then Margot McCarthy overtook Jane (not hard to do) and snatched Dazzle from Fliss's arms.

I looked for something that was going to help me prove Jane was responsible.

The medicine jar that had rolled into the road, and I recognised the label. It was printed with instructions from the same vet we take Bacon to – only we'd never been prescribed this medication.

**Diazepam**: *To be used to calm nervous dogs. One tablet only. WARNING: Excessive consumption will cause extreme drowsiness.*

Dog sedatives! The perfect way to stop Dazzle barking and giving away his whereabouts!

'He's been drugged,' I said, my hands shaking with anger as I held up the bottle. 'Jane was the one who took him from the kitchen. He's been hidden in her van this whole time and she lied that he was on the motorway, because . . . because . . .'

Why *had* she lied? Why steal Dazzle and then pretend to

everyone that he was in grave danger? I didn't know, but it didn't make her any less guilty. Not that Margot, Charlotte and Mum looked totally convinced of that.

Jane was pulling a horrified face. I knew she was going to pretend that I'd made the whole thing up.

'Sid. This has gone too far! I don't know how you got Dazzle from the motorway into the van, but we need to get him to a vet,' Jane said, still trying to take charge just like she had for Mum in Margot's living room.

'Sid, look!' Fliss said, her eyes wide as she passed me one of the crisp, new leaflets that had fallen on to the road with Dazzle's blanket.

*Waggy Tails: a new dog whispering, walking and watching service is back in your area. Call to join today, as demand is expected to be high.*

Waggy Tails? That was the name of Jane's old company. The one that went bust, unable to compete with the Dog House because of our incredible dog whispering, walking and watching services!

I fixed my eyes on Margot McCarthy. I had to make her believe me, and now that I knew what Jane's motive had been, I could.

'Jane wants the Dog House closed so she can reopen

Waggy Tails,' I said, hardly able to breathe. 'She framed me and then tried to make you think Dazzle was about to be squashed on the motorway. I bet that after you'd told everyone not to use the Dog House, Jane would have pretended to find Dazzle wandering the streets – she'd have been a hero!'

Margot looked from me to Jane, cradling Dazzle's head.

'I expect you would have got one of these leaflets through your door a few days later, when you and most people in the area would have been in the market for a new dog walker,' Fliss added, handing one to Margot.

Margot studied the leaflet, before backing away from Jane, towards me and Fliss. 'Somebody call the police!' she cried. 'This woman dognapped my dog!'

I was so relieved I wanted to fall into a heap on the floor. Margot believed me! We were going to be OK! The Dog House and Mum would be all right.

Then Dazzle stirred, yawned and drooled on Margot McCarthy's yoga pants. He was all right as well!

'Already on it, Mrs McCarthy,' Fliss said, dialling the number on her phone and flashing me that giddy look she gets when a criminal is finally brought to justice on *Crim-Catcher*.

Jane opened and closed her mouth a few times, but no words came out. Bacon growled at her, expertly displaying his investigative training (he's definitely part sniffer dog after all). Like a cornered pug, Jane turned to make her escape. Not a chance. Mum's hand was already gripping her jacket.

'You framed my son and did this to an innocent animal?' she asked. 'You aren't fit to call yourself a dog walker!'

I grinned. Mum had turned from lost stray back into the Dog House's pack leader.

Charlotte McCarthy, back to her usual fierce preened-poodle self again, leapt on Jane and placed her arm in a death grip. She glanced at me and Fliss, and then I swear I heard her say . . .

'Thank you.'

It was officially the most eventful and weird day of my entire career as Junior Assistant Dog Exerciser.

# POISON PLOTS

History is a dangerous place. Poison was everywhere – in food, in drink, in homes and in gardens.

These three stories feature criminals whose methods are ingenious and astonishing. Today's detectives should feel lucky that they don't have to pit themselves against such formidable adversaries . . .

# GOD'S EYE
## By Frances Hardinge

The first time that Ben was allowed aboard the balloon, he was terribly sick over St Katharine Docks.

For almost a year, London had been buzzing with excitement about the Great Exhibition. Eyes turned to the vast, glass-walled Crystal Palace which had been built to house it. Every day there were new rumours about the things that would be shown there – diamonds the size of duck eggs, strange new inventions, and curiosities from all over the world. Queen Victoria herself would be there to open it, they said.

And now a newspaper called the *Daily Trumpet* had decided to produce their own exhibit – a huge 'God's Eye View of London' picture, using sketches made from a balloon. Two artists had won the competition to produce it, but unfortunately they argued bitterly. It soon became clear

159

that making them share a balloon would be disastrous, and that they would have to work in shifts.

It was not so bad before the ascent began. In fact, it was exciting to watch the great balloon slowly fill with coal gas, its brown silk losing its wrinkles and filling out. The little London park was packed with people who had come to watch, and when Ben joined his employer, the artist Solomon Cork, and Mr Pickles, the balloonist, in the basket, the rapt attention of the crowd made Ben feel like a dashing aeronaut.

Even when Ben felt the basket lose contact with the earth, it still felt like an adventure. The ropes that tethered the balloon to the earth were let out a little at a time, and the ground dropped away in a series of soft swoops. Ben was small for his twelve years, and could only just peer over the edge of the basket, but he dared a heroic wave at the upturned faces of the crowds.

When they rose above the houses, however, the wind struck them with full malice. Tiny, panicky ripples chased each other through the balloon silk. The basket twisted this way and that, and the ropes creaked until Ben thought they would break.

The roofs were below them, in the way that roofs never should be. London dropped away in lurch after lurch, and spread out under him, in grimy, red-brick billows. The river gleamed like dull metal, scattered with a thousand model boats. The horizons were a haze, the far reaches of the city merging into the smoke-laden, jaundiced grey of the sky. But it was a sick city, a giddy city, rolling around like a drunk. The ropes that rose from the ground were supposed to hold the balloon steady, but instead left it twisting and struggling in the brisk breeze from the estuary.

On one side, beyond the Tower of London, he could see the grand old city made miniature. St Paul's dome was a blue-grey bell, the Monument was a pencil stood up on end and the parks were scraps of green cloth. On the other side lay the grey, energetic sprawl of the docklands, with its huge warehouses and walled-in harbours. One huge, half-built ship loomed over the surrounding shipyard, but even that was a toy seen from this height, caged by matchstick scaffolding. Here and there, the red-brick factory chimneys belched fat, wind-tugged gouts of smoke, so thick that the buildings behind them were ghosts.

Ben had never guessed that working for an artist would involve needing a head for heights.

'I told them we'd be fighting the wind!' called out Mr Pickles. According to his posters, he was 'The Great George Pickles Whose Aeronautical Exploits Have Delighted Europe'. In practice he was a grey-haired man with a calm, jowly face, and a bowler hat fastened to his head by a ribbon knotted under his chin. 'The balloon likes to float free – she doesn't enjoy being put on a leash like this.'

'This is not a pleasure trip!' snapped Solomon Cork, Ben's employer. 'The newspaper is hiring you and your balloon so that I can sketch a God's eye view of London! Do your job, and stop your contraption lurching!' He was already peering through his spyglass, his cravat and coat-tails aflutter in the wind.

Unlike Ben, Cork had already endured two flights in the balloon. As before, he had nipped into the Old Lion for a tot of gin just before the morning's ascent, and had emerged glossy-eyed, his face as red as his sideburns. Perhaps it had steadied his nerves, but it had done little to improve his temper.

'Hand me that board and the charcoal!' snapped Cork. Ben hurried to obey, swallowing and swallowing as he tried to keep his breakfast down. The sketches were pinned to wooden boards so that they did not blow away, and Ben kept catching his fingers between them. 'Quickly! Idiot boy!'

After an hour of this, the balloon lurched once too often, and Ben lost control. Cork heard the splatter, and turned to find that Ben's morning porridge had over-painted one of the sketches, a finely pencilled outline of the river as it weaved past the little enclosed harbour of St Katharine Docks.

Cork gave Ben a cuff about the head that knocked him to the floor of the basket. 'Look at this! Do you know how important this sketch was?'

Ben barely heard him, too busy retching and clutching his bruised eye.

·

When the balloon touched down, and Cork stormed out of the basket, dragging Ben by his ear, they immediately bumped into William Pother, the other artist, who was standing in the watching crowd. Pother was younger than Cork, with a constant smile that was half nervous, half mischievous. He looked more like a poor clerk than an artist, and blinked a lot behind his spectacles.

'Are you trying to pull the poor boy's ear off?' he asked, as Cork tried to barge past.

'This little vandal threw up over one of my pictures!' shouted Cork.

'That sounds like a perfectly natural reaction to me,' Pother remarked serenely. 'Probably improved it.'

The two artists brought out the worst in each other. Cork was never good-humoured at the best of times, but Pother's smiling jibes drove him insane with rage. And Pother, who was courteous to nearly everybody, became waspish when he talked to Cork.

Ben sometimes wondered what it would be like to work

for Pother instead. It would probably be easier on the earlobe. Secretly, he also thought that Pother was a better artist. However, Cork had told Ben many times that he was a useless cub that nobody else would hire, and Ben didn't dare leave Cork's employ in case it turned out to be true.

Cork let go of Ben's ear to wave a finger in Pother's face.

'That,' he snarled, 'is the last straw. You'll be laughing on the other side of your smug face by tomorrow!'

Towards the back of the crowd, Ben recognised a distinctive white top hat. A moment later, Cork noticed it as well, and began pushing his way towards it.

'Mr Whyte!' he called out. 'I need to speak with you!'

Mr Whyte, the owner of the *Daily Trumpet*, always seemed to be trying to live up to his name. His top hats and waistcoats were white. His neatly combed hair and carefully curled moustaches were white. At the moment he was showing his strong, white teeth in a smile as he answered the questions of some well-dressed ladies. This smile wilted a little as Cork approached.

Cork murmured something in Mr Whyte's ear, and the two men moved away together. Ben followed at a distance, not wishing to come within ear-grabbing range.

Cork was fiddling with his cane, a sure sign of agitation. The round metal knob at the top was always loose, and when Cork was angry or tense he unscrewed it, then tightened it again, over and over. On a couple of occasions, Ben had even seen him raise it to his mouth as if to gnaw on it. But it was also a sign that he was plotting something. Whatever the two men were talking about, Ben suspected that it did not bode well for Pother.

His curiosity overcoming his fear of another cuff, Ben ventured close enough to overhear snatches of the conversation.

'I will not work alongside that puppy Pother any more!' Cork was declaring. 'And I am not being paid enough for this! Consider the risks I run! I am worth ten times the fee you are paying me!'

Mr Whyte said something patient but inaudible.

'Nonsense – you do not need Pother!' snapped Cork. '*I* am the only one you need, and you know it! Replace Pother with another artist if you must, but unless you turn him away you must do without me. And you *cannot* do without me, Mr Whyte.'

'You should kill Mr Cork with candles,' said Susan, Cork's maid-of-all-work, as she dabbed at Ben's swollen eye later that day. Cork was still with Mr Whyte, and Ben could only hope that the newspaper man was calming the artist down.

Life in Cork's employ was not easy. Susan worked herself ragged cooking, cleaning and scrubbing out fireplaces. Ben did everything else: fetching, carrying, polishing boots, cleaning up the studio and helping his master home after he had drunk too much. The artist paid them both a pittance, and vented his foul moods on them. Susan sometimes talked about walking out, but that would have left her stranded and homeless in the middle of London, with no references to help her find another job. Instead, on bad days they imagined Cork dying in bizarre ways, which cheered them up no end. It was a game and nothing more, but rather satisfying. Susan read every crime story in the newspapers, and usually came up with the most ingenious murder methods.

'What, set fire to him?' asked Ben incredulously.

'No!' Susan snorted. 'I mean, swap his bedroom candles for the old sort made with arsenic. They'd poison him as they burnt.'

'Oh, "corpse candles"!' exclaimed Ben, who had read of them once. Susan was fourteen, and a treasure trove of macabre facts and rumours, so Ben was glad to show off his own knowledge when he could. 'I thought nobody sold them any more.'

'Well . . . maybe not.' Susan wrinkled her nose, then brightened. 'But I bet you could find some still tucked away in folks' cupboards, if you asked around.'

'I'd look suspicious as sin!' objected Ben. '"Excuse me, can I borrow some old candles? And can you make sure they're the poisoning sort?" Anyway, would candle smoke even do the trick? Some of his paints have arsenic in them too, and he's breathing their fumes every day. Hasn't done him a whit of harm.'

'Have you got anything better?'

'I read about a man who caught fire from the inside for no reason,' suggested Ben shyly. 'It burnt away everything except his hands and feet and clothes.'

'Ooh, that's a rum one.' Susan nodded with a connoisseur's interest. 'But how will you make him catch fire from the inside?'

Susan's wicked humour and no-nonsense kindness made the days bearable. It was like having an older sister. Ben had three younger siblings, none of them old enough to work. He felt a quiet pride in being one of the breadwinners of the family, and his mother sometimes gave him extra jam for it with his tea. Still, it was nice to have someone else make a fuss of him now and then.

Susan seemed to like having a stand-in younger brother, too. Unlike Ben, who lived with his family at home, she was a 'live-in' servant, with a room in Cork's house. She never talked about her family in Wiltshire, but Ben suspected that she missed them.

'You'll do.' Susan stopped dabbing and squinted at Ben approvingly. 'Now, I need to have dinner in the oven before Mr Cork gets back.'

Ben went up to Cork's studio to try to clean the vomit-spoiled drawing, which he had brought back from the balloon site along with Cork's other artistic paraphernalia. By the end it was better, but still slightly stained and smudged. Ben didn't dare throw it away, but he did not want to leave it lying around either, in case it reminded Cork how angry he was with him. Instead he hid it in his own satchel.

Ben was still tidying the studio when Cork returned home. Thankfully the artist was now in a calmer mood. He ignored Ben entirely, and settled down to work on a half-finished painting. Ben tiptoed around behind him, washing brushes and scraping paint from palettes.

Even when Ben crept close enough to collect the small, empty brandy bottle leaning against the foot of the easel, Cork paid him no attention. Instead he remained staring pensively at the canvas, the tip of his paintbrush between his lips to bring the bristles to a point. Glad that he was not being clobbered round the head this time, Ben slipped out again as quietly as possible.

The next morning saw Solomon Cork back at the park, Ben struggling along behind him, loaded down with sketches and drawing boards. Cork was just heading for the Old Lion for a pre-flight drink, when a hand grabbed his sleeve.

'Cork – what did you say to Mr Whyte?' For once Pother

was unsmiling and pale with anger. 'He has just told me that he is dispensing with my services!'

Ben was surprised. He had overheard Cork demand Pother's dismissal, but he had never thought that Mr Whyte would agree to it. If he had been Mr Whyte, he would much rather have sacked bad-tempered, drunken Cork instead of clever, friendly Pother.

'A good thing too,' growled Cork.

'I know you are behind this!' snapped Pother. 'What lies did you tell him?'

'Let go of me!' Cork was fiddling with the loose top of his cane, and Ben knew that he was getting angry again.

'We are ready for you, Mr Cork!' called the balloonist. Cork yanked his sleeve free. He cast a furious look at Pother, and a glance of mournful longing at the Old Lion, then strode to the basket.

When Ben started to follow, his master withered him with a glare.

'Give me those sketches – you wait down here. I cannot have you spoiling another drawing. I am still deciding how much should be deducted from your wages for the last one.'

Ben silently fumed as his master climbed into the basket. The day before Cork had bellowed about docking his wages to pay for the sketch, but Ben had hoped it was an empty threat. After all, he had already been belted round the head.

A second punishment was *not fair*. He hated feeling so helpless, and right then he hated Solomon Cork.

He watched the balloon rise. How frail it looked, as it rose above the houses! Just for a moment, he wished that it would burst, sag and fall. He wanted to see the terrible pull of the earth call loudly and unanswerably to Solomon Cork.

Only when the ropes were at full stretch, and the balloon at its greatest height, did he peer up at the two tiny figures in the basket, and realise that the one with the cane was behaving oddly. It was flailing wildly, and jerking to and fro.

And then the figure fell from the basket, with strange grace, towards the earth.

Ben spent the next ten minutes in a daze. He was aware of confused shouting around him, and the crowd surging this way and that.

*It's my fault*, he thought. *I wanted Mr Cork to fall. And then he did.*

The balloon slowly returned to earth and began to deflate, withering like an old plum. The balloonist, the Great George Pickles, dismounted shakily from his basket.

'Never lost a passenger before,' he kept saying, over and over. 'He went into some kind of fit, right in front of my eyes. Terrible smile on his face. Flailed around. Fell out. I couldn't do anything . . .'

The story of Solomon Cork's fatal nosedive appeared in all the newspapers the next day. Ben and Susan read them together in stunned silence. Susan was staying in Cork's house to keep his possessions safe and in order until his next of kin was found, and Ben dropped in to see her every day.

The day after Cork's demise, a policeman visited while Ben was there. He was fairly ordinary-looking in his long blue coat, apart from a certain sharpness in his ice-pale eyes. Two days later he was back again, with more questions for Ben and Susan.

'Can you tell me what your master ate and drank the morning of his death, and the night before?' He took slow and careful notes. 'And did he eat or drink anywhere else? A public house, perhaps?'

Ben shook his head. 'He wanted to step into the Old Lion for a drink, but he never got the chance.'

'Was he taking any medicine?'

'No.' Ben could not suppress his curiosity. 'Sir, why do you ask?'

'Because some medicines contain arsenic. And I am trying to discover why your master had arsenic in his stomach when he died.'

'What?' Ben and Susan stared at him.

'Oh, it is quite true, and will be in the news tomorrow. Mr Cork's "fit" seemed suspicious, so doctors examined the body, and performed the Marsh test – a test for poison. And there it was – arsenic. It was not enough to kill him, but maybe it was enough to make him go into convulsions and lose his balance. Where is the arsenic kept in this house?'

'It is locked away safe in a drawer,' answered Susan, hesitantly. As in most households, a small supply was kept for killing mice and rats.

'And who keeps the key to that drawer?' asked the detective mildly.

'Mr Cork had one . . . and I have the other.' Susan had turned as pale as her apron.

'But you can't suspect Susan!' Ben exclaimed.

The detective examined the kitchen, the scullery and Susan's little room. He raised his eyebrows when he found her stash of murder stories.

'You seem to have an interest in poisonings,' he remarked.

'They're mine!' Ben lied quickly. 'She collects them for me!'

But the detective did not believe Ben. He believed the Marsh test. He believed the neighbours, who told him that they had heard Susan complaining about her employer, and saying she wished he would 'drop dead'.

And nobody listened to Ben the next day, when two detectives came back to arrest Susan for murder. They ignored him even when he tried to kick their shins.

'She's innocent!' shouted Ben for the nineteenth time.

'If she is, then she's got nothing to fear from a fair trial.' The young policeman blocking the entrance to the station sighed, not unsympathetically. 'Sorry, son.'

'But I know why Mr Cork had arsenic in his stomach!'

There was a pause, and then the older detective with the ice-pale eyes appeared in the doorway, and peered out at Ben's fuming figure.

'Perhaps you had better come in.'

He led Ben into a cramped little office, and sat down.

'Well?'

'Mr Cork sucked the tips of his brushes. I've seen other artists do it too. It brings the bristles together, so the brush will paint a thin line. I clean those brushes, but I can never get *all* the paint off.

'Some paints have arsenic in them, sir.' Ben leant forward eagerly. 'I think Mr Cork has been eating arsenic off his own brushes, without knowing it.'

The detective's eyebrows rose, and he seemed to be considering Ben's words carefully.

'I'll make a note of that. Not a bad idea. But it doesn't sound like that would be enough arsenic to throw a man into fits.'

'Then perhaps it didn't! Maybe he *was* just taken dizzy!'

'That wasn't a mere dizzy spell, son.'

'Or . . . or . . .' Ben racked his memory desperately. 'One of the newspapers said the convulsions and the horrible smile sounded like something else – something that wasn't arsenic.' He struggled for the name. 'Strych . . . strychnine!'

The policeman shook his head, but at least Ben had the feeling that the man was taking him more seriously now.

'The doctors did talk of strychnine poisoning at first. The symptoms matched very well. And it's hard to spot after death – it might not have shown up on the Marsh test. But in the end strychnine didn't make sense. It's a *quick* poison, you see – you usually show the signs of it in less than twenty minutes. Your master had not eaten or drunk anything for over an hour when he died.

'Besides, even if it *was* strychnine, that wouldn't help Miss Susan Hooper, would it? It doesn't change the fact that Mr Cork ate and drank nothing that morning that wasn't prepared by her.'

Outside Mr Pother's house, Ben tried to muster his courage.

'Those fits weren't natural,' he said under his breath. 'Somebody did for Mr Cork.'

Ben was not short on suspects. George Pickles the balloonist certainly hadn't liked him, and he had been alone with Cork when the artist fell to his death. Mr Pother had argued bitterly with him, and even Mr Whyte had also seemed rather tired of the man.

Of course, Susan had disliked Cork too. For a horrible moment, Ben imagined his friend adding powdered arsenic to Cork's tripe and onions with a smile.

*No*, he told himself firmly. *She's innocent. I know she is.*

Instead, he thought of the people who had actually gained from Cork's death. And the most obvious suspect was William Pother.

Ben knocked on the door, gave his name to a confused young housemaid, and was shown into a little drawing room. Pother joined him a few minutes later. The young artist was dressed rather more smartly than usual. His cravat looked new.

'Good afternoon, Ben.' Pother seemed a little nonplussed by Ben's visit. 'Er . . . I understand you are looking for a job?'

'With Mr Cork gone, I find myself without a place,' Ben said humbly. It was the best excuse he could think of to talk his way into the house.

'I am sorry, young fellow, I really am, but I don't need an assistant right now.' Pother looked uncomfortable. 'Once I have finished working on the God's Eye picture, and have more time, I will ask around on your behalf –'

'I thought Mr Whyte sacked you!' exclaimed Ben,

forgetting to be humble.

'After Cork's death, he changed his mind.' Pother smiled slightly. 'In fact, I now have a permanent job, drawing illustrations for Whyte's newspaper.'

Glancing around, Ben could see more signs that Pother had come into money lately. There was a new hat on the table, still with the hatter's price tag. A small bottle of expensive-looking brandy stood proudly beside it. There was something about its black and gold label that was slightly familiar, but Ben could not place it.

*You have done very well out of Mr Cork's death, Mr Pother.*

'Can I see the God's Eye picture?' Ben asked boldly.

Pother hesitated. 'I suppose there is no harm in that.'

The young artist's studio was smaller and neater than Cork's. A large table was spread with familiar-looking sketches, and beside it stood a large canvas on an easel.

Pother had skilfully copied from the sketches on the table, and managed to combine them into one grand scene. Church spires, domes, towers and chimneys clustered beneath a writhing, smoky sky. The last time Ben had seen this vista, he had been in a jolting, wind-chilled basket.

Ben stared at the picture. Something was wrong. Something was missing.

'Where are the docks?'

'The docks?' Pother's eyebrows rose. 'Oh, those aren't

in the picture. Mr Whyte wanted us to draw *this* view, looking over the heart of the city. The docks are in the other direction.'

'But . . . Mr Cork made a sketch of St Katharine Docks! I saw it!'

'Are you sure?' Pother looked baffled. 'Why would he do that?'

Ben had no answer. Why had Solomon Cork sketched entirely the wrong bit of London?

When Ben returned home, he dug out the splotchy sketch that he had tried to clean. There was no doubt about it. The drawing showed St Katharine Docks, its high walls freckled with warehouse windows, its little harbour crowded with boats.

Now that he looked at it more closely, Ben started to notice other strange things about the sketch. There were tiny marks, numbers and symbols that did not seem to be part of the view of London. He had never seen anything like them on Cork's other drawings.

What were they? He had no idea, and he could only think of one way to find out. Ben would visit the places in the picture that Cork had marked with a squiggle, and see if he could work out what was odd about them.

He had not reckoned on the noise and chaos of the docklands, however. Brawny 'lumpers' heaved boxes and bales from boats on to the wharfs. Hogsheads and barrels were rolled into towering warehouses. Carts rumbled, barrows creaked, and Ben was in the way wherever he stood. He caught snatches of conversations in strange tongues, and smelt spices and salt on the wind. The riverside was a forest of masts, flickering with flags and bunting of every colour.

Ben had no idea what he was looking for. After two hours of getting jostled, ignored and told to move on, he was almost ready to give up.

Then, by chance, he happened to notice a skinny, blonde girl of about his own age slinking past with a tray of goods slung on a cord round her neck. The oddments in her tray seemed to be scraps and findings. There were shells and 'sea coal', lumps that had fallen off coal ships and washed up on the shore. Among them nestled a small, dented, metal ball with 'SC' engraved on it.

Ben stared at it for a moment, then realised why it looked so familiar. It was the top of Solomon Cork's cane.

What could it be doing out here? Ben realised that he had not seen the cane since Cork carried it with him on to the balloon for his final catastrophic journey.

'Um . . . excuse me!'

The girl stopped and turned at his call.

'Where did you get that?' Ben asked, pointing at the metal knob.

'Found it.' She looked defiant and wary.

'Listen, that used to be part of my master's cane . . .'

'It was just lying on the ground!' interrupted the girl. 'That means it's fair game. Rule of the docks. It's like sea coal.' She looked like she was getting ready to fight or run.

'You can keep it,' Ben said quickly, and she relaxed a little. 'Where did you find it?'

'Near Little Tower Hill.' She nodded back towards the Tower of London, and the place where Cork had made his last fatal flight. 'The cane was smashed to smithereens – only this part was worth picking up. Broken wood and glass everywhere.'

'Oh.' Ben supposed the cane must have fallen out of the balloon, and smashed when it hit the ground. Then he frowned. 'Wait a minute. Did you say *glass*?' He felt a tickle of excitement. 'Can you show me the place?'

The girl held out her hand, and Ben reluctantly put a ha'penny in it. She led him back along the waterfront, then up a couple of streets. In a narrow, shadowed alleyway the cobblestones were indeed scattered with shattered wood and glass shards.

Ben stooped and peered. He had wondered whether the glass might have come from some local drunkard's bottle, or even from Cork's own spyglass. As he looked at the fragments, however, these possibilities faded away. The shards were curved, as if they came from a glass tube, and they were at the heart of the splintered mess.

'The cane was hollow,' said Ben under his breath. 'And there was glass inside.'

At last Ben was starting to understand what had happened to Solomon Cork. Now he just had to work out why.

He shielded his eyes and stared up at the brilliant blue sky, trying to imagine the chocolate-coloured balloon hovering overhead. He thought of Cork, leaning out of the basket . . . looking at what?

'What are you doing?' asked the girl, giving him a funny look.

Ben hesitated. He didn't know the area well, but she clearly did.

'I'm trying to guess why someone would go up in a balloon to look at the docks.'

The girl narrowed her eyes in thought.

'You could look down into the harbours, past the walls, I suppose. My father's a lumper – one of the men who shifts cargo – and he says kings' fortunes are unloaded off the Thames every day. So . . . if you could see when the valuable cargos turned up, you might know which warehouses to rob.'

Ben tried to remember what else had caught his eye during his only balloon flight, and recalled the vast, scaffolding-covered hull of the half-built ship.

'I saw a very big boat in one of the shipyards,' he said. 'Do you know what it is?'

'Oh – you mean the new warship for the Admiralty!' the girl answered, with some enthusiasm. 'Are you interested in battleships?'

'Yes,' said Ben thoughtfully. 'And I think I'm probably not the only one.'

Ben waited on the bridge, his heart thumping. It was a damp, clammy night, with no hint of moon or stars. He shivered with nerves and the cold, but focused on the thought of Susan in her prison cell. Her fate depended on his success this night.

In the distant gaslight, Ben made out a glimmer of white. A pristine white top hat, a white waistcoat. Mr Whyte strode across the lonely bridge, and came to a halt not far from Ben's huddled figure.

'So it is young Ben. You sent me a letter, asking me to meet you here – saying that you had a certain drawing that you were willing to sell me. I suppose I can spare a shilling for it.'

'I think it's more valuable than that,' said Ben. 'At least, I fancy the police would think so.'

In the darkness it was hard to make out Mr Whyte's expression, but Ben saw him stiffen.

'You only needed one artist for the God's Eye picture, but the competition gave you an excuse to hire two. You could count on Mr Pother for decent sketches, but you needed Mr Cork for something else. He would do anything for money, so you had him spy out over the docks while he was up in the balloon. Finding out where the big cargoes were stored. Spying on the shipyard where the warship is being built. The wrong kind of people would pay a lot of money for that sort of information, wouldn't they? Thieves. Spies. Saboteurs. He gave you sketches of the docks, with little coded marks on them. You never knew that *I* had one of them.

'Then Mr Cork got greedy, and started asking for more money. So you had a nice chat with him, and told him *of course* he could have more money, and *of course* you would sack Mr Pother. And you gave him a little bottle of good brandy to take away with him. A bottle with a gold and black label – like the one you gave to Mr Pother later. But the brandy you gave Mr Cork wasn't just brandy.

'You didn't know when Mr Cork would drink it, but you didn't really care as long as you weren't there. In the end, he poured it into a glass flask hidden inside his walking cane. The next time he went up in the balloon, he didn't get a chance to go to the Old Lion first, so he took a nip from his flask to steady his nerves.

'And then he went into fits and fell out of the balloon. Because strychnine works really quick, doesn't it, Mr Whyte?'

Ben was watching the newspaper man like a hawk, but was still taken by surprise when the tall man lunged for him. Mr Whyte grabbed Ben by the collar, lifted him and pushed him backwards over the railing, until he was holding Ben out over the dark drop to the river.

'If you know all that,' snarled Mr Whyte, 'then you know how I treat those who try to blackmail me. Where is that drawing? Tell me, or they will be fishing you out of the Thames tomorrow!'

A sudden blaze of light bathed the pair. Two policemen had stepped out from their hiding place behind the pillar, uncovering their lanterns. Mr Whyte froze, then slowly lowered Ben, turning as white as his own name. Ben felt almost as sick and shaky as he had in the balloon, but this time with relief. Susan no longer sat in the shadow of the gallows.

'Thank you for your help, son,' said the pale-eyed policeman. 'And thank you for your confession, Mr Whyte. I am sure the two gentlemen that the Marine Police caught earlier tonight trying to sabotage one of Her Majesty's warships will be able to tell us the rest . . .'

# THE MYSTERY OF THE PINEAPPLE PLOT
## By Helen Moss

In the spring of 1751 I was delivered to Catchpole Hall from the island of Jamaica in a crate of pineapple cuttings.

Had I crawled in among the cargo as a game? Or had the plantation owner stowed me aboard the ship by way of a free gift with the order? I don't know. Whatever the case, Lord Catchpole had been disturbed all morning by his daughters, Eliza and Catherine, weeping over the death of the nursery cat. *Perhaps*, he thought, *this little stowaway might amuse them.* The expense of returning an unwanted infant was also scandalously high. My fate was sealed. Lord Catchpole gave me the name stamped on the side of the crate and a home in the servants' quarters.

Which is how I came by the curious label of Quality Fruit.

Ten years have passed since my arrival. Eliza is a young lady of sixteen, accomplished in the gentle arts of needlework, French and flower pressing. Catherine is twelve. The gentle arts have, by and large, failed to attach themselves to her. She is more often to be found with an adventure book in her hand than an embroidery needle. I have grown tall, and the young pineapple cuttings have also grown. They are now, at last, producing fruit fit for the table.

And that is where my mysterious tale begins: at the dinner table. The dessert course, to be precise. Picture me, waiting outside the dining room of Catchpole Hall, buckling under the weight of a silver salver piled with a pyramid of fruit.

'Prepare to be astonished,' Lord Catchpole bellowed from behind the door. 'Master Quality Fruit will shortly bring in an Arrangement of Tropical Fruits, all home-grown –' there was a slurp as he swigged from his glass of claret – 'yes, *home-grown* in our very own glasshouses. Melons, oranges, pomegranates and . . . you will not believe your eyes . . . even a pineapple . . . '

I pushed the door with my toe and peeped in.

Candlelight sparkled on a sea of silver soup tureens, sauceboats, cruets and carafes. Lord Catchpole sat at the head of the table, his back to the fireplace, watched over by a portrait of his late wife, Elizabeth, who was taken by the fever when Catherine was just three days old. At the other end was the guest of honour, Lord Percy Ponsonby. This sumptuous banquet was to celebrate his engagement to Eliza. Also at the table were Eliza and Catherine, of course, our neighbours, Lord and Lady Fitchett, and their daughter, Dorothea.

Footmen were whisking away the remains of roast swan, lobsters, beef à la mode and French ragouts. Others were setting out the dessert: all manner of ices, jellies and syllabubs, and the Taj Mahal sculpted from marzipan and spun sugar. 'Why, I pray, do *we* not have a French chef who can produce such a centrepiece?' Lady Fitchett demanded loudly of her husband. She fluttered her ivory fan. 'Our Italian can manage nothing but a Greek temple. So outdated!'

'This pineapple is the biggest ever grown in this part of England,' Lord Catchpole continued. 'Why, when my gardener placed it upon the weighing scale yesterday, it almost broke the pan! Seven pounds and two ounces!'

'Impossible, my dear Catchpole!' Lord Fitchett thundered. He was a small man with a large voice, and every bit as fanatical about growing tropical fruit as Lord Catchpole. 'You graced us with a tour of your pinery only yesterday. We all saw the pineapples growing in their hotbeds in the glasshouse. I swear there was nothing above a four-pounder –'

Lord Catchpole cut him off. 'That, my dear Fitchett, is because I *deliberately hid* the best fruit from view so that the surprise should not be spoilt!'

Catherine spied me peeping around the door and stuck out her tongue. I returned the favour by crossing my eyes. She stifled her laughter under the pretence of choking on a sugared wafer.

'Master Quality Fruit!' Lord Catchpole boomed. 'Enter if you please!'

I paraded into the room with the fruit tray, feeling like a prize pig in a show ring. Or, should I say, a prize *turkey*. My master had ordered that I be costumed for the occasion in a cloak of saffron yellow velvet and matching turban topped with peacock feathers 'as befits a Dark-Skinned Citizen of the Exotic East'. My ear was still smarting from the sharp cuff it had received from Mr Tripeworth, the head footman, for venturing to remark that I was, in fact, from the West Indies, which – as the name suggests – is rather less to the east than Catchpole Hall itself.

The Arrangement of Tropical Fruits produced gasps of admiration from all but Catherine, who was giggling merrily at the peacock feathers dangling in my eyes. Eliza smiled too, but she looked a little poorly. She had complained earlier of a toothache. Indeed, she had returned to the table only moments before I entered, having left in search of some cloves to chew on to ease the pain.

I set the salver down in front of Lord Percy Ponsonby. He was generally considered a handsome fellow. His enormous stomach, bulging eyes and lack of a chin might have worked against him, had it not been for one shining feature: the richest estate in the county. Lord Catchpole, who had recently suffered a run of bad luck at the card table, had been overjoyed when he'd shown an interest in Eliza. By snaring Ponsonby and his fortune for his daughter, my master could pay off his debts and even afford an extension to the pinery.

Lord Ponsonby clapped his plump white hands. 'How thoroughly thrilling!' he trilled. 'What a corker of a pineapple!'

Lord Catchpole puffed with pride. 'Is he not a bruiser? Young Sam Bradley, my garden boy, has dubbed him *King George*.' He roared with laughter. 'The King of Fruit named for the King of England!'

The pineapple was indeed a magnificent sight – a golden-armoured orb beneath a crown of green spikes.

'It is almost as beautiful as Eliza.' Lord Ponsonby took a scroll from his lilac silk waistcoat. 'I have written a poem on the very subject, entitled "My Love Is as Lovely as the Loveliest Pineapple".' He cleared his throat. 'Allow me to read it out.'

'No, I beg you, do not!' Eliza cried.

Everyone looked at her in surprise.

'What my sister means,' Catherine piped up, 'is that we find your poetry so very . . . *moving*, that the emotion would simply be too much for us!'

Eliza did indeed look close to tears. I feared that her toothache must have grown worse.

Lord Ponsonby patted his elaborate white powdered wig. 'Ah yes! My poetry is so powerful that I find it often has that effect on delicate young ladies.'

'Ponsonby, my good fellow!' my master cried. 'Cut the pineapple open!'

Lady Fitchett dropped her macaroon. '*Eat* the pineapple?' she shrieked. 'Whoever heard of such a waste? It could adorn your table for a month.'

Dorothea frowned. 'But think, Mama, when Eliza is Lady Ponsonby, she will be able to afford to eat pineapple every day if she pleases!'

'I wager it will taste bitter,' Lord Fitchett grumbled. 'It appears under-ripe.'

With a cry of 'Huzzah!' Lord Ponsonby plunged a long silver knife into King George.

We all leant close – but what horror was this? A stench filled the air. Shreds of bark and dried black dung spilt out over the white damask tablecloth, and a monstrous centipede, as long as a toasting fork, sprang out of the pineapple and landed squarely upon Lord Ponsonby's nose.

Eliza screamed and leapt from her seat. The villainous creature dropped wriggling upon a china plate, where, by means of swift action and an upturned breadbasket, I imprisoned it.

Lady Fitchett swooned into the Taj Mahal.

Lord Percy Ponsonby, meanwhile, staggered about, hands clapped over his face. 'The bounder has bit me on the nose!' he wailed, and then he fainted. As he hit the rug, his wig fell off to reveal his own hair beneath, as yellow and tufty as duckling down. 'You've killed him!' Dorothea howled.

Lord Fitchett beamed. 'I *knew* that pineapple was a rotter!'

Lord Ponsonby sat up. His smitten nose was now blazing red and had doubled in size. 'Brandy!' he murmured. 'I must have brandy!' He looked about him. 'Best cognac if you can put a hand to it.' His pale eyelashes fluttered and he fell back again.

'Tripeworth!' Lord Catchpole commanded. 'Remove Lord Ponsonby to a guest chamber and call for the physician.' He thumped his fists upon the table, rattling the best china. 'This outrage is the work of young Sam Bradley.' He glowered as Lady Fitchett extracted herself groggily from the Taj Mahal, a sugar-paste minaret protruding from her forehead like the horn of a unicorn. 'He is the owner of this vile worm! I'll have the boy horse-whipped for this!'

I exchanged a troubled glance with Catherine. The pale skin of her right cheek blanched whiter still. The left side of her face, which was entirely covered over with a purplish birthmark, blushed a deeper hue. Sam Bradley, the garden boy, kept a menagerie of small creatures, and the giant centipede was his. Like me, Leggy had arrived from Jamaica as a stowaway in a crate of cuttings.

'It is warm for the season, is it not?' Catherine said. It was the secret signal we had used since our nursery days. She dropped her napkin and we both dived beneath the table.

'Whatever shall we do?' she whispered to me. 'This was not Sam's doing. Leggy is his pet – he would not put him in danger!'

'Someone else must have taken him without Sam's knowledge,' I agreed. 'But if the real culprit is not discovered, Sam will be punished.'

Catherine clutched my hand. 'We must help him! Father will not let Sam off lightly.'

I hesitated. This could spell trouble for us both. But Sam had been our friend since Catherine and I first slipped away from her nursemaid and roamed the gardens together. 'Meet me at the pinery,' I breathed. 'We must warn Sam. Then we must uncover the truth.' I crawled out from under the tablecloth, snatched up the breadbasket and hastened to my master. 'My Lord, allow me to return the centipede to its home. The doctor may wish to examine it to determine the nature of its venom.'

'Yes, yes, good idea, young Quality Fruit. And bring Sam

Bradley back to the house with you. The scoundrel will regret the day he disgraced a Catchpole pineapple!'

I waited outside the pinery, the largest of the three glasshouses. I had arrived by way of the back stairs, the scullery and the walled kitchen garden. Catherine took a longer route to avoid notice, leaving by the French window from the drawing room and strolling about the terrace a little – as if the shock had made her light-headed, and she needed to revive herself – before ducking behind the maze to the back of the house. She came running up at last, as quickly as her hooped skirts would permit, her white linen cap flapping by its ribbons.

We stepped inside together and were transported, as if by a magical carpet, to the tropics. Heat and steam swallowed us up like the laundry room on washday.

'Sam! Where are you?' Catherine called. 'Something terrible has happened!'

I hastened after her along the path between the pineapple pits: raised beds filled with dung and tanner's bark, which give out heat as they rot and ferment. Standing in these hotbeds were large clay pots, each containing a single pineapple plant, their long leaves stained blood-red by the rays of the setting sun.

A barefoot boy in undershirt and breeches came flying

towards us. His red hair flamed doubly bright in the crimson light, like the copper pans that hung above the kitchen fire. 'Qually!' he cried out. 'Lady Kitty! Something terrible indeed! Leggy vanished in the night. He's done a runner!'

I presented him with the breadbasket. Eyes wide, Sam peeped inside. 'Qually! You gem! I feared the cold outside would've killed him.' He took the giant centipede from the basket. Seeming to know his master, Leggy curled neatly in Sam's palm.

'Has Leggy ever bitten you?' I asked.

Sam smiled fondly. 'Only the once, when I first found him in the crate. He didn't know me then, see? He was scared. But it was no worse than a bee sting. I was right as rain in no time.'

I looked at Catherine with relief. By the sound of it, Lord Ponsonby and his nose would soon recover.

At the end of the glasshouse, a number of boxes were arranged on a wooden platform. All were inhabited by spiders, beetles and lizards. Sam gently placed Leggy inside the one that stood empty. Then he crossed to a frame mounted on the wall to consult a thermometer of the very latest Fahrenheit design. Pineapples are finicky. They must be bathed in sunlight and coddled with warmth. It was Sam's duty to stoke the furnace that piped hot air around the glasshouse. 'Where did you find Leggy?' he asked.

Catherine explained how the centipede had appeared, without invitation, at the dessert course.

'Leggy bit Lord Ponsonby?' Sam's cheeks paled so that his freckles stood out like nutmeg on new milk. 'Lord help me,' he mumbled. 'They'll transport me to the colonies for this!'

'Not if *we* can help it,' Catherine declared.

I doubted that Sam would be deported to the Americas for damaging a pineapple and a nose, but he would certainly face a whipping and be dismissed from Catchpole Hall. 'You must lie low until we can prove that you were not to blame. Tell me,' I said, 'when did you first notice that Leggy was gone?'

'At dawn. He wasn't in his box. I've been searching all day.' Sam clutched at his hair.

'Didn't you hear anything?' Catherine asked. Keeping the pineapples warm required such constant attention that Sam slept in the shed at the end of the pinery.

Sam shook his head. 'The furnace whistles and crackles all night long. Anyone who knew where Leggy's box was could have taken him without waking me.'

'Which means anyone who has ever set foot in Catchpole Hall!' Catherine sighed. 'My father is so proud of his glasshouses that he gives visitors the tour whether they want one or not.'

'That's right,' Sam said. 'He was here yesterday with the

Fitchetts. Lady Eliza was with them . . .'

'Did anyone show a particular interest in Leggy?' I asked.

Sam shook his head. 'Lady Fitchett fainted clear away at the sight of him. I told her there was no need to take fright. Leggy wouldn't harm a fly.' Sam faltered, recalling Lord Ponsonby's swollen nose. 'Except if he's been roughly handled and half-suffocated in a pineapple.'

He began gathering his few possessions into a bundle. 'I have to hide! Before Lord Catchpole comes to find me . . .'

'Anyone else?' I pressed.

'Lady Dorothea asked me what Leggy likes to eat. "He's partial to gingerbread and plum pudding," says I.' Sam grinned briefly. 'She's one of those young ladies who'll believe any old hogwash. "Then I shall fetch him some next time I visit," says she.'

We set off quickly towards the door of the pinery. 'Lord Fitchett was only interested in the pineapples, of course,' Sam said. 'Spying on our methods to report back to his own gardener.' Sam pointed out a wooden partition as we passed. 'Behind that screen is where we keep the biggest plants. Nobody is allowed to see 'em except us gardeners.' He glanced at Catherine. 'And family, of course.'

I peeped round the screen. Sam indicated one of the hidden plants, its stem as naked as a beheaded neck. 'That was King George. Lord Catchpole cut His Majesty down yesterday evening with his very own hands.'

'What about this one?' I asked, pointing to another plant that was bare of fruit.

Sam blushed. 'That was the next biggest. Only a jot smaller than King George. I called it Queen Charlotte, after our queen. It wasn't meant to be cut for days yet, but this morning it was missing. I haven't dared tell Lord Catchpole.'

Catherine was already at the door. 'Hurry!' she called. She took out a package of bread and cakes from the folds of her overskirts – she must have concealed them there at dinner. 'Take these, Sam. Go to the ruined cottage beyond the lake. Stay until we send word it's safe.'

'Thank you, Lady Kitty! Thank you, Qually! Don't let them harm Leggy while I'm gone.' As Sam opened the door, I felt the cool air rush in. I pushed my yellow cloak and turban into his arms. Like Leggy, Sam was accustomed to the pinery. I feared he might not stand the cold.

'Now that we have heard Sam's account,' I said to Catherine, when Sam had melted into the shadows, 'can you deduce anything more about the crime?'

Catherine nodded vigorously. 'I am certain the wrongdoer did not intend to cause Lord Ponsonby any serious harm. A little arsenic in his brandy would have been a far surer method, if murder had been the aim . . .'

Sometimes I wonder whether some of those novels

Catherine reads are a little *too* adventurous. But I agreed with her point. 'It seems the intention was to shock and offend him. That would explain why they added the dung from the pineapple beds as well as the insect.'

'And to cause embarrassment to my father,' Catherine continued. 'What about Lord Fitchett? He has been at war with my father for years. When Father hired a gardener from Holland, Fitchett hired two. When Fitchett added pineapples to his coat of arms, Father built a folly with a roof in the shape of a pineapple. Lord Fitchett would love nothing more than for Father's pineapple to be a laughing stock.'

Catherine waved her arms for emphasis, and an object that she had tucked into her sleeve fell to the ground. I stooped – it was a small oval tortoiseshell snuffbox.

'Oh!' said Catherine. 'I forgot! I found that lying near the thermometer. Someone must have dropped it. I don't think it's one of Father's.' Suddenly her eyes sparkled. 'Ooh, Quality! Do you think it belongs to the culprit? They could have dropped it when they crept in to take Leggy . . .'

I held the snuffbox up to the light. The tortoiseshell was worn smooth with use, but I thought I could make out some faint scratches. I took up a handful of earth and rubbed it over the lid. Gradually, the dark powder picked out initials engraved into the surface.

*T.W.F.*

'T.W.F.' Catherine exclaimed. 'Thomas Fitchett! I was right! Lord Fitchett did it!'

I looked across the gardens at the house, its windows catching the last golden rays of the sunset. I agreed that the finger of suspicion now pointed to Lord Fitchett, but we could not yet be certain. 'He may have dropped the snuffbox during the tour yesterday afternoon,' I said.

Catherine frowned. 'But if not Lord Fitchett, who else could it be?'

'Perhaps Dorothea did the deed to shame the Catchpole family and ruin Eliza's chances with Lord Ponsonby. She sounded jealous of Eliza at dinner. She may have hoped to win his fortune for herself?'

Catherine's hand flew to her mouth. 'Dorothea could never do such a thing! She and Eliza are the best of friends.'

'How about *Lady* Fitchett?' I suggested. 'She dreams of a finer life. She could be scheming to win Lord Ponsonby's riches for her daughter.'

'I dare say,' Catherine agreed. 'But Lady Fitchett could not have hidden Leggy inside the pineapple. The very sight of him sends her into a fainting fit.' She paused for a moment. 'I suppose they *could* be working together . . .'

I laughed. 'You believe they are a criminal double act, like the highwaymen Dick Turpin and Tom King?'

Catherine had to admit that her notion was a little fanciful. 'I must go back before I am missed. The ladies will have retired to the drawing room by now.' She took the snuffbox. 'I will return this to Lady Fitchett and ask whether Lord Fitchett mentioned losing it, and if so, when. And while I am there,' she teased, 'I will keep watch to see if Dorothea and her mama pass coded messages with the sugar bowl!'

'In the meantime,' I told Catherine, 'I will follow another thread. I will visit the kitchen and discover who could have borrowed King George and operated upon him to conceal Leggy inside.'

On the way to the kitchen I called at the dining room and told Lord Catchpole that Sam Bradley was nowhere to be found. The men were still at table, drinking port and smoking their pipes.

'So, the rogue has fled, has he?' My master swung his glass through the air, slopping red drops across the tablecloth. 'That proves his guilt beyond doubt!'

My heart grew heavy. I confess I had not thought of this. By urging Sam to hide we had made things look worse for him. It was now more important than ever that Catherine and I prove his innocence.

I hurried to the back stairs. As I passed the butler's pantry – the little room at the top of the stairs where the footmen keep dishes warm, ready to be taken into the dining room – I glimpsed a gleam of gold. A delicate chain had become caught at the base of the door. I grasped it and pulled free a small locket.

I recognised it as a token given to Eliza by Lord Ponsonby some weeks ago. How had it come to be there? Then I remembered that Eliza had gone to fetch cloves from the kitchen for her toothache. The locket must have fallen from her neck as she rushed past the butler's pantry. I slipped it into my waistcoat pocket to return to her later.

I hurried down to the kitchen, where I was lucky to find Molly, the scullery maid, opening oysters. Being very small and very quiet, Molly was never noticed, but she noticed everything. When I asked her what she knew of the pineapple before it arrived at dinner, she gave me a full account. 'It was locked in the spice cupboard,' she said, 'from the moment Lord Catchpole brought it to the house yesterday evening, to the moment Monsieur Choufleur placed it on the salver for you to take up to the dining room.' She waved her sharp little knife. 'Not even a traitor in the Tower of London could've been under closer watch. One of the kitchen boys was on guard around the clock.'

'Have any of the guests come into the kitchen today?' I asked.

'Oh yes!' Molly dipped her red hands into the pail of ice and pulled out another oyster. 'That Lady Fitchett was down here this morning.'

My ears pricked up. 'Snooping around the spice cupboard?'

Molly shrugged. 'I only heard her talking to Monsieur Choufleur. Asking whether he is happy here at Catchpole.' Molly snorted. 'I would *hope* he's happy. He's paid more than the rest of us put together, and he gets a bottle of champagne a day to boot!'

I thanked Molly and returned upstairs to find Catherine. She hurtled out of the drawing room, almost knocking me off my feet. 'I am surer than ever that Lord Fitchett is our man,' she whispered. 'Lady Fitchett told me that he had his snuffbox with him yesterday evening. He cannot have lost it while on the tour of the pinery in the afternoon!'

I quickly told Catherine my information from Molly. 'Lady Fitchett was hanging about the kitchen. I believe she was waiting for a chance to get her hands on the pineapple.'

'Then it is *Lord and Lady Fitchett* who are working together!' Catherine gasped.

'But how could they have done it?' I asked. 'King George

was under lock and key.'

Catherine chewed at a fingernail. 'When you carried the pineapple up to the dining room, did you ever leave it alone?'

'I most certainly did not!' I said, incensed at the very suggestion. I retraced my steps in my mind. Then I remembered. There *had* been a moment . . . As I stood at the dining room door, I had heard a whimpering noise coming from the butler's pantry behind me. I rested the tray of fruit on a little side table, crossed the corridor and looked inside. It was only Princess, one of Lord Catchpole's favourite spaniels, trapped inside. When I opened the door, the little dog dashed away without so much as a lick, and I returned to my post. King George had been out of my sight for no more than half a minute. Even a master surgeon could not have cut out its heart and replaced it with a giant centipede in so short a time.

I was recounting this incident to Catherine when we were startled by a cry from one of the maids upstairs. 'Send for the priest! Lord Ponsonby has taken a turn for the worse. The physician fears he will not last the night!'

Catherine clung to my arm. I shared her terror. The crime might now be even worse than an assault upon a pineapple and a noble nose. It could be murder.

My thoughts in turmoil, I took out Eliza's locket and flipped it open. A pair of tiny eyes looked up from a portrait no larger than a penny. The artist had done his client a kindness and given him the suggestion of a chin, but the miniature was unmistakably of Lord Ponsonby.

I was about to close the locket when I noticed something else: poking out was a small lock of dark brown hair tied with a strand of red silk.

All at once I knew who had committed the crime. I also knew how and why it had been done.

But I wished with all my heart I did not.


'**Y**ou *know* who did it?' Catherine asked. We had shut ourselves in the butler's pantry to avoid being overheard and were now sitting on a warming shelf in the dark. 'It was Lord Fitchett, wasn't it?'

'No,' I said. 'Lord Fitchett *did* creep into the pinery during the night, but only to spy on your father's pineapple-growing secrets. That's why the snuffbox was found beneath the new thermometer, nowhere near Leggy's box.'

Catherine was silent for a moment. 'I see. So, it was Lady Fitchett?'

'I thought so for a time,' I said. 'But even if she could somehow have taken the pineapple from under its guard, she could not have placed Leggy inside without fainting. I believe her reason for snooping about in the kitchen was simply to try to poach Monsieur Choufleur away for her own household. And,' I added, 'I am sure it wasn't Dorothea. She may have wanted to marry Lord Ponsonby, but she is not spiteful enough to have scuppered Eliza's chances or clever enough to have hatched such a plot.'

'So who was it?' Catherine asked. 'You have ruled out *all* our suspects.' She caught her breath. 'You can't think it was Sam after all?'

'No, not Sam. It was . . .' I could barely bring myself to name the culprit. 'What colour is Lord Ponsonby's hair?' I asked instead.

'Why, it's blond,' Catherine said. 'What he has left under that wig. But what does his hair have to do with anything?'

'Do you think Eliza loves him?'

Catherine sighed. 'How could she? That poetry! But the marriage is what Father wants, and Eliza has always been a good, obedient daughter so she doesn't mind.'

I found a candle and lit it. Then I held out Eliza's locket and showed Catherine what I had found hidden under the portrait. 'I think Eliza *may* mind more than you think.'

'But that's not Lord Ponsonby's hair!' Catherine spun the lock of dark hair by the red thread. 'Eliza has a . . . *sweetheart?*' Her eyes were wide in the candlelight. 'You think *Eliza* put Leggy in the pineapple?'

'I'm sure of it,' I said. 'She didn't mean to hurt anyone. She had heard Sam say that Leggy was quite harmless. She merely wanted to disgust Lord Ponsonby with the insect and the foul-smelling dung. She hoped he would be so horrified that he would break off the engagement. No wonder Eliza screamed when Leggy jumped out and bit him. That was not part of her plan.'

'But *how* did she do it?' Catherine asked. 'Molly said the pineapple was under constant guard!'

'That was the clever part of the plot!' I said. 'I should have realised as soon as Sam told us that a second pineapple was missing. The pineapple Lord Ponsonby cut into was not King George. As a member of the family, Eliza was one of the few people who knew that there was an almost identical pineapple behind the screen in the pinery – Queen Charlotte. Eliza crept in during the night and stole both Leggy and Queen Charlotte. That gave her all day to secretly hollow out the pineapple in the privacy of her room and stuff the unpleasant contents inside. Then she came to dinner with it concealed in her hooped overskirts – just as you did to bring the bread and cakes for Sam.'

Catherine nodded slowly. 'Eliza didn't have toothache, did she?'

'No. Fetching some cloves was an excuse to leave the table. She put the dog in the butler's pantry to distract me. As soon as I left the fruit on the side table, she jumped out and quickly switched the pineapples – putting Queen

Charlotte on the tray, and hiding King George in her skirts. She then returned to the dining room. The two pineapples were so similar in size that nobody noticed the substitution.'

'Except Lord Fitchett!' Catherine exclaimed. 'He almost saw through the trick when he said that the pineapple looked a little unripe.' She sighed and closed her hand around the locket. 'Poor Eliza! We would never have found her out if she hadn't dropped this.'

And so the mystery of the pineapple plot was solved.

Catherine and I hurried directly to the dining room and gave Lord Catchpole our conclusion. At Catherine's pleading, my master agreed to keep Eliza's crime a secret. Nor did he insist that Eliza go through with the marriage. Sam Bradley and Leggy were quite forgiven, and Sam returned to his post in the pinery. By great good fortune, only days later Lord Catchpole won enough at cards to pay off his debts, and by even greater fortune, Eliza's crime did not turn out to be a murder. Lord Ponsonby recovered within the week.

It is now three months later – a quiet evening here at Catchpole Hall, as the family are dining away from home. They are at Fitchett Manor to celebrate Dorothea's engagement to Lord Percy Ponsonby.

I wonder whether pineapple will be on the menu?

# THE MURDER OF MONSIEUR PIERRE
## By Harriet Whitehorn

Long before Hercule Poirot paced the corridors of the Orient Express, or before Sherlock Holmes sucked his pipe in Baker Street, there was a girl who lived in Georgian London named Angelica. She was to become Lady Angelica Bulstrode, crime solver extraordinaire and cleverest woman in London. But when this story begins she was still plain old Angelica Beck, or Jelly to her friends.

The place is the corner of Greek Street and Old Compton Street, in Soho. The year is 1782, the season is early autumn and the time is eight o'clock in the morning. A small, slight, blonde girl, dressed simply in a pale cotton dress and cap, is hurrying along. You might not notice her immediately, but once you spot her, there is something intriguing about the determined tilt of her chin, her intelligent blue eyes and the way her small feet step with such surety on the dirty pavements.

Soho is a rag bag of an area, where the very rich live alongside the very poor. Immigrants like Angelica's family, who arrived from France a few years before, are crammed into tall houses, several families to a floor. Later in the day, the streets will be a bustling mass of fops and pickpockets, street sellers and drunks, tradesmen and fine ladies, all dodging between the carts and carriages and sedan chairs. But for now, all is quiet in the bright morning sunshine.

'Good morning, Angelica,' Doctor Mason, Soho's finest physician, called to her. Angelica returned his greeting with a ready smile and a small bow of her head.

'Morning, Jelly!' Burt, one of the street urchins, called from a doorway, and she waved back.

Angelica was making her way to Monsieur Pierre's Hairdressing and Beautification Salon, where she worked among towering, ridiculous hairstyles as Monsieur Pierre's apprentice. Monsieur Pierre's supremacy was rivalled only by his bitter enemy, Monsieur Leonard of St James's. But Monsieur Leonard was a ghastly snob, whereas Monsieur Pierre was entirely charming. He was small and chubby, with a nondescript face in which only his small periwinkle blue eyes stood out, but he knew how to make women laugh, and so society women, raised on a diet of stuffy English men, adored him.

Monsieur Pierre had first hired Angelica three years before, when she was just eleven, and since then she had proved the perfect apprentice. She seemed to know instinctively the size of comb, the colour of rouge or the length of false hair that he needed. Likewise, his clients only had to wish for a glass of wine or a plate of cakes and they would appear at their elbow. The shop was immaculate, Monsieur Pierre's accounts were in perfect order, and his appointments were managed with tact and discretion.

Outside Monsieur Pierre's shop, Angelica was just reaching into her pocket for the key to open the door when a voice shrieked behind her, 'Have you seen my wretched husband?'

Angelica turned around to see a dishevelled Madame Pierre, Monsieur Pierre's wife, lurching towards her. She was still in evening dress and jewels, but her make-up and hair were looking the worse for wear and her eyes were slightly crossed.

'He never came home last night,' she complained furiously. 'I waited until I was so bored that I just had to go out to the assembly without him. But now he still isn't back. Where is he?'

Angelica had seen many of Madame Pierre's tantrums, so

she replied calmly, 'I am afraid, Madame, I have no idea. I left him at the shop last night with Lady Osborne.'

Madame Pierre let out a furious gasp.

'Not her!' Just wait until I get my hands on them . . .' And she stormed off.

Angelica smiled to herself; Lady Osborne and Monsieur Pierre were simply old friends. But she did wonder where Monsieur Pierre was. It was unlike him not to go home each night.

She tried to turn the key, but the door was already unlocked. *How strange*, she thought as she opened the door and gasped. The shop had been turned upside down: the chairs lay on their sides, the wall cupboard hung open, and the floor was strewn with papers and spilt hair powder.

But worse still, the body of Monsieur Pierre was lying on the floor, his periwinkle blue eyes staring at the ceiling. It was Angelica's turn to shriek.

'Madame Pierre, come back! Burt, run for Doctor Mason immediately!' she cried.

As soon as she realised what had happened, Madame Pierre set up such a caterwauling that a crowd gathered. Doctor Mason arrived moments later. He rushed into the shop and bent over the body, searching for a pulse. Tears began to cloud Angelica's eyes, but she blinked them away.

'I'm sorry,' Doctor Mason said after a few minutes of

examining the body. 'He's dead. And I'm afraid that it may not be a natural death. His dilated pupils and the rash on his chest suggest poison.'

Angelica cried, 'No!' as Madame Pierre, raising a hand to her forehead, spiralled down in a faint. The doctor only just caught her before she hit the floor.

'Madame Pierre, let me get you home,' he said. 'I will have the body moved back to my house after the constable has seen it. Angelica, please wait for him.'

After the doctor left, Angelica had no desire to stand on the street, where the newsboys were already crying, 'Monsieur Pierre was MURDERED!' Nor could she bear to be near the body, so she went into the shop's little backroom. It was part storeroom and part office, and almost entirely hers. It was where she sat most mornings, perched on a stool, doing the accounts and other paperwork, and as often as not, creating all the creams, make-up and other beautifying aids that Monsieur Pierre sold to his customers. He found the work boring, whereas it was Angelica's favourite part of the job. She loved pulling the different jars and bottles down from the crammed shelves above her, and the hours would fly by as she mixed up flower waters, herbaceous balms, hand cream and rouge.

Poisoned, Doctor Mason had said. Angelica immediately thought of the powdered arsenic, an ingredient in their bestselling face whitener, and the small blue glass bottles of belladonna that they sold to ladies to make their eyes darker. They had been down to their last bottle of belladonna the day before; Angelica had made a note to buy some more from the apothecary. She checked the shelves. The arsenic was all there but the belladonna was gone!

'Hallo?!' She was still reeling from her discovery when a voice summoned her to the front of the shop. It belonged to a man of about thirty, scruffily dressed. Angelica recognised him as Nathaniel White, one of the most well-known of the Bow Street Runners. With him was a boy of Angelica's age and the Soho nightwatchman, Tom.

'Morning, Jelly,' Tom greeted her. 'What a sorry business this is. Mr White, Fred, this is Angelica, Monsieur Pierre's apprentice.'

'I am pleased to meet you, Angelica,' Nathaniel White said to her, bowing slightly and looking at her intently. 'I am sorry for the terrible shock you must have had.'

'I was just telling Mr White, Jelly,' Tom said, 'that I saw a lady leave the shop at about nine o'clock last night. She was wearing a green cloak.'

'That sounds like Lady Osborne,' Angelica said. 'She always wears green. She says it's her lucky colour. She was here last night – when I left at six, Monsieur Pierre was still finishing off her hair.'

Nathaniel was about to reply, but Fred grabbed his arm. His fair skin had turned a queasy grey and little rivulets of sweat were running down his face.

'I'm terribly sorry, sir, but I can't be in here with that . . .!' He gestured at Monsieur Pierre's body.

'Honestly, Fred!' Nathaniel sighed. 'You will have to get used to the sight of a corpse if you want to continue in this job. Go back to Bow Street and make yourself useful there. Tom, you can go too.'

Fred rushed out, his hand over his mouth. With a kind smile for Angelica, Tom also took his leave.

'So,' Nathaniel turned back to Angelica, 'you say you left at six and didn't return until morning?'

Angelica nodded. 'That's right.'

'Is there anyone who can confirm that?' Nathaniel asked evenly.

Angelica gave a start. Surely he couldn't think that *she* had anything do with it?

'Of course,' she replied. 'Half of Soho saw me walking home, and when I got there I was with my aunt and cousins all evening.'

'I see,' he replied slowly, still studying her. 'So tell me, did you get on with Monsieur Pierre?'

'I l-liked him very much,' Angelica stammered. She could feel tears in her eyes as she remembered poor Monsieur

Pierre lying on the ground. 'He was very kind to me.' She turned away from Nathaniel, and furiously wiped her face. He began to examine a bottle of wine and some glasses that were sitting on a side table.

'I must tell you something,' Angelica said nervously.

'Go on,' he replied.

'Well, Dr Mason said that Monsieur Pierre was poisoned, and I noticed, when I was in the storeroom just now, that there was a bottle of belladonna missing.'

Nathaniel's eyes drifted disconcertingly to the ceiling. Did he really suspect her still, Angelica wondered? How could she stop him? But then, suddenly he looked straight at her, with a bright smile.

'Angelica, that could prove very useful. You know, Tom told me you were a good girl who was fond of her employer and I can see that he is right. I don't believe that you had anything to do with the crime. Now you can help me. Who else knew that you kept belladonna here?'

'Madame Pierre did, and a few of our regular customers. Lady Osborne did, I know,' Angelica replied, relieved to be out of suspicion.

Nathaniel nodded. He continued to examine the room. 'This cupboard has been forced open. Is this where Monsieur Pierre kept his money?'

'No, he always kept his money at his house. He just

stored papers and letters in there.'

'Papers and letters,' Nathaniel repeated. 'Which are now strewn all over the floor. I suppose some may have been stolen.' He bent down. 'So we have a poisoned victim and a possible burglary.' He paused. 'Tell me about Monsieur Pierre. Did he have any enemies?'

'Just Monsieur Leonard,' she replied. When Nathaniel raised his eyebrows in query, Angelica explained about the two hairdressers' fierce rivalry. She winced as she remembered the scene only the week before, when Monsieur Leonard had discovered that one of his favourite clients, the Duchess of Argyll, had come to see Monsieur Pierre. Monsieur Leonard had stormed into the shop, threatening terrible revenge.

'Interesting,' Nathaniel replied. 'Did he argue with anyone else?'

'Only Madame Pierre,' Angelica replied.

'Really? Did they argue a lot?'

'Well, yes,' Angelica conceded. Hardly a week went by without Madame Pierre causing a scene.

'And Lady Osborne? Was Madame Pierre jealous of her?'

'Terribly.'

'With reason?' Nathaniel raised his eyebrows.

'No, they were just friends.'

'Tell me about her.'

Angelica thought. Blonde Lady Osborne was gracious and

beautiful, and always kind to Angelica, taking an interest in her and her family. She had been born penniless in the Covent Garden slums but had become a famous actress. Now that she was married to Lord Osborne, she moved in the highest part of society. But there was something slightly melancholy about her – some part that didn't belong with the rich people she lived among now. Angelica didn't know how to explain that to Nathaniel, so she just replied, 'She's nice.'

'Where does Lady Osborne live?'

'Nearby, in Soho Square,' Angelica said.

Nathaniel paused, his eyes drifting to the ceiling again.

'Can you write, Angelica?' he asked a minute later. She nodded, and he said, 'Since I am missing an assistant, would you mind coming with me to take notes of what the witnesses say? We can start with Lady Osborne.'

Angelica hesitated; it sounded awkward, especially if he was going to question Lady Osborne in the same way he had questioned her. All she really wanted to do was go home, have a cup of tea and cry about poor Monsieur Pierre. But then, she told herself, if it would help Nathaniel catch the murderer, perhaps she should.

'Very well then,' she agreed.

Nathaniel handed her a pencil and notebook. 'You never know, you might enjoy it,' he said.

Outside, the crowd had dispersed except for a gaggle

of street urchins, who called after Nathaniel, 'We know whodunnit, sir! Give us a penny and we'll tell ya!'

Lady Osborne's carriage was just pulling up outside her grand house as they arrived.

'Angelica.' Lady Osborne smiled warmly at her. 'Why are you coming to see me? Did I leave something in the shop last night? Or have you brought me some more of your amazing hand cream?'

'No,' Angelica faltered. Although she had agreed to help, she felt uncomfortable about being there, and she could feel a lump forming in her throat.

Nathaniel stepped in. 'Lady Osborne, allow me to introduce myself. I am Nathaniel White, of the Bow Street Runners. Would it be possible to talk inside?'

Lady Osborne paled.

'Yes, of course, come in, both of you,' she replied.

They followed Lady Osborne inside, nearly colliding with a small, dark lady, whom Angelica recognised as Lady Osborne's sister-in-law, the Honourable Felicity Osborne. She had come to Monsieur Pierre's for a while but found his 'mixed' clientele too distressing. Now she went to Monsieur Leonard's, where all of the customers had titles. There were rumours that she was still angry at her brother for marrying an actress.

'Are we entertaining the servants now?' her cold, sharp voice rang out. Lady Osborne ignored her, ushering them into quite the grandest room Angelica had ever seen. She stood while Nathaniel perched awkwardly on the edge of a silk-covered chair and began, 'I am very sorry to tell you that Monsieur Pierre was found dead this morning.'

Lady Osborne raised her hands to her face in horror.

'How terrible. How did he die?'

'I am afraid, Your Ladyship, it appears that he was murdered. As you were the last person we know of to see him alive, may I ask you some questions? Is Lord Osborne in? He should probably be present.'

'My husband is away for another week. But do not trouble him – I'm happy to answer your questions now.'

'I understand from Angelica that you and Monsieur Pierre were old friends.'

Lady Osborne nodded.

'So, Your Ladyship, what time did you leave Monsieur Pierre's last night?'

'About seven. But he was alive and well then!'

'I see. And what did you do afterwards?'

'I dined alone, here. My husband is away, as I said, and my sister-in-law was out.'

'Did Monsieur Pierre mention that he was expecting anyone else after you left?'

'He told me he was shutting up the shop and going home to dress for an assembly at Lady Fawcett's. Tell me, was it a robbery? Was anything taken from the shop?'

'Perhaps some papers. It is hard to tell.'

A look of concern passed across Lady Osborne's face that both Angelica and Nathaniel noticed.

'How did he seem when you left him?' Nathaniel asked. 'Did he talk of arguing with Monsieur Leonard or his wife?'

'Yes,' she replied distractedly. 'He was upset with both of them.'

'Lady Osborne, a lady matching your description was seen leaving Monsieur Pierre's shop at nine last night. What do you say to that?'

'Nonsense! I left at seven, and besides, why would I murder Monsieur Pierre? He was my oldest friend,' Lady Osborne exclaimed, rising to her feet. 'Please leave, both of you, at once.'

'I had better speak to Madame Pierre next,' Nathaniel said as they walked into the square. The leaves on the trees were turning from green to gold, but the sunshine was still warm enough to feel hot on Angelica's arms. They walked down Greek Street, heading to Meard Street where the Pierres lived. As they were crossing over Queen Street, a carriage swerved in front of them, making them jump back.

Lady Osborne's face, looking agitated, appeared at the open window as it clattered to a halt.

'Please get in!' she told them and they climbed up into the carriage.

'I think I know the reason why someone might murder Monsieur Pierre,' she blurted out as they sat down opposite her.

'Go on, please,' Nathaniel said coolly, showing no amazement at what had happened. Angelica was open-mouthed.

'Monsieur Pierre and I have been friends since I was just starting out as an actress. He knows my secret – that many years ago I had a baby, a little boy named Henry. Henry's father and I couldn't marry, and so I had to send him away to live in the country, with an aunt of mine. I used to go and see him regularly, and all was well until Lord Osborne asked me to marry him. I knew I could never tell him about Henry, so I arranged with my aunt that she would keep the boy with her and write to Monsieur Pierre's address with news of him. Pierre kept the letters safe for me and I read them when I came to the shop.'

'And now you think someone has taken the letters?' Nathaniel said.

Lady Osborne nodded. 'Yes, because I received this just now,' she said, producing a folded sheet of paper. 'I know your secret' was written across it.

'And do you suspect anyone?'

Lady Osborne sighed. 'It must be someone who wants to discredit me or Monsieur Pierre.'

'And was Madame Pierre aware of the letters?'

'No, I don't think so,' Lady Osborne replied.

Angelica wasn't so sure. She remembered Madame Pierre demanding the cupboard's key from Monsieur Pierre, yelling that she knew it contained love letters from Lady Osborne. He had refused to give her the key, making her even angrier.

'I think she suspected something,' Angelica said. 'She was shouting at him about letters.'

Nathaniel nodded. 'Come, Angelica, we must go and see Madame Pierre at once.'

The Pierres' house was halfway along Meard Street. The housemaid showed them up to a first-floor bedroom. Madame Pierre was in bed, propped up on a mound of cushions. She looked terrible, with a pale puffy face and red swollen eyes. However, her face brightened at the sight of Nathaniel, Angelica noticed, and she began to pat her hair, and smooth her clothes.

'I am pleased to meet you, Mr White,' she said, giving him her hand as if they were at a party. But when she saw Angelica, she asked rudely, 'What are you doing here?'

'My usual apprentice is unwell, so Angelica is helping

me,' Nathaniel replied.

'I see,' she replied tersely. 'Have you apprehended the murderer yet?' she asked, and dissolved into noisy sobs that Angelica was sure were false.

'Not yet, madam. May I ask you a few questions?'

Madame Pierre's expression changed.

'Questions? Me? What for?'

'Just to straighten a few things out,' Nathaniel replied soothingly.

'Very well,' she said with a sniff. 'But not too many. My health is very precarious.'

'Thank you,' Nathaniel replied, all charm. 'If you could just tell me what you did yesterday evening from six onwards.'

'Well, I was here getting ready for an assembly at Lady Fawcett's. I waited and waited for Pierre, feeling so . . .' she paused, choosing the correct word, '. . . so worried.'

*So furious, more like*, Angelica thought.

'Then Mrs Giddon's carriage came for me at eight-thirty and I felt it would be rude not to go with her. I came back at about seven this morning,' she added, a little sheepishly.

Nathaniel considered this for a moment.

'And you saw nothing of Monsieur Pierre in that time?'

Madame Pierre shook her head.

'What colour cloak were you wearing last night?'

'My new scarlet one, with the fur trim,' Madame Pierre

replied, proudly. 'It was much admired.'

'Madame Pierre, who do you think might have murdered your husband?'

'He was . . .' she paused dramatically, '. . . very close to Lady Osborne. I wonder perhaps whether they quarrelled. I know she is fearsomely jealous of me. Oh my poor husband . . .' and she dissolved into sobs.

Angelica had to stop herself from rolling her eyes.

'You have been most generous at this terrible time,' Nathaniel said, taking her hand with mock gallantry. 'We will leave you now.'

'Thank you,' Madame Pierre sighed, sinking back into her pillows.

*Well, it cannot have been Madame Pierre if she was at the assembly at nine, and wearing a red cloak*, Angelica thought as the front door shut behind them.

'Before we question Monsieur Leonard, I would just like to have another look in the shop,' Nathaniel said, striding off.

The shop seemed to be wrapped in a veil of sadness, mourning its master.

Nathaniel went over to the bottle of wine and glasses that he had been examining before.

'Were Monsieur Pierre and Lady Osborne drinking this?'

he asked Angelica.

'No,' she replied. 'It wasn't that wine.' She looked around the room. 'It was this Moselle.' Nathaniel picked up the half full bottle and examined it carefully. Then he bent down to look at the glasses. Angelica looked at them too.

'They both have lip rouge on them,' she remarked. 'Monsieur Pierre never wore it so Lady Osborne must have drunk out of both of them, which is odd. Or perhaps there was a third person here.'

Nathaniel looked at her, impressed.

'Go on, tell me what else you can see,' he urged.

Angelica blushed a little and looked again.

'I would expect belladonna would leave a sour taste.' She dipped her fingertip into the sediment at the bottom of the glasses, cautiously tasting it.

'But there is only the taste of two different wines. The one in that glass is sweeter. And there is a smell of . . .' she paused, trying to place it, 'frankincense and orange blossom. From that glass only.' Nathaniel was looking at her with such amazement that she felt she must add, 'I make all the toiletries for Monsieur Pierre, so I have a good nose.'

'Excellent. But if Monsieur Pierre drank from another glass, it is missing.'

They both began to look around the room. A glint

of glass under a sofa caught Angelica's eye. 'Here, I think I've found something,' she said. Nathaniel bent down with her to examine the shards. 'A third glass! But it has been smashed to pieces, so will tell us nothing.'

'But look what's underneath here too,' Angelica said, pulling out an empty blue bottle. It was the missing bottle of belladonna! Again she caught a whiff of frankincense and orange blossom. This time she could place it.

'The smell is Monsieur Leonard's Magical Hand Salve,' she announced.

'I think we have our man! Let's go!' Nathaniel cried.

*Monsieur Leonard must be the murderer*, Angelica thought as they walked across Soho to his shop in Bond Street. She remembered his furious face as he threatened Monsieur Pierre the week before. She could just imagine him coming to the shop, and pretending to make friends with Monsieur Pierre, insisting they had a drink together . . .

Monsieur Leonard's distinctive shop, painted bright pink, was in front of them.

The smell of frankincense and orange blossom hit them as soon as they walked in. His apprentice informed them snottily that Monsieur Leonard was much too busy to see them and that they would have to return later. But as they were about to go, the door to the private salon opened. The hairdresser himself, in his elaborate wig and make-up, appeared, brandishing a pair of curling tongs. He gave a curt nod to Angelica as Nathaniel introduced himself,

'I had heard about Monsieur Pierre's death, and I cannot say that I am sorry,' Monsieur Leonard said with a shrug. 'But it was nothing to do with me.'

'Can you prove that?' Nathaniel asked.

'Most certainly. I was here all yesterday afternoon with the Honourable Felicity Osborne. The Duchess of Gloucester came afterwards, and stayed until nine-thirty, and then I went straight to Lady Bath's house, two minutes' walk away in Hanover Square, for a late supper.'

Angelica scribbled it all down as she felt her heart sinking. Monsieur Leonard had an alibi! But if it wasn't Monsieur Leonard, who could it be?

They walked out of the shop feeling very dispirited.

'I think we should go back and speak to Lady Osborne,' Nathaniel announced. 'Since it is clearly neither Madame Pierre nor Monsieur Leonard, she is still our main suspect.'

'But what about the letter she received?' Angelica asked.

'She could have sent it herself this morning!'

'But why would she lie?' Angelica asked, unconvinced.

'To try to divert us from suspecting her of Monsieur Pierre's murder.'

'But she has no motive!'

'She does if he was blackmailing her,' Nathaniel argued.

228

'What if they quarrelled and he threatened to expose her?'

'Monsieur Pierre would never do such a thing – they were friends,' Angelica protested. 'What about the second glass with rouge on it? Don't you think that suggests that someone else was there? If it wasn't Monsieur Leonard himself, it was someone who uses his hand cream.'

'Lady Osborne could have just as easily drunk out of both – she could have changed glasses when they changed wines. And perhaps she does use that hand cream as well as yours. We know that someone in a green cloak like hers was seen leaving the shop at nine, and she has a motive, as well as the means. She knew that you kept belladonna here.'

Angelica was about to protest but they were interrupted by Fred, charging up to them.

'Sir, I've been looking for you everywhere. A note came to Bow Street for you. It says it's very urgent!'

Nathaniel read the letter, his brow furrowing.

'Lady Osborne has received another letter from the blackmailer, telling her to meet them at Monsieur Pierre's shop at eleven o'clock tonight, or they will expose her. Well, I must be there to watch. All will be revealed tonight. Perhaps Monsieur Leonard or Madame Pierre were lying about their alibis. Or perhaps my theory is correct, and Lady Osborne is bluffing, in which case no one will turn up.'

'Can I come too? Please?' Angelica asked.

Nathaniel thought for a moment.

'Yes, as long as you promise to stay out of the way. Now I had better get back to Bow Street. Will you meet me at the shop at ten-thirty tonight?'

'Oi, Jelly, have they caught the villain yet?' Burt called across to her, as Angelica was walking home.

'No, not yet,' she replied. Then something occurred to her. 'Burt, did you see Lady Osborne leaving last night?'

'Course I did. She gave me a penny.'

'And what time was it?'

''Bout seven. And then the other lady came after, wearing a green cloak just like hers.'

Angelica could hardly believe her ears.

'Which other lady? Do you know her?'

'Nah. But she were small and dark. Now, buy us a bun, Jelly, will ya? I'm starvin'.'

That evening, Angelica was hidden in the back room as instructed by Nathaniel, while he hid behind a curtain in the front of the shop. Lady Osborne was waiting there too, pacing nervously.

Angelica wondered if her new theory about the blackmailer's identity was right. Everything had fallen into place after her conversation with Burt, but when she told

Nathaniel her theory, he had been dismissive.

'You shouldn't trust the word of a street boy. I have thought about this carefully,' he said, 'and my money is on Lady Osborne.'

The blackmailer had arrived!

'Get your hands off me!' Angelica heard a familiar voice cry as she peered out from behind the door. Nathaniel grabbed the cloaked figure who had just come into the shop.

They struggled furiously but Nathaniel was stronger. A few seconds later, he pulled the hood back to reveal, as Angelica had suspected, the Honourable Felicity Osborne!

'I can't believe it!' Lady Osborne cried to her sister-in-law. 'Why would you do such a thing?'

'For the honour of my family!' Felicity spat back. 'It was bad enough that my brother chose to marry a common actress, but when some gossip told me about your child, that was it. I had to force my brother to divorce you.'

'But why didn't you just tell Lord Osborne?' Lady Osborne said.

'Because I knew I would need evidence to make him believe me. And it didn't take me long to work out your little arrangement with Monsieur Pierre.'

'So will you tell us what happened last night?' Nathaniel asked her.

'Why would I?' Felicity replied with a laugh. 'You'll never

prove it was me.'

'I wouldn't be too sure about that,' Nathaniel said. 'I have an extremely reliable witness who saw a woman exactly matching your appearance arriving at and then leaving the shop.' Angelica smiled at his description of Burt.

A look of doubt passed across Felicity's face. 'You're bluffing,' she replied.

'Am I? I also have an expert perfumer,' he said, again making Angelica smile, 'who has matched the fragrance of the hand cream that you wear to the poisoned glass.'

Felicity blanched.

'So if I were you, madam, I would confess,' Nathaniel continued. 'I'm sure the magistrate will be more lenient if you do.'

Felicity let out a cry of fury. 'Oh, very well. If only the stupid man had taken my bribe and handed over the letters sensibly, then everything would have worked out perfectly. But he refused and so I had to kill him. I knew he would have arsenic or belladonna in his storeroom, so I made an excuse to use it and slipped the belladonna into my pocket. I then insisted on us having a drink to show there were no hard feelings and added the poison when he wasn't looking. It was all incredibly easy.'

'And then you ransacked the shop for the letters as he lay dying?' Nathaniel added.

'How clever you are, constable,' Felicity said angrily.

'I didn't work it all out on my own, I can assure you,' he replied with a wink to Angelica. 'Now, madam. I would be grateful if you would accompany me to Bow Street.'

A week later, Nathaniel and Angelica were sitting outside a confectioner's shop on Dean Street, eating brown bread ice cream and enjoying the unseasonably warm weather.

'So have you seen Lady Osborne?' Nathaniel asked.

'She came to my house yesterday, and was very kind.' Angelica would never forget her family's faces as Lady Osborne told them she had paid their rent for ten years. 'Lord Osborne and she are going travelling in Europe shortly, to wait until the scandal dies down.'

'And so he won't divorce her?'

'No. She said he was angry at first, but he has forgiven her now.'

'Good. And what did you think about Sir Sampson's offer?'

Angelica still couldn't quite believe it. Sir Sampson Wright, the head of the Bow Street Runners, had asked to see her personally and had offered her an apprenticeship with Nathaniel. It had been decided that Fred was better suited to being a messenger.

'It is an unusual job for a woman,' Sir Sampson had said

to her. 'But if you would like to do it, we could use someone with a first-class mind like you, young lady.'

'I accept,' Angelica replied happily.

'Excellent,' Nathaniel cried. 'But promise me you won't start fainting at the sight of corpses!'

'I promise,' she replied. 'So tell me, what is our next case?'

'Luckily there isn't one yet,' Nathaniel replied, but then, just as he was sitting back to relax in the sun, Fred appeared.

'You've got to come quick, sir, miss. There's been a robbery on Dean Street . . .'

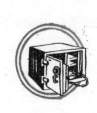

# CLOSED-SYSTEM CRIMES

Some of the most interesting crimes take place in closed systems – a place where no one but the suspects can get in or out.

These three cases feature an office, a hotel and a theatre – but the question is always the same. Whodunnit?

# SAFE-KEEPING
## By Sally Nicholls

They arrested Mr Conrad on Tuesday.

Billy and me was going round with the afternoon post. We've got a kind of trolley thing, and it's our job to drop all the ingoing post into everyone's 'In' trays and take the outgoing post out of the 'Out'. We'd done the main room where the clerks and the typists sit, and we was on to the offices what belonged to the three solicitors. They all got private offices where they can talk to clients without everyone else earwigging. We'd just knocked on Mr Conrad's door, what were off the main room, when Mr Conrad and Mr Mathieson come out, with two men from the police.

Billy and Arnold and me, we was rather disappointed with the policemen. When the necklace got nicked from Mr Mathieson's safe last week, we thought they'd send a proper Scotland Yard detective to investigate. We thought it'd all be alibis and interviews and 'Where was you on Wednesday lunchtime?' (We was in the Office Boys' Room by the door. All three of us together, all lunch. So our alibis was A1.) Billy and Arnold and me gets all the story papers, so we know all about 'tecs. Billy likes the Gem and the Magnet, which is school stories, Billy Bunter and them, but Arnold and me think school stories is wet. We like the Nelson Lee Library and the Union Jack, what have Nelson Lee and Sexton Blake stories in 'em. 'Tec stories. The two men they sent to investigate the robbery wasn't 'tecs. They wasn't detectives at all. They was local bobbies!

So no wonder they got it wrong.

When we saw them taking Mr Conrad away, we didn't realise what were going on at first. We thought arresting someone would be like it is on the pictures – guns and police chases and 'Stop in the name of the law!' At the very *least* we thought there'd be handcuffs. But the policemen was just leading him out, and Mr Conrad were saying, 'P-p-p-please d-don't w-w-w-worry, M-M-M-Mathieson.'

Mr Conrad's stutter always gets worse when he's worried. He were twitching too, which he always do when he's upset. Mr Mathieson were looking upset too. Mr Mathieson's kind of big and amiable, like a teddy bear in a suit, and when he feel something, it show all over his face. He said, 'Really, I think there must be some mistake. I *can't* believe it could be

238

Conrad. It *couldn't* be.'

Billy and me looked at each other. That's when we
figured out what were going on. I said to the bobbies, 'Mr
Mathieson's right, sir. Mr Conrad ain't a thief. He's a war
hero!'

He is too. That's why he walks funny, with a cane like,
and why all down his left side is sort of slurred, like melted
rubber. He nearly got blown up in the Battle of Mons, going
back to rescue a wounded comrade from the jaws of death.
He got the Military Cross for it and all. Mr Mathieson told us
boys about it, after he caught Billy doing an impersonation
in the Office Boys' Room. Mr Mathieson hardly ever gets
angry, but he got hopping mad with Billy then. He told Billy
it were unpatriotic and unBritish to make fun of a war hero,
and Billy ought to be ashamed of himself. Mr Mathieson is
the senior partner in Mathieson and Conrad. Mr Conrad
used to work for him before the War, and they always been
good friends. When Mr Mathieson come back from France
in 1919, he started up the business again, and made Mr
Conrad junior partner. So naturally, Mr Mathieson didn't
think Mr Conrad done it.

When I said he were a war hero, Mr Conrad gave his
funny smile, which *do* look a bit rum, because his mouth
only goes up on one side.

'Th-th-th-thank you, St-t-t-Stanley,' he said. It made me

feel right peculiar when he did that. I'd thought the robbery were something exciting, like a story in the Union Jack. It were only then I realised what it actually meant.

Nice Mr Conrad going to prison.

Mr Mathieson said, 'Don't you worry, old man. I'll get a lawyer – the very best. We'll sort this out, I'm sure.' But he were kind of twisting his hands, like he weren't sure at all, and he looked rather ill. I thought it were funny that Mr Conrad had told Mr Mathieson not to worry, and Mr Mathieson had said the same thing back to Mr Conrad. Then I thought about it a bit more, and I knew it weren't funny at all.

Mr Mathieson went downstairs with Mr Conrad and the policemen, and Arnold come out the Office Boys' Room, and said, 'What's up?' so Billy and me told him. Then all the big office – Mr Vernon, and the typists, and the clerks, and us boys and everyone, we all just sort of stood around talking about it, all gormless, like nobody quite knew what to do.

Billy said, 'But why does they think it's Mr Conrad?' which were just the sort of dumb question you'd expect a kid like Billy to ask.

Arnold said, 'Ain't it obvious? Cos there's only two people in the whole office what knows the combination to that safe – Mr Mathieson and Mr Conrad. And Mr Mathieson's hardly going to nick his own necklace, is he?'

It weren't actually Mr Mathieson's necklace, of course. It belonged to his mother-in-law, and Mr Mathieson were going to take it to the jewellers on the high street to get the clasp fixed. But obviously he were going to have to pay his mother-in-law back now because it'd been stolen from his office. Sixty quid, it were going to cost him, Miss James said.

Billy went bright red, so you could see he were upset, like. Ever since Mr Mathieson told us that story about the Battle of Mons, Billy's been a bit soft on Mr Conrad.

I said, 'There must be other ways to open a safe. Master criminals does it all the time in the story papers. Why! I bet Waldo the Wonderman, or Monsieur Zenith, or Professor Moriarty could open that safe just by blinking.'

'Yeh!' said Billy. 'Or mebbe with dynamite, like.'

And I said, 'Dynamite!' dead scornful. It weren't dynamite. We'd have noticed if it were. It'd have gone 'Boom!' for a start.

Miss James, who's one of the typists, and a bit prissy, sniffed, and said, 'I hope you don't think any of us are master criminals, Stanley.' Me and Arnold looked at each other. We had to admit it were a bit unlikely. This lot looked like the most nefarious thing they ever done were scrimping on the tea kitty.

'Miss James is right, old chap,' said Mr Vernon. He were the third solicitor, after Mr Mathieson and Mr Conrad. He were all right. He didn't condescend to us boys, like some of the clerks did. Only, Arnold tended to be a bit sniffy about him, cos he wore his hair slicked back with pomade, like someone in an American picture. 'We had a safe like that in my old office – bought it myself, actually. It's one of the best on the market. You really would have to be Professor Moriarty to break into one of those.'

'Well,' said I, rather desperate, like. 'Perhaps Mr Conrad or Mr Mathieson told someone the combination. Or they wrote it down and it got nicked. Or – I know! Mebbe someone come in while one of them were opening it up and saw him.'

'But,' said Mr Vernon gently, 'Conrad says he didn't do any of those things – I heard him myself, and so did you, last week, when we found the necklace was gone. And I'm sure Mathieson said the same.'

He were right. Mr Conrad were ever so distressed when he found the necklace had been nicked.

'I d-d-d-don't *understand* it,' he kept saying.

'But,' said Arnold suddenly, 'don't you see? That *proves* he didn't do it! I mean, if you *had* done it, you'd come up with as many ways as you could to try to pin it on someone else, wouldn't you? You'd say you'd written down the combination in your notebook, and someone'd nicked it. Or that you'd forgotten to close the safe door properly. You wouldn't go out of your way to make yourself the only suspect, like what Mr Conrad did. You *know* he did.'

There were an awkward silence. Then Mr Kettleworth, who were one of the clerks, said, 'Look here, lads. Mr Conrad had an awfully rough time in the War. Sometimes – well, sometimes that can make you go a bit peculiar. I'm not saying he *knew* he'd done it – but – well – maybe he had a funny turn, and then forgot. Or . . .'

Arnold flushed. Billy opened his mouth like he were about to say something *really* rude to Mr Kettleworth.

Miss James said, hasty like, 'Don't you boys have work you're supposed to be getting on with?'

And I grabbed Arnold's arm and said, 'Come on, lads.' And we all stalked off to the Office Boys' Room, and sat round the table sticking stamps on all the outgoing post and fuming.

Billy said, 'I bet that's what them bobbies thought. That Mr Conrad's a loony. Or a simpleton! Only a simpleton would nick a necklace out of a safe that only they knows the combination of. I bet they took one look at him and thought Mr Mathieson made him a partner out of charity. The cheek of it!'

'I bet you's right, and all,' said Arnold.

But I'd thought of something else. I said, 'You do realise, don't you, that it's our evidence what got Mr Conrad put away? We's the ones what said no one come in, all that lunchtime. If we'd never said that, it might've been a criminal gang or summat. It's thanks to us they know it were an inside job.'

It were true. Mr Mathieson put the necklace in the safe in his office when he come in on Wednesday morning. He worked in his office till twelve o'clock, when he went out to lunch. He come back at one. At two, he opened the safe again, to put some papers in. And that's when he found the necklace were gone.

So the police knew it had to have been nicked between twelve and one, just like something in a 'tec story. And we was the ones what said no one but folk what worked here had come in and out in all that time. Visitors has to walk up the stairs to our floor, then they rings the doorbell, then one of us office boys has to let them in. Then they come into the big office, what Mr Conrad and Mr Vernon have their offices off of. But Mr Mathieson's office is down the corridor, next to the lavatories and the kitchen, which were dead convenient for the criminal, cos he could've just pretended to be going to the lavatory, when really he were nipping into Mr Mathieson's office and nicking the necklace. When visitors rings the doorbell, we has to take them to see whatever solicitor it is they got an appointment with and show them out when they goes. If it's a delivery man, or something like that, we has to deal with them too, sign for the parcel and what have you. So we *knew* there weren't anyone in the office that luncheon except the people what was supposed to be there.

And we'd told the police so too.

There were an awful silence.

'I reckon we ought to investigate,' I said furiously, tearing a stamp off the sheet so hard I ripped it in two. 'Do it properly. Motives and alibis and all that.'

'Yeh!' said Billy. He put on a 'tec voice. 'Where was you on the night of the murder?'

'Chuck it,' said Arnold. 'How could we find out folk's motives? We can hardly *ask* them, can we?'

'Mr Kettleworth's got a motive,' I said. 'His little boy's got pneumonia, and he's ever so worried about how he's going to pay the doctor's bills. I heard him telling Miss James about it.'

'Miss James's got one too!' said Billy. 'She's always saying how men like Mr Conrad shouldn't have jobs when so many folk are out of work. Maybe she done it out of politics.'

'I don't think you'd send someone to *prison* just cos you thought they didn't ought to have a job,' I said doubtfully. 'What about Mr Vernon? Them fancy suits he wears look proper expensive. And mebbe he were jealous of Mr Conrad, being the junior partner and that.'

'He gets the suits cheap cos his landlord's a tailor,' said

Arnold. He were frowning. 'Thing is,' he said, *'everyone's* got a motive, ain't they? That necklace were worth sixty quid. Who *wouldn't* want to nick it?'

He had a point. It weren't like a murder. You need a thwonking great motive to murder someone. A necklace worth sixty quid . . . well, it's sixty quid, ain't it? That's a lot. It's about what me dad earns in a year. And it weren't like anyone at Mathieson and Conrad's was millionaires or anything. Business were bad after the War. If this were a 'tec story, someone would turn out to have a shameful love child, or gambling debts, or a dark past they was being blackmailed about. I didn't suppose anyone in our office had anything like that. All they had was leaking roofs, and shoes with holes in them, and their kids' birthdays coming up. But Arnold were right. That were enough.

'Mr Mathieson don't have a motive,' I said. 'He can't even get it back on the insurance, Mr Vernon said so.'

'Maybe he wants to get rid of Mr Conrad,' said Billy hopefully. ''Cos he puts off the clients, like, looking how he does, and talking funny.'

But Arnold and I didn't believe it. Mr Mathieson and Mr Conrad . . . they wasn't just partners. They was friends. You just knew if Mr Mathieson had asked Mr Conrad to go, he'd have said, 'D-d-don't w-w-w-worry about it, old th-thing,' and he'd be gone. I were sure he would. And Mr Mathieson had seemed properly upset about Mr Conrad being arrested. I didn't think it were guilt. I thought it were someone being worried about their friend.

'Alibis then,' said Billy. But Arnold didn't need to answer. We all knew alibis was no good. Some folk had gone out for lunch, to one of the cafés on the high street, or the King's Head on the corner. But none of them was gone the whole hour like Mr Mathieson were. Mr Kettleworth had had lunch at the King's Head with some of the other clerks, but he come back early cos he had some work what needed finishing. Mr Vernon had a pie what he bought at the butcher's, but he brung it back and ate it in his office, so he weren't gone hardly at all. And Miss James just ate her sandwiches at her desk, like always.

'I reckon them policemen was right,' said Arnold. 'It's not about *why* they done it. It's about *how*. If we could only work out *how* that thief got into the safe, we'd be there, I know we would.'

We finished sticking the stamps on the letters and sat staring at them in gloom. Being a 'tec were a lot harder than Sexton Blake and Nelson Lee made it look. I were beginning to think them 'tecs in stories had an awful lot of luck. They was always stumbling across pages from important letters, or walking past an open window, just exactly when the murderer were discussing something revealing with his accomplice.

247

And they had all sorts of equipment too, like cameras, and callipers, and magnifying glasses, and whatever it were 'tecs used to take fingerprints. Not that fingerprints would be any good in this case. Criminals always wore gloves, everyone knew that. The only fingerprints on that safe had been Mr Mathieson's and Mr Conrad's, just like they ought to be.

'I bet you can learn how to safe-crack,' I said, rather desperately. 'Mebbe we should look through everyone's drawers after they's gone home, and see if they's got lock-picking tools or safe-cracking books or summat in there.' But even as I said it, I knew it were a pretty hopeless idea.

'I dunno . . .' said Arnold. 'I read a story once, with a bloke what were a robber in it. He said, the easiest way to do it were to know the person what chose the combination. Like, if they's romantic, they'd probably pick their wedding anniversary. But if they's mathematical, mebbe they picks one of them mathematical numbers. And so on. Mebbe the thief just figured out what combination Mr Mathieson would pick and tried that.'

We all sat and thought about what combination Mr Mathieson would choose for a safe, but it weren't easy. He weren't mathematical. He were married, but he weren't soppy about his wife or anything. He didn't have kids. I suppose he must've had hobbies, but none of us knew what they was.

'I don't reckon Mr Mathieson bothered that much about security,' I said, eventually.

'Mebbe . . .' said Billy. But just then Miss James put her head round the door.

'What *are* you boys doing in here?' she said. 'Shouldn't somebody be taking the tea trolley round? And why hasn't anyone collected the waste-paper yet? Stanley, don't just sit there looking like a wet weekend. Off you trot.'

So then, of course, we had to get back to work. Billy and Arnold went off to the kitchen to fill up the tea urn, and I started going round doing the paper.

The paper at Mathieson and Conrad goes into waste-paper trays. There's four big ones in the main office, and little ones in all three little offices. Every Tuesday, one of us goes round and collects it up in a sack, and it all go off to the paper-mill.

Normally, this were a dead boring job, but today I were taking a bit more time over it, cos I were still thinking about Sexton Blake, and how he always finds useful clues on bits of blotting paper and what have you. I don't know if you's ever tried reading old bits of blotting paper, but it ain't easy, and it *particularly* ain't easy when you's doing it in a big office with lots of folk watching. Still, I did me best.

It were easier when I got to Mr Vernon's office, cos it were separate like, and Mr Vernon were in a meeting with

Mr Mathieson, so I could take me time. I went through everything properly, then I has a look through Mr Vernon's waste-paper tray.

And that's when I found it.

I didn't think it were anything at first. It were a narrow bit of paper with instructions on it, like what you gets when you buys a gramophone or something. I were about to chuck it in the sack when I sees what it were the instructions for.

Mr Mathieson's safe.

I started to get excited then. Why did Mr Vernon have the instructions for Mr Mathieson's safe? Perhaps they would tell you how to break the safe open!

Except, they didn't. Them instructions was dead boring. They just told you how to change the combination to one what you could remember, and how to open the door, and so forth. There weren't anything that would help you crack the safe *at all*.

Still, I put them in me pocket, and went and showed them to Arnold and Billy, what was in the kitchen, emptying the tea urn.

'It must be a clue,' I said. '*Mustn't* it? Why else would Mr Vernon have 'em? He must have done it!'

'Course he must,' said Billy. 'We should tell him we's on to him!' He put on his 'tec voice again. 'We knows you done it, mister! Tell us everything, or we'll blow yer kneecaps off!'

'But we don't know he done it,' I said. 'Anyway, I bet he'd just come up with some excuse for why he had them. Like, he just found them in a drawer or summat.'

'Hmm,' said Arnold. He took the instructions from me and frowned at them. 'I wonder . . .'

'What?' said Billy. But Arnold didn't answer. He turned and set off down the corridor towards Mr Mathieson's room, still holding the instructions.

'What?' I said, just like Billy had. 'You wonder *what*, Arnold?'

But Arnold just rapped on Mr Mathieson's door. Then, without waiting for an answer, he barged right in. Mr Mathieson and Mr Vernon was sitting at the desk, reading through some papers. They looked at us in astonishment.

'Boys? Is everything all right?' Mr Mathieson said. Arnold ignored him. He went straight to the safe under Mr Mathieson's desk, and started turning the dial.

Mr Vernon said, 'Arnold! What in *heaven's* name do you think you're doing?'

Arnold didn't bother to reply. I figured, since Mr Vernon were prime suspect number one, that meant we didn't have to do what he told us no more, so I got down on the floor beside him. He were putting the numbers in, one after another.

Two – five – five –

'Oh!' I said. Suddenly, I got it. 'Oh, Arnold!'

Zero – two – five –

He turned the dial with a flourish.

And the safe opened.

'Coo!' said Billy.

Mr Mathieson said, 'Good heavens! How the devil did you know the combination?'

Arnold sat back on his heels, looking pleased with himself.

'It's the standard combination, sir,' he said. He saw Mr Mathieson looking puzzled, and added, 'When you buys the safe new, sir. That's the combination it comes with. That's why the instructions say you's supposed to change it, sir.' He flapped the instructions at Mr Mathieson.

Mr Mathieson said, 'By Jove!' For the first time since he found the necklace were gone, he started to laugh. 'Goodness, I'm not even sure I know *how* to change it. Dear, oh dear. You mean anyone who knew that could just walk in, and take whatever he liked?'

'Yes, sir,' said Arnold.

Billy said, 'Coo!' again.

I burst out, impatiently, 'But don't you see, sir? Mr Vernon, sir! He said he bought a safe just like this one in his last position! He knew what the combination it come with were, sir! And . . .' I hesitated. 'And, no offence, sir, but he'd know you ain't the sort to worry too much about security, like. And –'

But Mr Vernon interrupted me.

'Now, hang on a second,' he said. 'Are you suggesting I stole Mr Mathieson's necklace? That's rather a dramatic leap of logic, isn't it?' He turned to Mr Mathieson. 'See here, Mathieson,' he said. 'I'm quite willing to admit we used to have a safe like that, but I honestly couldn't tell you what combination it came with. I think we used the King's birthday, if I recall correctly.'

'Oh, *yeah*?' said Billy. He were practically hopping up and down, he were so excited. 'Then what about *these*? What was they doing in your office?' He grabbed the instructions from Arnold and thrust them in Mr Vernon's face. 'Explain them away, mister!'

Mr Mathieson said, 'Billy!' but rather weakly, like his heart weren't in it.

Mr Vernon had gone white. He said, 'Is that piece of paper supposed to mean something to me?' But he didn't sound so sure of himself either.

I said, 'Them's the instructions to the safe! They got the combination the safe come with on them and everything! Mr Vernon's lying if he says he don't know the standard combination, sir. *I found them in his waste-paper tray!*'

'So there!' said Billy triumphantly.

'Good Lord!' said Mr Mathieson.

'And!' I said. 'Mr Vernon's got a motive too, ain't he? Besides the sixty quid, I mean. If Mr Conrad goes to prison, you'd have to make him junior partner, wouldn't you?' Mr Mathieson stared. 'Well, wouldn't you?'

Mr Mathieson shook his head slowly.

'Vernon,' he said. 'Is this *true*?'

'It most certainly is *not*!' said Mr Vernon. But he didn't sound that convincing. He were sort of blustering. 'I don't know what this is about – if it's some sort of a practical joke – but let me tell you, boys, it isn't a funny one!'

'No,' said Mr Mathieson. 'It isn't funny at all.' I'd never heard him speak like that before, all cold, and hard, and unforgiving. Even Billy were quiet. We all just stood there, kind of staring, until Mr Vernon dropped his eyes, and looked away.

# THE MYSTERY OF THE PURLOINED PEARLS
### By Katherine Woodfine

I'm not usually a great one for writing things down. It reminds me a jolly sight too much of school for my liking – ink-stained fingers and boring old compositions and awful Miss Pinker droning on. Billy is the one of us who likes writing things: he always seems to have an exercise book and pencil somewhere about his person. In fact, after the peculiar adventure of the clockwork sparrow in the spring, he spent ages writing down what happened, quite as if he thought himself Dr Watson in one of Sir Arthur Conan Doyle's stories. (Though of course he didn't like it a bit when I said that – he'd much rather imagine that he's Sherlock Holmes, or maybe Montgomery Baxter, that schoolboy detective he's always jawing on about.)

'It's *important* to write things down,' Billy told me, looking indignant. 'That's what *real* detectives do, so they can keep a record of the cases they solve.'

This particular case, as it happens, is one that I solved all on my own – without any help from Billy or Joe, or even my closest friend Sophie. Afterwards I started thinking about what Billy had said, and I decided that after all I probably ought to write down what happened, because unless I did there would be no sensible record of it at all, only the idiotic made-up version that everyone got told afterwards. And also, Billy isn't the only one who can behave like a proper detective. I get jolly tired of boys thinking that they are the ones who do all the important things, as this story will soon show you.

It all began one ordinary afternoon, when I was going to a rehearsal at the Fortune Theatre. I'm a chorus girl, you see – much to the horror of my parents, who think it is dreadfully improper. At present, I sing and dance in the chorus line of rather a silly show called *The Shop Girl*. The story really is a lot of rot. When I'm not performing, I also work at a department store, Sinclair's in Piccadilly, and I can tell you for certain that the things that happen to the heroine in *The Shop Girl* aren't even the tiniest bit like anything that would happen to a shop girl in real life.

So there I was, off to rehearsal, but in all honesty, not looking forward to it much. Some people think that being a chorus girl must be terrifically glamorous, but the truth is it's mostly plain hard work. We do a simply ghastly amount of rehearsing – every step of every dance has to be quite perfect, which is all very well for the girls who are properly trained dancers, but jolly difficult for me (my old school being the sort that went in for French and lawn tennis rather than tap-dancing and so forth).

On this particular day I was looking forward to rehearsal even less than usual. Our ticket sales had begun to drop off as a new show at the Palace Theatre was drawing in the big crowds, so Mr Mountville was determined to add more of what he called 'razzmatazz' to our production. Mr Mountville is the producer of *The Shop Girl*, and frightfully smart and important: everyone is a little afraid of him and always does exactly what he says. He had decided to make our final number extra splendid, but the new routine was tricky – and the last time we had rehearsed it, Miss Sylvia had been frightfully scornful about my high kicks. Miss Sylvia is in charge of all the dancing in the show. She is very severe, and wears her hair scraped up into a topknot and regularly has one or the other of the chorus girls in floods of tears. (She really can be jolly rude sometimes: I may not be the best dancer in the chorus line, but I do think that saying I am 'a danger to myself and others' is too much by a long chalk.)

So when I arrived at the theatre, I was rather pleased to discover that rehearsal seemed to be cancelled. Neither Miss Sylvia, nor Mr Mountville, nor Mr Simpson, who is the manager of the Fortune Theatre, were anywhere to be seen. The other chorus girls were all in the dressing room we share, tucking into a big box of caramels that had been left by one of the Stage Door Johnnies – young men who like to hang around the stage door and give chorus girls presents.

'I say, whatever is going on?' said I.

'Ooh, there's been ever such a row!' said Eliza.

'Miss Shaw's pearls have gone missing,' explained Letty. 'Stolen from her dressing room! She's having a blue fit!'

'Says she won't stir a step on to the stage until they're found,' reported Millie, importantly (and it must be admitted that Letty, who as well as being a chorus girl is also Miss Shaw's understudy, looked rather thrilled at this).

Miss Kitty Shaw is the star of our show and the darling of the West End. She's awfully famous and the absolute picture of glamour – I really think she must have a different fur coat for every day of the week! She always has the most terrific queue of admirers waiting for her at the stage door after every show, all clutching photographs for her to sign. But it isn't just Stage Door Johnnies dangling after her – Maurice, who is Miss Shaw's dresser, had told me that Mr Frederick

Whitman, the American Broadway star, had been paying her visits in her dressing room (of course, she's far too important to share a dressing room like we chorus girls do). I knew that he always arrived with an armful of hothouse flowers, a bottle of champagne, and an invitation to eat oysters in one of London's most elegant restaurants. Apparently he had proposed to her a dozen times at least, but in spite of the flowers and champagne and glorious food, Maurice said that Miss Shaw was still 'in two minds' about Mr Whitman. (Maurice says Miss Shaw told him it was because she was 'wedded to her art', but *he* thought it was really because she had a secret fancy for Mr Edward Sinclair, the owner of Sinclair's department store.)

Anyway, what you need to understand is that Kitty Shaw is a jolly important person – in the world of the Fortune Theatre at any rate. If she was saying that she wouldn't go on stage that night – well, it was nothing short of a disaster. Everyone was in a dreadful flap: Miss Shaw was weeping in her dressing room; Mr Mountville was trying to coax her out again; Mr Simpson was fussing about, offering cups of tea and smelling salts, and generally making a nuisance of himself; and Miss Sylvia was striding around saying things like, 'This is the last straw!' We girls enjoyed it all immensely.

After a while, Mr Mountville stormed out of the dressing room in a temper and came to fetch Letty. He began running her through some songs, in case Miss Shaw was still refusing to go on when it was time for the evening show. Of course, we girls went to watch too. At first, Letty looked delighted with her chance to play the starring role, but as soon as they began to rehearse, she went to pieces. Eliza said she had stage fright, and perhaps she did, but whatever the reason was, Mr Mountville began to look crosser and crosser. (I was simply itching for him to give me a turn: I felt quite sure that, whatever Miss Sylvia had to say about my high kicks, I could do a far better job than poor old Letty.)

'This is impossible!' exclaimed Mr Mountville after a while. 'The show can't go on like this. That's it, I'm calling the police. If Kitty really won't budge then this necklace must be found at once.'

Mr Simpson was looking very agitated. He is a small, rather round man with a face that is very pink at the best of times, and now he was pinker than ever. 'No, no, don't you trouble with that, Mr Mountville. I'll take care of it directly!' And he scuttled off to the telephone in his office, as if he was in a terrific hurry.

'Well, we'd better hope the police can find out who took it, and get it back,' said Eliza. 'Otherwise tonight's show is going to be a right old mess.' Beyond, on the stage, Letty was looking rather green. Miss Sylvia had stormed over and was having what looked like a dreadfully stern conversation with her. I distinctly heard the words 'hopeless', 'disgraceful' and 'pull your socks up at once!' Letty and Miss Sylvia have known each other for years: Miss Sylvia taught Letty to dance, and she was the one who helped Letty get the understudy job. Now, she seemed jolly determined that Letty was going to keep it. 'Oh, I'm sure the police will soon solve it,' said Millie confidently.

But I wasn't quite so sure. The thing is that I have had encounters with the police before, and I know that they are not always what you might call helpful (sometimes in fact, they are quite the opposite – but that, as they say, is another story). At that moment, it came to me that having recently helped to solve a mystery myself, perhaps there might be something I could do to help sort things out. I got up at once, and slipped through the pass door that leads backstage.

I must say that I never get tired of the thrill of being backstage at the theatre. It's so frightfully exciting: the smell of greasepaint and chalk, stagehands lugging bits of scenery around and Emmanuelle, hurrying by, her arms piled high with tulle and sequins. (Emmanuelle is our wardrobe mistress, which means she is in charge of all the costumes in the show – she usually looks as though she is wearing a costume herself, she's so fond of bright colours and sparkles.) Today there seemed to be even more backstage commotion than usual, and as I went down the passage to Miss Shaw's dressing room, I could hear Mr Simpson on the telephone in the office talking very fast: 'Yes, that's right, Tommy! Kitty Shaw's treasured necklace! Priceless pearls – stolen, right here in the theatre!' I must say, I was rather surprised to discover that Mr Simpson was so chummy with a policeman. He made it all sound *most* dramatic.

I tapped on the door of Miss Shaw's dressing room and a tearful voice said, 'Come in!'

'Oh it's *you*,' she said, when in I came – now sounding not so much upset as rather annoyed. I must explain at this point that Kitty Shaw does not like me very much, on account of the time that I barged in on her talking to Mr Sinclair at the Sinclair's opening party (I do think that anyone with a bit of sense would be jolly well grateful since that conversation very probably *saved her life*, not to mention everyone else's at the party, but that really is another story). 'I thought it might be Mr Simpson, with news from the police,' she went on in a plaintive voice. 'What do *you* want?'

'Er . . . I thought I'd just come and see if you or Maurice needed anything,' I said, rather weakly. 'You know, in your time of need.' I wasn't all too sure how Miss Shaw would respond to this, so even as I spoke, I was taking the opportunity to have a good look around the room. (This is what Billy would call 'examining the scene of the crime'.) Her dressing room was large, comfortable and about a hundred times nicer than the dressing room we chorus girls share. There was fancy wallpaper on the walls, and a chaise longue with an embroidered shawl over it, and an enormous dressing table, with bottles of scent and pots of rouge and face powder all neatly laid out. The walls were plastered with dozens of photographs of Kitty Shaw herself in various attitudes: looking soulful with flowers in her hair; peering coquettishly over her fan; posing as a Grecian nymph holding a harp; and goodness knows what else besides. An enormous bouquet of roses and lilies was accompanied by a card that read, in scrawling handwriting: 'To darling Kitty, from your devoted Frederick.'

Miss Shaw herself was reclining on the chaise longue, while behind her Maurice bustled about, shaking out the ruffles in her first-act costume, and hanging up her silk kimono in his usual fastidious way. As dresser, it was his job to look after Miss Shaw and her dressing room and all of her clothes – only the biggest stars have their own dresser of course. We all like Maurice, who is rather a dear; even Miss Sylvia is passably nice to him, although she's as cross as two sticks with the rest of us.

'All I *need* is for my pearl necklace to be found!' Miss Shaw was saying dramatically. 'It's my most precious possession – it brings me luck. I can't possibly go on stage without it!'

Half the girls in the theatre have some sort of trinket they believe brings them luck – a four-leaf clover or a rabbit's foot or some such nonsense – and they are fearfully superstitious about them. I had supposed that if Miss Shaw's necklace had been stolen, it was because it was worth a lot of money – but now it occurred to me that if it was her good luck charm, perhaps someone might have taken it to upset her.

'When did you realise your necklace was missing?' I asked, getting into the stride of the thing now and rather enjoying performing the role of detective.

For a moment, I thought that Miss Shaw was going to tell me to scram – but I looked at her as sympathetically as I could manage, seeing that she was so eager for an audience that even I would probably do in a pinch. Evidently it worked: 'Oh, it was only an hour ago – no more!' she began, rather dramatically. 'The pearls were here this morning, in my jewel box, just as usual. Emmanuelle was admiring them. Then I put them away in my dressing table and locked the drawer, just as always,' she went on. 'I went out to luncheon and when I returned the box had been put here on the dressing table, just as you see. Everything else was there – but the pearl necklace had gone!'

'How dreadful,' I murmured compassionately. 'And whereabouts do you keep the key to the drawer?'

Miss Shaw blushed. 'Well . . . it's usually just here on my

dressing table. I really never thought that anyone here in the theatre would . . . Oh *who* could have done such a dreadful thing?'

At this, she began to weep all over again, and Maurice rushed over with a lacy handkerchief, looking almost as upset as Miss Shaw herself. Meanwhile, I was thinking. If she had left the key lying about like that, why anyone in the theatre might have sneaked into the dressing room while she was out, and helped themselves to the necklace!

I opened my mouth to ask another question, but at that moment the door opened, and Mr Whitman swept in. 'My poor Kitty!' he exclaimed at once in his booming voice. 'My dear! Mr Simpson has told me everything! How awful – how perfectly awful for you! Come with me – I'm taking you for some tea.'

'But, Frederick, I can't possibly,' she fluttered. 'I must be here to talk to the police.'

'Oh, Maurice can take care of that, can't you?' said Mr Whitman, looking winsomely at Maurice. (It must be admitted that Mr Whitman is jolly handsome.) 'Besides, we'll only be at the restaurant next door. Look, you can't sit here *dwelling* on this, Kitty. It isn't good for you. I absolutely insist.'

Even as he was saying this, he was whisking Miss Shaw into her little fur, and leading her out of the room, leaving Maurice and I gawping after him. (Mr Whitman does generally have rather that effect, but on this occasion it was mostly because I was thinking hard.)

'I say, Maurice,' I asked suddenly. 'Have you been at the theatre all day?'

Maurice said he had.

'But you weren't here in the dressing room while Miss Shaw was out to luncheon, I suppose?'

Maurice shook his head. 'No – I was here for a while, tidying things up, and then I went up to see Emmanuelle in the wardrobe department about one of Miss Shaw's costumes. We had a cup of tea, and then I left her to have my own lunch.'

'Who else was in the theatre at that time?' Maurice frowned. 'Well . . . there was Emmanuelle, of course. And Miss Sylvia, and Mr Simpson.'

'Anyone else? What about Mr Mountville?'

'No, he didn't arrive until later. But I think I saw Letty on my way to wardrobe.'

I began prowling around the room, in case the thief had left behind any sort of clues. (This is another thing that I know from Billy that detectives like to do.) But I couldn't see anything even remotely unusual: the whole dressing room was terribly neat, and everything was in its proper place, apart from the empty jewellery box – not at all like our dressing room where there are always stockings and hair ribbons and tins of greasepaint strewn about everywhere. Maurice obviously looked after Miss Shaw very well indeed. I had a look at the jewel box where the pearls had been kept, and then thought of something else:

'Did Miss Shaw say that Emmanuelle had been here earlier, looking at the necklace?' I asked.

'That's right,' said Maurice. 'You know Emmanuelle. She loves jewellery.'

That was true – everyone knew that Emmanuelle was like a magpie when it came to anything that glittered or sparkled. She was always simply plastered with costume jewellery – the shinier the better. She was also given to doing rather eccentric things, like the time she had suddenly decided to dye the costumes of all the chorus girls bright green without telling anyone. Perhaps she hadn't been able to resist 'borrowing' the pearl necklace?

But even as this idea crossed my mind, I caught sight of something white lying on the carpet, close to the dressing table. Bending down, I found a small crumpled piece of paper. Could it possibly be a clue?

Unfolding it, I saw to my surprise that it was a theatre ticket – but not for *The Shop Girl*. Instead it was a gallery seat for the previous night's showing of *Miss Flora*, the new musical comedy at the Palace Theatre – the very show that was luring away our audience.

'Miss Shaw didn't go to see the show at the Palace last night, did she?' I asked in surprise, scrutinising the ticket – punched, too, which showed it had been used.

Maurice looked astonished. 'No – how could she? She was on stage here!'

'What about Mr Whitman?'

'Mr Whitman was here too – he came to see her perform and they had dinner together after the show.'

'And I don't suppose *you* . . . ?'

'Oh heavens no! I'm always here, whenever Miss Shaw is performing!' he exclaimed. 'Not that *I* would have any money to spend on the likes of theatre tickets anyway,' he added, rather bitterly. 'Not with poor Mother taking a turn for the worse and all those awful doctor's bills to pay.'

Everyone in the theatre knew that Maurice was terribly devoted to his mother, who had not been well. It was not surprising he looked so upset; I said that I hoped she would be much better soon, then I turned my attention back to the crumpled ticket.

'Could anyone else have dropped this here?' I asked. 'Has anyone else been in the dressing room since yesterday?' 'Mr Mountville and Mr Simpson came in just now – to comfort Miss Shaw,' said Maurice, perplexed. 'But that's all.'

'And Miss Shaw was sitting over here, on the other side of the room,' said I, pacing over to the chaise longue and back again.

'Did either of them come over here, to the dressing table?'

'Why no, I suppose they didn't,' said Maurice, looking more baffled than ever.

I was beginning to feel a little baffled too: this detective business was jolly hard work. What's more, there was still no sign of the police – who were, after all, the ones who were really supposed to be investigating the theft. After a little more general chat, I said goodbye to Maurice, who seemed to want me out of his way so he could get on with the tidying up, and retreated to the empty chorus girls' dressing room to ponder further. It seemed to me that the crumpled theatre ticket *must* have been dropped by the thief. But if it was true that the thief had been at the Palace Theatre for *Miss Flora* the night before, then I knew that it couldn't possibly be Emmanuelle. She had been at the Fortune all evening. I knew that because I'd had to go and see her in the interval of our show myself – Letty had put her great hoof on my frock and torn it.

Just then, Eliza came back in.

'Whatever are you doing sitting in here all by yourself?' she asked. Then: 'Oh honestly, Lil! Have you polished off *all* of those caramels? Why, there was almost half a box!' (It is true that detective work is a very hungry business.)

'How's Letty getting on?' I asked, quickly changing the subject.

'Much better. Miss Sylvia gave her a real talking to. That made her pull her socks up, all right.'

Letty! Of course! Maurice had said that he had seen her around the theatre earlier in the day – and Letty was Kitty Shaw's understudy. She stood to benefit the most if Miss Shaw refused to go on stage! Might it just be possible that she had taken the pearl necklace to deliberately sabotage the star of the show – so that she would have the chance to step into the spotlight in her place?

But then I remembered the ticket, and I knew at once that couldn't be right. Because of course, *Letty* could not have been at the Palace Theatre the night before either. She'd been dancing in the chorus line next to me, just like always. I sighed, and mentally scratched Letty off my suspect list.

'Of course, Miss Sylvia wasn't going to allow Letty to ruin her chances,' Eliza was saying. 'She's always loathed Kitty Shaw, you know – and Letty is her favourite. The two of them are as thick as thieves.'

*Thick as thieves.* That was it! I jumped up from my seat. *Letty* couldn't have been at the Palace theatre last night – but *Miss Sylvia* could! Now I thought about it, I didn't remember seeing her anywhere at the theatre the previous evening. In fact, she was about the only person I *hadn't* seen the night before – apart from Mr Simpson, of course, but he had probably been tucked away in his office as usual.

And it would have been easy for her to slip into the dressing room and take the necklace to upset Miss Shaw, giving her protégée Letty the chance to be the star! 'I've got it!' I exclaimed, feeling tremendously pleased with myself.

I rushed out of the room in a terrific hurry, Eliza staring after me as if she thought I'd gone quite mad. But when I got to Miss Shaw's dressing room, I found that there was a commotion going on outside. A young man with a notebook, and another carrying a camera, who I at once recognised as the photographer for the *Daily Picture*, were in the passageway. Mr Mountville seemed to be haranguing them: 'Look here, what do you think you're doing? You can't just come barging in here, taking photographs! For heaven's sake, the police haven't even arrived yet.'

'Well that's news to us,' said the photographer, grinning at me in a chummy sort of fashion. 'That other fellow we spoke to said we could do as we like.'

'*Which* other fellow?' demanded Mr Mountville in astonishment.

'Your theatre manager,' said the reporter. 'He's got some sense – this could be big news. Star's pearls stolen from her own dressing room! It could make the front page. With that sort of publicity – why, you'll be sold out!'

I left them arguing and pushed forward into the dressing room. When I got inside, I found a quite extraordinary sight awaiting me. Mr Whitman was holding Maurice by the collar, evidently furious. Miss Shaw, Miss Sylvia and Mr Simpson were all looking on in horror.

'What on earth is happening?' I asked.

'What's happening?' repeated Mr Whitman angrily. 'What's happening? I'll tell you what's happening! We came back from tea to find this little rat with his paws in Kitty's purse, that's what! There's no doubt about it – *he's* the one who took her pearls!'

I stared at the scene before me in astonishment. Maurice was obviously terrified: Mr Whitman looked like he might punch him in the nose at any moment. Behind them, I could see Miss Shaw's purse lying open on the dressing table, a few coins spilling out. But something about this just didn't add up; I thought about how upset Maurice had been about the missing pearls, and how devoted he was to Miss Shaw. 'Look here, that can't be right!' I burst out. 'I don't believe it – you've got the wrong man!'

To my astonishment, Miss Sylvia spoke up too. 'The girl's right,' she said curtly. Gosh! Was she about to confess, I wondered? Then she added: 'Tell them, Maurice.'

Maurice had managed to wriggle out of Mr Whitman's grip. He seemed to be in a terrible state. 'I-I'm so sorry, Miss Shaw...' he choked out. 'I know what I did was wrong! But you must believe that I would never steal from you – never! It's just that, well . . . you haven't paid my wages yet this week, even though I've asked you for them twice. And with poor Mother so ill, I simply must have the money to pay the doctor's bill today!' He looked as though he might burst into tears, but Miss Sylvia put a hand on his arm. 'There, there, Maurice,' she said, in an unexpectedly gentle voice. 'Your mother is doing fine. When I went to see her last night, she seemed much better.'

My mouth fell open. So Miss Sylvia *hadn't* been at the Palace the previous evening after all! I must say I was rather astonished: I hadn't thought of Miss Sylvia as being at all the type of person who visited people's sick mothers. But perhaps there was another side to her than the brute who shouted contemptuous things about people's dancing, I thought, seeing how kind she was being to poor old Maurice.

Meanwhile, Kitty Shaw had melted: 'Maurice dear, why didn't you tell me you needed the money now? I had no idea! You know I would have given you whatever you needed!' Together, she and Miss Sylvia began to comfort Maurice, and in their eagerness to make him feel better, the two of them suddenly seemed not like mortal enemies at all, but rather quite good friends.

All this time, Mr Whitman was pacing around, muttering to himself. 'But if *he* didn't take the pearls, then gosh darn it – who did?'

But I saw at once that if it wasn't Miss Sylvia – or Letty, or Maurice – well, then there was only one person left that it could be. And suddenly it all made perfect sense.

'Oh for heaven's sake,' I said, feeling rather cross with myself that I hadn't worked it out sooner. 'It's perfectly obvious who took them.'

Mr Whitman was the only one listening. He looked over at me, his handsome face terribly confused. And this is where I made my big mistake:

'*It was Mr Simpson,*' I hissed to him, jerking my head in the direction of the theatre manager. 'He took Miss Shaw's pearls! It's all because of that new show at the Palace. He went to see it last night – that's why I didn't see him anywhere here. He's worried about us losing audiences to them – and he thought that if Miss Shaw's necklace appeared to have been stolen at the theatre, it would be in the papers and give our show lots of extra publicity. That's why the police aren't here yet – he hasn't even called them! He was *actually* telephoning those journalists, to make certain that the story would make the newspapers.' As I spoke, I noticed that Mr Simpson's large pink hand was resting anxiously over a lump in his waistcoat pocket. 'Why, I'm quite certain that the pearls are in his pocket at this very moment!' I finished. Mr Whitman gaped at me for a second or two, and then at Mr Simpson, and then he suddenly puffed out his chest.

'Stop!' he boomed out. 'The real culprit is amongst us!' He turned to Mr Simpson. 'You are discovered, sir! The game is up – confess at once!' he declaimed. I began to suspect he must have played a detective in a Broadway play – he was frightfully good at it, even if it was all rather over the top.

'I-I don't know what you're talking about . . .' began Mr Simpson.

I stepped forward and opened my mouth to say that it was quite obvious the pearls were in Mr Simpson's pocket, but Mr Whitman strode in front of me. He shot out a hand and seized the pearls right out of Mr Simpson's waistcoat. 'Then how do you explain *these?*' he demanded, holding them aloft.

Mr Simpson turned pinker than I would have believed possible. 'Oh . . . er . . . now I know how this must look, but . . . but . . . you must understand – it wasn't a *real* theft. I always meant to give them back before curtain-up, Miss Shaw. It was all for the good of the show, you see! I mean, think of how much publicity Sinclair's department store got when Mr Sinclair's treasures were stolen!'

'Well I never!' exclaimed Maurice.

'I'm fetching Mr Mountville at once!' announced Miss Sylvia, outraged.

'Oh, Frederick darling, you're so marvellously clever!'

said Kitty Shaw, falling into Mr Whitman's arms. (I had never seen anyone actually fall into someone's arms before, but I promise you she really did it.) 'My precious pearls! How on earth did you work it out?'

Mr Whitman did not even flinch. 'Oh it was nothing, my dear,' he said. 'Just a little cool logic and intelligence, that's all.'

'*I say!*' I began indignantly, but it was no use. No one was paying the least bit of attention to me: I might just as well have been talking to myself.

After that of course, there was quite a to-do. Mr Mountville was frightfully angry with Mr Simpson, and shouted at him so loudly that the girls said it made the whole stage set rattle. Kitty Shaw forgot all about Mr Sinclair and made up her mind then and there that Mr Whitman was the only man for her. A great big picture of the two of them appeared on the front page of the next day's *Daily Picture* under the headline 'Broadway Star Turns Detective'. It was accompanied by a very long article all about how Mr Whitman had been terribly clever and found Miss Shaw's missing pearls, which somehow managed to avoid mentioning anything about Mr Simpson.

Meanwhile I had to go back to rehearsing my high kicks, feeling tremendously annoyed because not one of the girls would believe that it was really *me* who found the missing pearls, and not Mr Whitman! But I do believe that if he was to read this account of it, even Billy would agree that I solved the Mystery of the Purloined Pearls quite as well as any real detective.

*

*Read more about Lil and her friends in* The Mystery of the Clockwork Sparrow *and* The Mystery of the Jewelled Moth, *available from Egmont now!*

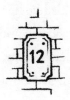

# THE MYSTERY OF ROOM 12
## By Robin Stevens

I know that our hotel is supposed to be haunted, but that's just a story. The woman in Room 12 wasn't a ghost, and I didn't make her up, either. She was real, and I always knew it, before anyone else believed me, because I was there when she checked in.

The night she arrived was a Tuesday. That's my dad's quiz evening at the pub, which means that Mrs Hughes was covering the front desk, with Alfie and me to keep her company. Before Mum left last year, there used to be more staff in the hotel, but now it's just my dad and Mrs Hughes, and a few weekend people. Before Mum left, a lot of things were different. But this is the way it is now. I'm James Kahn, by the way, and Alfie is my dog. He's big and hairy like a carpet, as big as I am small – even though I'm twelve I don't look it.

Then Mrs Hughes got a migraine. When Mrs Hughes gets a migraine, she says it's like her whole head splits open. She can't see, and she goes grey and has to lie down in one of our empty rooms upstairs. That day, luckily, there were lots – it was the off-season, so we only had three guests in the whole hotel. The off-season means that we don't get many guests because the beach is cold and the pier's half-closed and the donkeys are in their winter stables.

'James, you'll have to cover for me!' gasped Mrs Hughes as she staggered upstairs. 'I'm sorry – you'll be all right, won't you? It'll be quiet!'

I nodded, because I knew it was no good saying no. And then a door slammed and Mrs Hughes groaned and, just like that, I was in charge of the whole hotel.

It was sort of amazing, at first. I sat up on the high stool with the guest ledger open in front of me and felt like all four floors of the hotel and every corner of it belonged to me. But after a while I began to feel a bit bored. There was nothing to do, and no one was coming in.

Alfie was curled around my feet and I was yawning, and then the front door of the hotel opened and *she* came in. Alfie surged up to put his paws on the desk (Dad taught him the trick – guests love it) and I sat up too, surprised, and looked. The woman who came in wasn't particularly interesting-looking – she was sort of young for an adult, with pretty hair and nice clothes that weren't too bright or weird. She had a suitcase with her, a little brown one with a tag on it, and a bag on her shoulder. But she looked . . . worried, I guess, and that made me curious.

She came up to the desk, and I smiled, trying as hard as I could to sound the way Mrs Hughes does when she greets someone new. 'Hello and welcome to Hogarth House Hotel. *Do* you have a reservation?'

'Hello,' she said. 'Can you get the receptionist, please? I need a room for tonight.'

'The receptionist isn't here at the moment,' I said, feeling like I'd been playing a game, and she'd caught me out. 'But I can put you in Room 12 if you'd like. The hotel manager will be back soon. How would you like to pay?'

She frowned. I remember thinking that she was definitely worried about something. She seemed nervous. 'Cash.'

I was glad about that. I had no idea how to use the card machine. 'Write your name in the ledger,' I said, 'and I'll take you up to your room. Breakfast will be at eight o'clock tomorrow morning.'

There was a pause while she pulled out cash from her purse, then she wrote her name, 'Stella Smith'. Then I folded back the divider on the front desk and stepped through to take her upstairs. Alfie whuffled his nose against Stella Smith's legs, and I bent down to take her suitcase, but she said, 'No! I'll take that.'

I saw the tag on her suitcase then, and it didn't say 'Stella Smith' at all. It said 'Andrea Sandford'. I thought that was odd, but I couldn't ask her about it, so I just led her up the stairs, to Room 12.

Our hotel is tall and thin, with a winding staircase up through the middle, and lots of narrow corridors leading to the rooms. I could hear someone on the stairs above us as we climbed – actually, that wasn't the first noise I'd heard. I was sure that there had been someone above us all the time, ever since Stella had come in. I wondered which of our three guests it was.

Room 12 is at the very end of the corridor on the second floor, beyond a grandfather clock and a lamp with purple glass on it and a pile of antique luggage. It's one of the nicest rooms, all in blue with paintings of waves and seagulls hung on the walls. It even has a gold telephone (which doesn't work, but is brilliant anyway – it's one of my dad's best antique-shop finds). Stella didn't say anything about the room, though, just stood in the doorway and looked at me as though she wanted me to go. So I did.

I walked away down the corridor and turned, just once, to look back at her in the lamplight. Then . . . well, then I never saw her again.

Because it was late and Mrs Hughes was still groaning in her room, I tucked Stella's money away very carefully under the ledger, closed up the desk and carefully locked the front door. I knew my dad could let himself in – he has the only other set of keys to the outside, so guests have to ring the doorbell if they're late back. And then I went to bed.

When I came down to breakfast the next morning, the other three guests, Mrs Illingworth, Mr Pearse and Miss Heaven, were all in the dining room, ignoring each other. Stella Smith, though, was nowhere to be seen. That made me feel a bit worried, because I *had* told her about breakfast, hadn't I? After I'd checked her in last night, Stella Smith felt like *mine*. Mrs Hughes was up again, still looking pale, but cooking breakfast in the kitchen.

'Thank you for being good last night, James,' she said to me. 'You're a nice boy. Who are you looking for?' I kept on staring at the door, waiting for Stella to appear.

'A woman came in last night,' I said. Mr Pearse rustled his paper, Mrs Illingworth coughed and Miss Heaven sneezed. 'I checked her in. Has she come down yet?'

Mrs Hughes looked shocked. 'A new guest?' she asked. 'Oh, James! Why didn't you come and tell me?'

'I didn't want to worry you. I put her in Room 12,' I said. Suddenly I got a sick feeling. Had I done something wrong?

A timer pinged, and Mrs Hughes turned towards it. 'Go

speak to your father, James,' she said. 'I'm sure he'll know.'
So, not feeling hungry at all any more, I went to find Dad.

Dad was doing the accounts, and I could tell he was in a
don't-disturb mood.

'Dad,' I said nervously, 'has the woman from Room 12
come down yet?'

'What woman from Room 12?' asked Dad, and he
scratched his beard absently.

'A woman came in last night. I checked her in, but she
hasn't come down this morning. Her name's Stella Smith,'
I said. I grabbed hold of the ledger and spun it around, to
point at Stella's name.

But it wasn't there.

I couldn't believe it. I stared at the ledger, as hard as I
could. There were Mrs Illingworth's, Mr Pearse's and Miss
Heaven's names, just the way they had been last night – and
below them, nothing apart from a little smudge, that *could*
have been rubbed-out pencil, or just a stray mark on the
page.

'Are you sure, James?' asked Dad, frowning. 'And what
was Mrs Hughes doing, letting you check in a guest on your
own?'

'She had one of her migraines,' I said. 'I had to. But look,
she gave me money and I put it –'

But then I lifted up the ledger book, and Stella's money

had gone. I couldn't believe it. 'But she was here!' I said. Everything suddenly felt like a bad dream. There really had been a woman – hadn't there?

'James,' said my dad, 'are you sure about this? Hey – maybe you saw the hotel ghost!' He smirked, like he'd said something funny.

I glared at him. There's supposed to be the ghost of a woman who haunts our hotel, but I know it's not true. 'She wasn't a ghost!' I said. 'I put her in Room 12! Here, come on, I'll show you.'

I grabbed Dad's hand and dragged him up the stairs, past the mirrors and the china display and the suitcases and the clock and the lamp to the door of Room 12. I knocked, but there was no answer. Then I threw it open – and it was empty.

The bed was neatly made, the floor was clear and the lights were off. The window was just a little open, and the blue curtain breathed softly in the draft. It didn't look like anyone had been in there for days, not since Mr Thorne left the week before.

But I knew it wasn't true. Stella Smith had been there, last night. I had *seen* her. And I knew someone else had as well. I remembered the person I'd heard on the stairs. It couldn't have been Mrs Hughes, or my dad. It had to be one of the other three guests. I had to work out which one it was, and make them tell my dad the truth.

I turned and ran back down the stairs.

Breakfast was over, and Mrs Hughes had cleared the guests away. Mrs Illingworth and Miss Heaven had gone to their rooms, but Mr Pearse was in the sitting room with a paper and his cup of coffee. 'Excuse me,' I said to him. He blinked up at me. He was thin and thoughtful, and he had messy black hair. He had the crossword on his lap, which I thought only really old people did – but Mr Pearse was younger than my dad. 'A woman checked in, late last night. Did you see her?'

'Do you mean the old woman at breakfast this morning, or the younger one?' asked Mr Pearse, frowning. I could tell that he wanted to get back to his crossword.

'Neither,' I said. 'Another one. She had dark hair, and she was wearing a blue dress.'

'Sorry,' said Mr Pearse. 'The only women I've seen are the young one in jeans, and the old one with the jacket on. And the one with the apron, in the kitchen. That's it.' He absent-mindedly fiddled with one of the fingers of his left hand, then glanced down and frowned again, as though that finger had annoyed him.

So maybe it hadn't been Mr Pearse on the stairs. I went upstairs, where Miss Heaven was just coming out of Room

15. She was wearing jeans and a very neat bright-green top. 'Excuse me,' I said to her.

'What do you want?' asked Miss Heaven, raising her eyebrows at me.

'I'm James,' I said. 'My dad runs the hotel. Did you see a woman on the stairs, last night? She had a blue dress on, and she went into Room 12.'

Miss Heaven shook her head. 'I was in my room,' she said. 'I never saw anyone. Now excuse me, I have to go.' And she pushed past me down the stairs.

Maybe it hadn't been her, either.

Mrs Illingworth came by then, from Room 16. 'Hello, dear,' she said, as though I was six, not twelve. 'How are you?'

'I'm very well,' I said. 'Thank you. Did you see a woman come into the hotel, late last night? She was staying in Room 12.'

'I went to bed early, I'm afraid,' said Mrs Illingworth. 'I was dead to the world. Why do you ask?'

'No reason,' I said, because the way Mrs Illingworth was looking at me *did* make me feel six years old. I was beginning to wonder if I had made the whole thing up.

'Well,' said Mrs Illingworth, 'then there's nothing to worry about,' and off she went down the stairs after Miss Heaven.

I stood there, staring at the carving of the dolphin that Dad had stuck halfway up the landing, just above the green glass cat, and felt the hairs creeping on the back of my neck. I suddenly realised something. According to Mrs Illingworth, Miss Heaven and Mr Pearse, no one had been on the stairs the night before. But I had heard someone – and I couldn't be imagining *two* ghosts. I couldn't really even be imagining *one*. It was impossible. And that meant that someone had to be lying. But why? And what had happened to Stella Smith?

Back in my room, I opened up my computer. If Stella Smith was real, maybe I could prove it by finding her on the internet.

I googled 'Stella Smith' but all I got were hundreds of women who weren't her. Some of them looked a little like her, but only if I narrowed my eyes. I was just about to give up and go back to my list when I remembered the name I'd seen on her bag. Andrea Sandford. 'Andrea Sandford', I typed.

And this time I got the opposite of nothing.

*Preston Woman Steals Millions!* read the first link.

*You Won't Believe How This Woman Tricked Her Employer.*

*'I never knew she had it in her,' says best friend of cupcake-con woman.*

*Baking entrepreneur loses millions as employee goes on the run.*

*'Tricked by my own wife!' Cupcake-con husband speaks out.*

I opened about thirty tabs, until they clustered up and stopped showing properly, and then I flicked through them. They were all about Andrea Sandford, a woman who had taken all the money from the baking company she worked for and ran away with it, leaving her husband and all of her friends behind. There were pictures with the articles, of her husband, and her best friend, and her boss. And they looked a bit like Mr Pearse, Miss Heaven and Mrs Illingworth. Except – not quite. The man in the pictures had a beard, and Mr Pearse was clean-shaven. The young woman in the pictures had blonde hair, and Miss Heaven's hair was red. And the old lady had big jowly cheeks and a round stomach, and Miss Illingworth was thin. Their names were different, too. *Was* it them? I couldn't be sure.

Suddenly I felt scared. Stella Smith – Andrea Sandford – *was* real, or she had been. Now she was missing. What if the person I'd heard on the stairs had come down to Room 12 afterwards – what if they were the reason she was missing now?

'Alfie,' I said. 'I have to find out about this.'

I went back down past the grandfather clock and the lamp with purple glass in it and the pile of antique luggage to Room 12. I moved as quietly as I could, although Alfie panted noisily behind me. If I was going to work out what had happened to Andrea Sandford, I had to think like a detective. What did detectives need? I made a list in my head. There was a *crime*. I thought I had one. There were *suspects*. I had three of those. There were *motives*. I had those, too, from my googling. So now I needed *clues* – hairs, or footprints, or fingerprints, or dropped bits of paper. I had seen Andrea go into Room 12. She must have left a trace.

I stared around the room, but I couldn't see any hairs on the bed, or the carpet, or any fingerprints on the mirror or the windowpane. There were no footprints, either, or papers. I had no clues to go on at all.

Then I wondered if I could work out *how* she might have left the room. The window was still open, the way it had been this morning – but when I pushed it open enough to stick my head out, I saw a straight drop down, two floors, with only a thin plastic pipe that didn't even look like it could hold me. There was no way an adult, even a small one like Andrea, could have climbed down it. At the bottom was our garden, with Dad's flower bed, undisturbed and blooming. So she couldn't have got out that way – or been pushed out. I knew that the only doors outside had been locked (whenever Dad came in he always locked up behind him again), so she couldn't have gone out that way. Guests can ring the night bell to be let out, but no one had done it yesterday, or I would have heard.

So . . . she must still be in the hotel. And if no one had seen her . . . I turned and looked at the wardrobe, and my heart sped up. People don't just disappear. Not real people, anyway.

Before I could give myself time to get really scared I walked straight up to the wardrobe door and pulled it open.

It was empty. Three metal hangers jangled on the rail, and the door boomed a little as it swung back against the wall. My knees turned to water and I had to lean against Alfie.

She wasn't there. But I knew what I had to do next. I had three suspects – I could look for clues in their rooms.

Miss Heaven and Miss Illingworth had left the hotel for the day, so it would be safe to go into their rooms. I looked into the sitting room for Mr Pearse – he wasn't there either. Perfect. I snuck the master set of room keys into my pocket while Dad was away from the front desk, took a cloth and a squirty bottle of cleaner in case anyone saw me, and went upstairs, feeling like a proper undercover detective.

I went into Room 16, Mrs Illingworth's, first. The sheets were crumpled, and a dress lay across the floor. Things were spilling out of her suitcase, and the room smelt powdery and sweet. It made me sneeze. I marched straight up to her wardrobe and pulled it open. Nothing. Then I checked under the bed. Nothing there either.

I waited for my heart to stop beating in my ears, and then I checked Mrs Illingworth's case. Stretchy white knickers (embarrassing). A book (*4:50 from Paddington*. A murder mystery! I could hear my heart again). And a crumpled-up letter.

*Sue,*

*I want to make amends for what I did. If you come to the Hogarth House Hotel in St Jude's-by-the-Sea on the 15th of next month, I will be there. I can explain.*

*Andrea*

I felt dizzy. So Mrs Illingworth *was* the old woman from the internet articles! And Andrea had asked her to come here to meet her, today. She knew Andrea would be here – Mrs Illingworth had lied to me!

It was my first clue. I got out my phone and took a picture of it.

Then I went into Room 15, Miss Heaven's.

It was tidy – so tidy that I couldn't believe she had slept there. But there was her suitcase in the corner. The bed was made with the same neat corners that Dad always manages when he does the rooms. I looked under it (nothing), and then stepped towards the wardrobe.

What if Andrea *was* there? What would I do? Would it be just like a TV show? Bodies never look really dead, on TV shows. Sometimes you can see them breathing as they're lying on the pavement, or the coroner's slab. But real life isn't like that.

I pulled open the door. There were two dresses, one green, one pink, and one pair of white shoes. But there was no body.

I breathed calmly for a while, and then turned to the rest of the room. When I pulled open the dresser drawers, I saw one pair of knickers (much littler and lacier than Mrs Illingworth's - super embarrassing), a make-up bag and a two-pack of thin rubber gloves. One pair of them was missing. That was strange.

Was that why I hadn't seen any hair or fingerprints in Andrea Sandford's room? I took photos of the gloves with my phone. My clues were building up.

The last room was Mr Pearse's, Room 8. It was down the stairs, and as I walked down I was scared, more than ever. The lamps were still on in the hallway - it never gets really light in the hotel, not even in the day, because the corridors are so narrow and there aren't any windows on to the main stairs, except the skylight at the top of the house. Suddenly everywhere - the clock, the trunks, the tables and the sofas

– looked creepy.

I clicked the door open, and saw my hands shaking in front of me.

Mr Pearse's room wasn't as tidy as Miss Heaven's. There were pieces of paper all over the place, all ripped out of newspapers. Lots of them were half-done crosswords, but the rest were all articles about Andrea and what she'd done. And on the bedside table was a thick gold ring. So that was why Mr Pearse had been fiddling with his finger this morning! He really was Andrea Sandford's husband. I took a photo on my phone.

I had thought Mrs Illingworth must be guilty. Then I was sure it was Miss Heaven. But now I knew. It had to be Mr Pearse. Andrea had to be here. Blood booming in my ears, I pulled open Mr Pearse's wardrobe.

There was nothing inside it but a suit.

That was three empty wardrobes, and three suspects, each of whom seemed guilty.

I was so confused. I had lots of clues – and they made all of my suspects seem as though they had done it. Wasn't I supposed to be narrowing them down? Instead, what I had found had made them all seem more guilty.

Andrea had worked for Mrs Illingworth and run away with her money, and then had written a letter to her, asking her to come to this hotel so that she could apologise. And

Mrs Illingworth read murder mysteries.

Andrea had been best friends with Miss Heaven, and Miss Heaven had rubber gloves – just what you'd need if you wanted to tidy a hotel room and leave no trace.

Andrea had been married to Mr Pearse, and Mr Pearse had articles about her all over his room, as though he was still angry at her. He was very logical, too – all those crosswords proved that – and wouldn't you need to be logical, to make a body disappear like Andrea's had?

I frowned. I thought about the room, and all of the clues I'd gathered. I thought about my three suspects, and about Andrea going into Room 12. Who had been the person on the stairs? Who had taken revenge on her? I couldn't narrow it down.

I had to find Andrea, and to do that I needed to make another list. Where could you hide a body in a hotel? I wrote down 'rooms'. Then I crossed it out. All of the rooms were locked unless there were guests in them. I wrote down 'our flat' and crossed it out. I'd been there all night, and this morning, and so had Dad. I wrote down 'kitchens'. That was a better idea. The kitchens are big, and we have one of those industrial freezers. 'The sofas in the sitting room'. Another good idea. 'Broom cupboard'. I jumped up. I had to go check my theories right now.

'What are you doing, James?' asked Mrs Hughes, as I ducked past her, Alfie trotting behind me. She was beginning lunch for me and Dad.

'I want ice cream,' I lied. Mrs Hughes looked worried.

'Don't ruin your lunch!' she said, and I had to pretend I hadn't heard her. But the only things in the freezer were the ice-cream, tubs of peas and slabs of frozen meat. I felt stupid. No one hides dead people in freezers apart from in films.

I ran away as Mrs Hughes flapped her tea towel at me. 'The sofas in the sitting room' were next, and I was so glad that the room was empty when I went in. I could get down on hands and knees (stomach churning) and peer.

Nothing.

'Broom cupboard' was the last place on my list. Out I went to the front hall, and up the little half-stairs that led to it. My dad was on Reception, and he stuck his head round after me.

'James?' he called. 'Are you all right? You're not still upset about the ghost, are you?'

Then he laughed at himself. I ignored him. Something real had happened, not a ghost story at all, and I had to prove it. I pulled open the broom cupboard door – and there was no body.

Again!

I didn't understand it. My nose itched, and my eyes went blurry. I didn't want it to be true that Andrea was dead, but I knew it was. I just had to prove it to everyone.

I felt my dad's hand on my back, and I jumped and hit my head on the broom cupboard door.

'James!' he said. 'Hey, Jamie! Come on, what's all this?'

'She was here,' I said. 'She was!'

'All right, so what if she was?' said my dad. 'Maybe she took back her money and left this morning, before any of us got up. That happens sometimes. Sometimes people just pack up and leave. You and I both know that.'

I tensed my shoulders. Adults always do that – bring up things that don't belong. They've been around too long, and that means they can't see what really has happened because they've seen too much other stuff already.

What Dad was saying had nothing to do with this mystery. Andrea Sandford hadn't *packed up and left*. She'd never *unpacked*. She –

And then I knew where Andrea was, and what had happened to her.

'Dad,' I said. 'Come with me. Quickly!'

I dragged Dad upstairs again, to the second floor corridor, and I went past the grandfather clock and the lamp with purple glass on it – to the pile of antique luggage just in front of Room 12.

But now that I looked at it properly, I saw what I should have seen all along – that one of the pieces of luggage on the top of the pile wasn't antique at all. It was a little brown suitcase, the one I'd seen the night before. The tag was gone, but I knew what it was.

All I had to do was point. And when I pointed my dad saw what *he* should have seen all along – that the suitcases were all piled up wrong, in a different formation, as though someone had pulled them apart and built them up again without knowing the way they should go.

'Who's done that?' he asked – but of course *I* knew. I pulled at them, and suitcases fell around me ('Careful!' said Dad), until I was left with just one, the biggest trunk, sitting fat on the floor and not moving at all when I shoved at it.

'There's something in there,' said Dad. 'Funny! Who's gone and –'

And then he opened it. And the mystery of where Andrea Sandford had been hidden was solved.

'But who did it?' my dad kept saying, while we waited for the police to arrive. 'Who could have done it?'

I knew that too. It had been easy, really, once I'd stopped trying to make things fit.

'They *all* did,' I said, breathing deeply. 'All three of them – Miss Heaven and Mr Pearse and Miss Illingworth. They all helped, anyway. Mr Pearse was logical, so he organised everything. He got rid of the money she paid me, and rubbed out her ledger entry. I bet he killed her, too, because he was so angry with her. Mrs Illingworth worked out what to do with the body by using the murder mystery she was reading. *4:50 from Paddington* is all about a disappearing corpse, and a body hidden in something a bit like a suitcase – I read the plot on Wikipedia. And Miss Heaven is tidy – she cleaned the room, so it would look like Andrea had never been in it.'

'Jamie, how . . .' My dad looked really upset. 'How did you . . . How did this *happen*? How did you know?'

I couldn't figure out how to explain it to him in a way he'd understand. So I just said, 'I worked it out. And I did tell you. You just didn't listen to me.'

It turned out that I was right. Andrea Sandford had invited all three of them to our hotel, saying that she wanted to apologise to them for what she'd done. Only, when they all saw each other, that evening, and realised what was happening, they decided that they didn't want to forgive her after all. When she arrived, Mr Pearse had been on the stairs and heard that she was paying cash, and realised I was the only person who had actually seen her come in. He thought that they could get rid of her and no one would believe me. It was a stupid plan, because once they'd done it they were stuck with a body inside a hotel, and no way to get it out – but actually, if it hadn't been for me, they might have got away with it. It's funny: even though they pretend to be so serious, adults are good at believing in ghosts, but bad at believing in anything else.

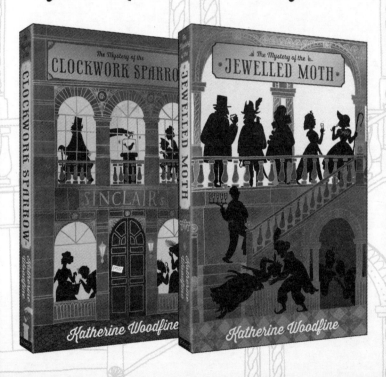

Join **MEL FOSTER**
and the
**RAG-TAG HEROES**
of the
**MONSTER
RESISTANCE**
in these **exciting
fantasy adventures**
from AWARD-WINNING
author Julia Golding.

**MEL FOSTER**
and the
**DEMON
BUTLER**

A monstrously big adventure!

**JULIA GOLDING**

**MEL FOSTER**
and the
**TIME MACHINE**

Back in time, back in trouble...

**JULIA GOLDING**